TEMPTING THE RECLUSIVE EARL

Taken by Destiny, Book 2

By Aurrora St. James

Text by Aurrora St. James
Cover by Kim Killion

Dragonblade Publishing, Inc. is an imprint of Kathryn Le Veque Novels, Inc.
P.O. Box 23
Moreno Valley, CA 92556
ceo@dragonbladepublishing.com

Produced in the United States of America

First Edition July 2023
Trade Paperback Edition

ARE YOU SIGNED UP FOR DRAGONBLADE'S BLOG?

You'll get the latest news and information on exclusive giveaways, exclusive excerpts, coming releases, sales, free books, cover reveals and more.

Check out our complete list of authors, too!

No spam, no junk. That's a promise!

Sign Up Here

www.dragonbladepublishing.com

Dearest Reader;

Thank you for your support of a small press. At Dragonblade Publishing, we strive to bring you the highest quality Historical Romance from some of the best authors in the business. Without your support, there is no 'us', so we sincerely hope you adore these stories and find some new favorite authors along the way.

Happy Reading!

CEO, Dragonblade Publishing

Additional Dragonblade books by Author Aurrora St. James

Taken by Destiny Series

The Earl's Timely Wallflower (Book 1)
Tempting the Reclusive Earl (Book 2)

Chapter One

Present Day
New York City

Bellamy Bennett paced her Park Avenue apartment, biting her manicured thumbnail as the phone rang. When she realized the bad habit, she stuck her hand in her pocket.

Come on. Come on, Archer. Pick up.

After the fourth ring, she ended the call, then immediately redialed. Her older brother would get tired of it eventually and answer. He had to.

She spun back toward her dining table which was currently covered in the pages of her new contract. *Vivant*, one of the bestselling perfume brands in the world, had just signed her to a four-year contract worth millions of dollars. Bellamy frowned at the contract and turned back to the window overlooking the city. The bright lights normally brought her peace. Tonight, they gave her a headache.

She hung up and redialed.

On the third ring, a gruff voice answered.

"What do you want, Bells?"

"I'm doing well, thanks. How are you, Archer?" She put as much sugar into her words as possible.

He grunted. "How are you, Bellamy?"

"I'm worried. I can't reach Lily." Of the three of them, their middle sister tended to be the most reliable. She answered her phone, returned their calls, and she never gave up on them.

"Maybe she's just out. People do have lives, you know."

Bellamy rolled her eyes, even though he couldn't see it. "Like watching television and not leaving your couch unless your stomach demands it?"

"I have a valid reason not to go out."

Don't bicker with him, Bells. He's still healing. "That's not why I called. If Lily is out, then she's been out for a week. I've left her four messages in the last seven days and she hasn't called back. That's not like her."

He was silent for a moment. "Did you get into another argument?"

She ground her teeth and bit back a sharp retort. It was a valid question. She and Lily hadn't been on the best of terms for the last eight years. "No. Last time we talked it was…fine." Stilted, but not argumentative. It was progress.

"Hm. I'm sure she's just been busy."

"Have you heard from her?"

Archer sighed and she could hear the self-recrimination in it. *Oh, Archer. What happened to you on that last mission?* He'd never tell her. All she knew was that he was medically discharged from the military after the vehicle carrying his SEAL team was hit with an explosive. He'd come back to the States after months in the hospital with a limp and an aversion to everything and everyone, including his sisters.

"She called a while ago. I didn't answer."

Bellamy straightened. "She called today?"

"Shit. No. It was…" his voice sounded farther away from the phone as if he was scrolling through his recent calls, "two weeks ago."

Two weeks! "That was when I talked to her." She heard something thump on his end of the line. It sounded like a fist hitting a wooden table. "My contract starts next week, so I don't have a whole lot of time. But we've got to go to Kentucky and try to find her."

"Bells, I'm sure she's—"

"What if something happened to her, Archer? Do you know anyone out there that can check on her?"

"No."

"Neither do I. Please. I owe her."

Archer muttered a curse. "I...I can't, Bellamy."

She gripped the phone until the edges cut into her fingers. "Can't, or won't, Archer?"

He blew out a harsh breath. "Does it matter?"

Damn him. How could he sit back and pretend everything was fine? "What the hell happened to you that you won't even leave your house when your sister might be in trouble?" she yelled.

"Lily can look after herself. She has since Mom and Dad died. Since she started taking care of you. She's *fine*."

"What if she isn't?"

"What if she's just avoiding you?" he shot back.

Bellamy sucked in a sharp breath and pressed her lips together until they hurt. "Then she can avoid me in person. At least I care enough about her to make sure she's okay."

Archer sputtered.

Before he could reply, Bellamy disconnected the call. And immediately regretted it. Archer was dealing with his own physical and emotional wounds. Maybe it wasn't fair to put the expectation on him to help, but this was *Lily*.

She tossed her phone onto the couch and sank beside it on the cushions, head in her hands. She *knew* something was wrong. For all their arguments and the years of strained tension, Lily had always been open to talking through their problems. No matter how mad she'd been at Bellamy or what harsh words were spoken, Lily cooled off quickly and didn't hold a grudge. Even if they had argued the last time they'd talked, Lily would have been ready to talk again the next day. Two weeks of silence wasn't like her sister.

Damn Archer.

Bellamy grabbed her phone and went to her bedroom. The large windows overlooking Park Avenue, with its war-era buildings and crowded streets below, let in a faint light. Cars honked and the noisy hum of the city couldn't be contained by the glass. She loved the energy of Manhattan. She'd been lucky to find this apartment on the Upper East Side, with its beautiful architecture and the security of a doorman. It was also close to the Madison Avenue boutiques, which she loved to browse, and Central Park when she needed the fresh feel of grass under her feet or the smell of fall leaves. Of course, it was outrageously expensive. Fortunately, her modeling career paid the bills and provided the security she desperately needed after losing her parents and their family home.

She'd left college in her first semester to start modeling and she didn't regret most of her choices. Only one truly bothered her—she'd been so caught up in grief over losing her parents that she'd pushed Lily away at every opportunity.

We have to work this out. I can't lose anyone else.

If Archer wouldn't go to Kentucky, then she'd just go by herself. She retrieved her suitcase from the closet and laid it open on the bed. She'd catch the first flight out to either Kentucky or Tennessee, whichever was closest, and find her sister.

If Archer was right and Lily was okay, then great. She'd spend time with her sister and make some new, good memories. But her gut told her something was wrong and she had time to go. The Vivant photo shoot started in ten days at the old chateau in France.

Please let it be enough time to find Lily.

She tossed a shirt into her suitcase, then reached for her tablet. A flight to Knoxville, Tennessee left at 8:30 a.m. Bellamy booked the flight, then called for a car service.

By the time she hung up, she was sniffing back the tears that clogged her throat. She wouldn't cry. Not until she knew what happened to her sister. If Lily was okay, she was going to mend their relationship and be the sister that she should have been all along. She owed Lily everything.

April 1814
London, England

THE *TINK-TINK-TINK* OF hammer against metal soothed Christian Albury's nerves as little else could. He hunched over his cluttered, wooden worktable, and tapped the jewelry hammer against the silver petal. He glanced at the full pink rose in the vase on his left to double-check its formation, turned the piece in his hand, and shaped the other side.

Blast. It didn't look quite right. Christian wiped the back of his hand across his brow. Half a dozen completed petals sat on the table near his elbow, all slightly different from the one in his hand. When assembled, they would recreate the garden rose, though his version would last forever. He could see it clearly in his mind. The flower would sit in a delicate glass vase with a silver pedestal to conceal the timepiece mechanism which would slowly open and close the petals to simulate the bloom.

The idea had come to him a few months back as he prepared to depart the house party his best friend, Gabriel Hawthorne, the Earl of Rothden, had forced him to attend. Under normal circumstances, he enjoyed spending a few days at Hawthorne Hall. Gabriel was one of only two men Christian considered his friends. But dozens of additional guests had attended the house party for the lavish suppers and balls. Being amid so many people made his pulse hammer and his lungs close until he fought the urge to barricade himself in his chamber.

Christian rubbed the bridge of his nose. He didn't quite have the social skills required to carry on a conversation, which often led to whispers behind his back or even a cut direct. Something about him put people off. His conversations were stilted, at best, and talking to a woman made his insides quake until he was reduced to single-word responses.

Gabriel understood that better than anyone. He dragged Christian to the events anyway, under the guise of it being good for him. Or at least, a way to improve his social skills. He usually snuck out to find solace the first moment he was able. Far better to be alone than the subject of derision. He was happier on his own.

He'd spotted a delicate rose in a vase outside his guest room while visiting Gabriel, and its strong fragrance brought a smile to his face. A flash of desire to capture that moment hit him, and his mind spun with ways to implement it. Once home, he'd barreled into his workshop and rifled through his tools and clock pieces, looking for the parts he'd need to begin.

Unfortunately, Parliament began session several days later, and he'd had to abandon the project to return to London. The miserably cold winter, one of the worst the country had in decades, meant he was unable to return home until the House of Lords session broke for Easter.

Christian shuddered. Now, the families of the lords joined them in London for months of theater, balls, and dinner parties that made up the Season. It all made his head throb.

He traced a finger over the silver petal and turned back to his project. The tightness in his lungs from thinking about the Season eased and allowed him to draw a full breath, scented by the garden rose. Now if only he could devise a way for the silver flower to release a similar scent into the air when the petals opened. Once he had the mechanism and design complete, he wanted to make this on a grander scale. An entire garden. He adjusted his grip on the hammer and tapped on the silver. Perhaps if he used a narrow tube that ran up the inside of the stem and connected to a small bellows in the bottom that squeezed when the gears turned to open the petals…

Tap-tap-tap.

Christian stilled and looked down at his hammer. He hadn't

made that noise…

"Lord Albury?" a muffled voice called through the wooden door. It opened and the dark head of Malcolm, his butler, appeared. "The mail has arrived, my lord." He entered the workshop, stepping over a stack of scrap metal pieces that tilted precariously. He held a small tray, with a single cream envelope upon it.

Christian set the hammer and the silver petal aside and turned in his seat to eye the letter. Surely Gabriel wasn't already harassing him to ensure he would attend the next ball. Christian pressed his lips together. This was Gabriel. In all likelihood, that was exactly what the letter contained.

They'd been friends for years, since schooling together at Eton. Circumstances had brought them together, and though Christian didn't understand why, Gabriel had insisted on becoming his friend, a fact he would forever be grateful for. If not for Gabriel, he might not have survived Eton.

He reached for the envelope. "Is it impolite to admit that when Lord Hawthorne married, I had hoped he would be so taken up with his lovely wife that he would hound me less about attending parties?"

The butler's brown eyebrows shot up to his hairline and disappeared beneath the thick locks that permanently waved across his forehead. "Very likely, my lord."

Hmm. "When Rothden met a charming woman at his house party and asked her to wed him, I was delighted. He deserves every happiness." Christian liked Lily immensely. He didn't fumble his words around her because her natural charm seemed to put him at ease. He couldn't think of another woman of his acquaintance with whom he could speak so easily. Not even his housekeeper.

"I suspect many a young lady is disappointed by the news," Malcolm said.

Indeed, they would be. Gabriel had avoided the marriage mart with the same dedication as a pickpocket avoiding police patrols. But when his sister Violet had nearly run over a poor woman in the street with her carriage, she'd done the sensible thing and brought the dazed woman back to their home for care. The woman, Miss Lily Bennett, was different from any lady of their acquaintance and quickly captured Gabriel's attention.

Certainly, there were any number of delightful qualities to appreciate about Lily. But as the days of the house party continued, Christian had continued to note oddities about her, until the conclusion he'd reached shocked him: Lily Bennett was from the future, and she'd used one of his inventions to journey over two hundred years through time.

The little time travel clock sat on his shelf above the workbench with a couple of his other past projects. How could the device modify time? He'd set its hands to every hour to confirm each chimed properly and none shifted the century he found himself in. Perhaps it wasn't something he'd done yet, but something he would do in the future. If he adjusted the balance wheel and the escapement…

Malcolm cleared his throat.

Christian realized that his hand still rested on the envelope on the tray Malcolm held. He felt the heat of a flush move up his neck to his cheeks. He picked the letter up, expecting to see the fluid script of his best friend. Instead, the monogrammed seal of his solicitors, Forester, Morrister, and Lamb was pressed on the other side. He cast about his workbench, snatched up a wing divider, and used it to open the envelope.

Malcolm muttered something as Christian removed the heavy paper from within and scanned the brief letter.

"My lord?" Malcolm cleared his throat, and Christian realized he was waiting for a response.

He frowned. "Sorry, Malcolm. What was that?"

The man's lips twitched. He'd been in Christian's employ for nearly nine years. He was well accustomed to Christian's wandering thoughts. "Tea? Or shall I wait for your reply?"

Christian read the letter once more. "My man of business

wishes to see me about the accounts. I shall call on the solicitors tomorrow. Have Dale gather the needed books." His steward ran the Huntington estate well. Christian quite happily left the man to the job to pursue his love of automatons.

Perhaps if the solicitor's meeting took a few hours, he would have a suitable reason to avoid Lady Barlowe's ball. He hated the crowds, the parties, the dancing, the polite conversation, and most especially the simpering young ladies and their marriage-minded mothers. What he wouldn't give to send a proxy to take his place for the Season, as he could for Parliament.

"My lord, you may recall that Mr. Dale left two days past to attend to a family emergency," Malcolm said patiently.

"Of course." Christian had no recollection of such, but it made little difference. "Could you—?"

"I shall see to it, my lord. I will also send tea up. Supper is in two hours. Cook will be displeased if you miss for the second day in a row."

Had he missed supper yesterday?

A small smile touched Malcolm's lips. "Shall I return when it's time for supper, my lord?"

Christian felt his cheeks heat again but agreed. Cook could be as maddening as Gabriel when he missed a meal. Accounting to both of them in the same week made him feel like a child being scolded by his parents.

Malcolm departed. Christian folded the letter from his solicitors and tucked it into his jacket pocket. If he worked a few more hours tonight, he could finish the last petals. Maybe even begin assembly of the rose.

He picked up his jeweler's hammer and grimaced. London was cold, dank, dark, malodorous, and noisy. His only respite for the long months of the Season was this small workspace he'd set up for himself in the family townhouse.

After the meeting tomorrow, I'll stay home to work on this. Let Gabriel try to force my attendance at Lady Barlowe's ball.

Christian reached for the silver petal and shook his head.

Despite his bravado, he knew in his heart that if Gabriel wanted him to go to the ball, he would. There was nothing he wouldn't do for his friend. Once, a long time ago, Gabriel had saved his life. Christian owed him everything.

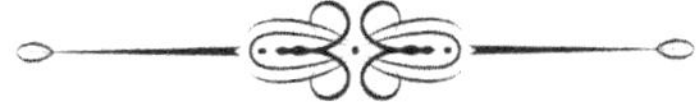

CHAPTER TWO

BELLAMY STOOD IN the center of a tiny efficiency apartment in Corbin, Kentucky, and tried not to cry. She'd arrived at the airport in Knoxville just before noon, then rented a car and driven an hour and a half north to a small town of less than ten thousand people. A ball of worry had lodged itself in her stomach when she still couldn't reach her sister. Now that she stood in Lily's efficiency, she could add shame to the fear.

She lived in an upscale apartment with a doorman and a car service. Lily lived...*here*. The apartment building was dirty, with stacks of mechanical parts outside that probably should have been inside something important, like the air conditioner which seemed on the brink of failure. Cigarette butts lined the stairs in the outdoor stairwell and there was no lightbulb in the fixture to illuminate the stairs at night. The door had a deadbolt, but Dennis, the sleazy landlord who'd let her into Lily's apartment, said that sometimes it stuck and wouldn't lock.

How could Lily even *pretend* that she was safe in a place like this?

And then there was the efficiency itself. The foldout bed, the small table with two chairs, and the bookshelf took up every inch of space. God, the kitchen was the size of a dime. There wasn't even a real stove. It was like someone had cut a stove in half and left two burners and a crooked door. The refrigerator was a step up from a mini beer fridge and the microwave would barely fit a bag of popcorn.

"If it smells weird in here, it's 'cause she left something in the microwave. It molded, but I didn't throw it out. Couldn't be sure the cops wouldn't be searchin', you know?" Dennis rasped from the doorway.

Bellamy spun to find him leaning against the door jam, thumbs hooked in the belt loops of his filthy jeans. He wore a stained white tank top and smelled like beer and cigarettes. Total. Class. She tucked her hands into her pants pocket where she'd moved the dispenser of pepper spray after meeting him for the first time.

"I didn't realize you'd been in here after Lily went missing. How long ago was that?"

His eyes widened. "Well, I uh…I was worried about her when she didn't pay rent. Thought maybe she tripped in the shower and needed help or something."

The man was hoping to catch Lily naked *and* helpless? Gross. Maybe she'd pepper spray him for that alone.

"What did you do when you hadn't seen her?" She knew the answer, just wanted the jerk to say it.

"Well, I figured maybe she was staying with that guy who's always hanging out in the parking lot, waiting for her. Of course, that was before I seen him come back after she was gone."

"Who is he?"

Dennis shrugged. "Lily said he was an ex who wouldn't leave her alone. Pretty women like you and her always have lines of men like that."

God, her sister had to contend with this guy *and* a stalker? The moment she found Lily, Bellamy was going to insist that she move somewhere safe. If not to New York, then somewhere else. They'd passed plenty of nice-looking apartments in town. Why wasn't Lily living there? Why *here*?

She pressed a hand to her temple. "I need to look around." Not that there was anything to see. The entire efficiency was smaller than the bathroom in the house they'd grown up in. The tiny bathroom here held the only closet in the apartment, and it was barely wide enough for a folded towel.

"Her purse and phone are here. The phone was dead, so I plugged it in," Dennis said. He gave her a slow smile. "Come find me when you're done. Maybe I'll buy you dinner."

Five years of interacting with paparazzi kicked in. *Give them what they expect to see.* She pasted on a polite smile. "I'll let you know when I'm finished." She closed the door on him, forced the deadbolt to engage, and sagged against it. Lily's purse and phone were here, but Dennis didn't find that suspicious enough to call the police? She *should* have pepper-sprayed him.

"I'll be waiting for you," he rasped from the other side of the door. Then his footsteps retreated.

Bellamy found Lily's purse by the bed. Her wallet had her driver's license and a debit card, but no cash. Had Dennis helped himself while he was here? There was no way to know. Her phone had twenty-three missed calls—nineteen from her and four from Archer. At least he'd tried to call.

She ground her teeth together and pushed thoughts of her brother aside. She'd deal with him once she found Lily, even if she had to turn up on his doorstep next. God, her family drove her crazy.

At least you still have them.

She scanned the small room again. There were some tools spread out on the table. She moved closer and realized that they were tools for small, intricate work. Like jewelry.

Her stomach dropped. Several months back, Lily tried making jewelry to sell online. At the time, she thought it was just a hobby that her sister did for fun. It never occurred to her that Lily might have been trying to make extra money. Her sister never complained about being low on funds or lacking basic comfort and safety. She'd assumed that whatever job Lily held was enough to pay her bills. Where did Lily work? Bellamy thought about it and was ashamed to admit she couldn't remember.

Wherever it was, it wasn't somewhere that paid much. And she'd never bought so much as a twenty-dollar bracelet from Lily.

Now her sister was missing. God, no wonder she'd had the old nightmare again last night.

I should have supported her. Mom and Dad would be so disappointed in us.

Before she thought better of it, she called Archer. He picked up on the second ring. She glanced at the phone screen. Did she dial the right number? Archer never answered the first time she called.

"She's okay?" he said in greeting.

"Hi, Archer. I got here just fine. Thanks for asking."

He blew out a hard breath and growled.

That brought a brief smile to her lips. "She's not here but her purse and phone are. Her landlord says she hasn't been here in a week. He thought she'd gone with some guy that was following her but saw the guy still looking for her later."

"He didn't call the police?"

"He was too busy going through her apartment," she huffed. "I think he took money from her purse. Her wallet is empty." Saying it out loud didn't make her feel any better, but he needed to know what they were up against.

Archer swore.

"Y-you should see this place. Or maybe you shouldn't. It's bad, Arch. I don't know how she felt safe here. Back alleys offer more protection than her apartment door." Bellamy rubbed a hand across her forehead.

"I should have come with you."

Damn right, he should have. Instead, he hid in his house like a grumpy hermit, favoring his injuries and avoiding everyone. He pretended the world outside didn't exist rather than helping find his sister like the hero she knew that he was. She bit back the words she knew she'd regret.

"I've been avoiding her calls," Archer muttered. "What if she was trying to reach me about one of these creeps, and I didn't answer? What if one of them took her, Bells?"

She heard the guilt in his voice, but she couldn't offer any absolution. She felt too much guilt herself. "God, we're the worst siblings in the world."

"After the folks died when I couldn't come back to help because I was on missions for the Navy, I was secretly glad. I didn't want to look at that house again. I didn't want to see it when they weren't there. I told myself I was helping you two by sending money back home to pay the bills."

The weariness in his voice made her heart hurt. "It helped. She still sometimes worked two jobs, like at Christmas, so that we could have a tree and gifts. I was such a brat, Archer. I know that I was a hormonal teen and that I was hurting, but I took it out on her. We didn't talk for months after I went to college. She gave up so much for me, and I couldn't be bothered to *talk* to her." She wrapped an arm around her waist and swallowed past the hard lump in her throat.

"We'll find her, and then we'll make everything right, okay?"

God, this was awful. What if Lily was just fine, sitting in a coffee shop somewhere, reading a book? What if she wasn't and something had happened to her? She didn't know what to do. "I'll do one last look and see if I find anything that might tell us what happened to her. Then I'll call the police and file a missing persons report."

"I'm sorry I didn't come with you, Bells."

"Yeah. Me too."

Bellamy hung up with her brother and tossed her phone onto the bed. She started a new search in the kitchen and then looked around the bed and bookshelf. A dark brown smudge on the corner of the bookcase caught her eye. Was that blood? She knelt to look closer and ran her fingers over it. The mark was dry.

Bellamy reached for her phone to call the police when something shiny on the floor by the foot of the bed caught her eye. She reached for that instead and picked up an enameled egg about the size of her palm. Red and gold filigree made it look like a Fabergé egg. It was beautiful, and too complex a creation for a home jewelry maker. She glanced back at the table with the tools. Was her sister repairing it? Why was it on the floor?

She stood and held it under the dim light of the bedside lamp. As she turned it over, one of the panels fell open on a little hinge. How curious. She opened the other panel and her breath caught in surprise. Inside lay a small clock face and beneath, two little golden dancers. The clock made a tinny chime. Then another.

Before she had more than a glimpse, white light burst out of the egg and filled the space around her hand.

"What the…?" Before she could form the thought, the clock chimed again and the whole world turned white.

"As you can see, Lord Huntington, these investments totaled over seventy thousand guineas. Seventy-three thousand, eight hundred, to be exact." Mr. Forester, of his solicitors, Forester, Morrister, and Lamb, gestured at the account book opened before Christian. The man cleared his throat. "Of course, we would have brought the matter to you sooner, but it took some time to investigate the investments to provide you the most with accurate information."

Christian's gaze flicked from the pages of neat columns up to the older, rotund man stuffed into a tight, gray suit. He'd come to the solicitor's office on Lombard Street this morning and had been shown into an office with dark-paneled walls and comfortable chairs before a large wood desk. It looked much the same as his own study at home, but here he felt uncomfortable. He swallowed past the sudden, sour taste in his mouth. "How many investments?"

Mr. Forester adjusted his spectacles. "Fourteen over three years."

Christian bit back a curse.

"Mr. Lamb discovered it quite by accident. When the account books were submitted for review, he found an investment in a cotton mill recently discovered not to exist. The others were much the same. Depleted mines, ships never built, land already entailed..."

"The records...?"

"Everything we found was signed by your steward, William Dale. Of course, we are not accusing the man of any wrongdoing...but he could answer how he chose these investments and possibly where the money went." Forester cleared his throat. "Not that I presume to tell you how to conduct your affairs."

Christian gripped the back of his neck and felt a headache forming behind his eyes. Seventy-three thousand guineas was nearly half his yearly income. An enormous fortune to a man like Dale. *Blast!*

"Thank you for bringing this to my attention, Forester. I shall see to it at once." He stood and gathered his hat, great coat, and gloves. "I should like a report of all your findings...and your discretion. Any future investments will be made solely by me."

"Very good, Lord Huntington."

It wasn't good. Not at all.

A blast of cold air hit his cheeks as he left the solicitor's office. He tipped the brim of his hat against the wind. The people around him were similarly huddled in their cloaks and great coats as they hurried past.

The chill in the air was no match for the frost that had taken hold in his chest during the meeting with Forester. Dale, his steward, had come with excellent references when Christian hired him four years past. The man had seemed competent in managing the Huntington estate. How had he misjudged the man? Had he heard complaints and ignored the warnings? How could he have let this happen?

The answer was clear. It had been easier to turn over the management to someone else than to concern himself with the many duties required to keep the Huntington estate profitable.

He'd allowed Dale full access to his money and investments, all so that he could focus on the projects that occupied his mind. As a result, he'd put the welfare of the people he provided for in jeopardy.

What the devil had happened with Dale? Why would the man embezzle funds from an employer? That would see him sent to prison. Unless he thought that he could escape the law. Christian blew out a terse breath that fogged white in the air. His butler, Malcolm, said that Dale had departed to tend to family. Was that a thinly veiled lie? Was the man, even now, steaming across the Atlantic for the West Indies with Christian's money tucked firmly in his pocket? The possibility infuriated him.

He nodded to his driver who pulled the carriage up. "The bank on Threadneedle," he said and then climbed into the welcoming warmth of the conveyance.

The Bank of England was a few blocks over. The slow journey only gave him more time to think back over the last three years, searching his memory for any sign that Dale meant to steal from him. Christian was not the sort of man to meet regularly with his staff, so the few interactions they had were fuzzy at best. Dale had seemed amiable, intelligent, and good with numbers. What other qualities could a steward need?

How about loyalty? Or integrity?

His head began to throb. Would his father have dealt with the matter differently? He couldn't say for certain. His parents had been largely inattentive throughout his upbringing and were happy when the time came to ship him off to boarding school. When his father died and the estate and title passed to Christian, he'd been unprepared for the responsibility.

I'm still unprepared.

He pressed his hand over his eyes and rubbed against the pain. Regardless of the outcome of his meeting with the bank, he could no longer allow others to see to Huntington land and finances.

Hopefully, Gabriel could help. When his best friend inherited the Rothden title, he'd built the estate back up from near destitution through smart investments. Investments that *existed.*

The carriage rocked as it stopped, and a footman opened the door. Thin, gray light spilled into the cab, spearing pain in his eyes.

Christian held back a groan, stepped down, and entered the bank. Large windows let in the light of the overcast day and highlighted the wooden panels the bank clerks stood behind. His heels clicked across the marble floor, nearly drowned out by the murmurs of dozens of people milling about the great hall. He moved along the edge of the room, avoiding the eye of any acquaintances in the Ton, and sought out a gatekeeper.

An hour later, his fears were confirmed. Dale had signed for the fraudulent investments. He also had signed a bank note for an additional five thousand pounds, drawn last month. As the banker talked, showing Christian the records on file for the transactions, the pounding in his head grew and it felt like a vein pulsed in his temple.

"May I be of any additional service, Lord Huntington?" the banker asked.

He clenched the brim of his hat in his fist and stood. "From now on, no one but myself may make any withdrawals from my account, and I will do so in person," he said in a clipped tone.

The man nodded.

Christian accepted the documents relating to the withdrawals and departed. Much of his cash had been depleted by Dale and the embezzled funds were putting stress on his remaining resources. He directed his driver to Mayfair, climbed into his carriage, and threw himself into his seat. London was a large city but if Dale was foolish enough to stay there, hoping to hide among the masses, he would soon regret it. Christian would find the man if he had to look under every bridge and every rock. He wouldn't rest until he recovered the lost funds.

It was one thing to threaten Christian's livelihood, but Dale's actions could put people out of work. Without the money to pay their salaries, his people would struggle to keep up their homes and sell their goods. They would suffer. He refused to allow that. Dale would pay for this transgression by languishing in prison for years. Christian intended to see to it himself.

Nearly eighty thousand guineas gone! Christian clenched his fist on his knee as the carriage drew near to Gabriel's townhouse in Mayfair. What could drive a man to destroy the lives of the people he worked with? He knew well the evil men could enact against one another, but he could hardly conceive that his steward would betray those around him, and for three years no less. He wanted to throttle William Dale.

With effort, he relaxed his fist and rubbed his hand on his trousers. A few steady breaths and he wrestled his anger under control. Tomorrow he would call upon the people who'd given Dale references. He didn't expect the man would return to their employ, but they may know places he might frequent when in London. If he remained in town at all.

Chapter Three

THE COACH SLOWED to a stop in front of a red brick residence at the end of a row of townhouses, each with iron fence work, and pillared doorways. The footman opened the door and stepped back to let Christian exit. He tugged his great coat closed to block out the icy wind and stepped out of the carriage. It was too damned cold for April. He settled his hat on his head and turned towards Gabriel's townhome.

A slim woman stood on the sidewalk just in front, with her arms crossed tightly over her bosom, and her shoulders hunched against the cold. As he approached, he realized that her attire was quite odd, and nowhere near warm enough for the chill in the air. She appeared to only be wearing boots, a thin blouse, and… he blinked…trousers?

Christian paused a few steps away. She faced the opposite side of the street, looking about as if she were lost, and hadn't seen him yet. Should he offer his assistance? A man of good breeding should do no less. Yet his feet seemed rooted to the sidewalk and his stomach dipped. A strong part of him wanted to hurry past, to avoid the interaction entirely.

What kind of man are you, Albury? It is clear she needs help. She will catch cold, standing there in such thin garments. Offer your assistance.

It shouldn't be so difficult to speak to someone and he hated that it was.

He willed his feet to move forward and searched for something to say. He cleared his throat. "Good day…" He mentally cringed at the rasp in his voice. "Miss?"

The woman wobbled on her feet as she turned and looked up at him with wide, deep blue eyes the shade of sapphires that were framed by long lashes several shades darker than the blonde hair that flowed unbound down her back. A fine tremble went through her, drawing his gaze down. She was taller than most women of his acquaintance, willowy, and so beautiful she stole his breath.

He put his hand on her arm to steady her as she swayed and immediately felt her chilled skin through the silky fabric. How long had she been standing here? He removed his greatcoat and held it aloft, then hesitated. "May…May I?"

Her chin dipped in the smallest nod. Christian kept his movements slow as he wrapped the coat around her shoulders. A shudder went through her, and a soft sigh escaped her lips. He rubbed her arms through the thick wool. The need to care for her, to see to her needs, rose sharply, startling him. The feeling was quite uncomfortable. His cheeks burned as he released her and stepped back.

Regardless, she couldn't stay out in the cold dressed as she was. They stood in front of the steps to Gabriel's door. Would she enter with him to get warm?

"Thank you," she said. "I…I don't know how I…*where* am I?"

Her voice was low, with a hint of panic. It drew his gaze back to her face. She looked up at him with those wide eyes that had an unnerved expression in their jewel-like depths. Her skin was flawless, her features near perfect. She had the ethereal beauty of Helen of Troy. Men would wage war for her.

Christian felt his cheeks flush harder at his romantic thoughts and tried to think of something to say that wouldn't sound foolish. She…she didn't know where she was? "You are standing outside the home of the Earl of Rothden on Hill Street. In

Mayfair." Did he sound too formal? Too stiff? He rolled his shoulders to release the tension there.

"Mayfair?" Her tone said that she didn't recognize the name. She was American. He could hear the accent now that she spoke more.

"London," he added.

"London?" She frowned and looked around, then pressed a palm to her forehead. "It looks a little like…but that's impossible. The last thing I remember, I was standing in my sister's apartment…"

She trailed off as a carriage rolled by, the *clop-clop* of the horses' hooves loud on the quiet side street. Across the way, two women walked down the sidewalk, huddled in their capes and bonnets. She went still as she watched them as if she'd never seen women walking before.

Christian cleared his throat, unsure of what to do next. Perhaps he should inquire if Lily was home and have her help the woman. She would no doubt be of far more assistance than he.

The woman's eyes misted and finally, she looked back up at him.

He saw her panic deepen. He wanted to reach for her and soothe her somehow. Should he? He had no experience comforting a woman. By the devil, he couldn't stand to see her looking so lost and vulnerable. Acting on instinct, he slowly reached out and laid a hand on her shoulder. The muscles beneath his hand relaxed a fraction.

She edged a step closer.

Emboldened by her response, he drew her into his arms. She shook slightly, then nestled closer. "I—I'm sorry. I don't normally hug strangers in the middle of the street."

His natural inclination was to rub a hand on her back, so he followed it and felt her calm further. "Might I enquire your name?"

"It's Bellamy. Bellamy Bennett."

Christian's stomach flipped over. He scanned her, taking in

the thin blouse and trousers. Her unusual clothing, the style in which she wore her hair, even the way she spoke...*Of course. Why had he not seen it before? This was Lily's sister...* He stilled as another realization hit him. *Lily's sister... who should not be in their time. She too had time traveled.*

"I am Christian Albury," he said. Should he give his title? He preferred not to use it, still uncomfortable in the role of the earl, even after all these years. Did he want her to use it? Christian felt that painful awkwardness that came when speaking to a woman. "I am calling on friends here." He gestured toward Gabriel's front door. "Would you...I should like you to join us. Warm yourself by the fire."

She stepped back and stared at him, shifting from foot to foot.

No doubt she weighed the consequences of entering an unknown place with a stranger. He wanted to assure her, to tell her about Lily, but the words wouldn't come. Finally, he settled on, "You are safe with me."

She tugged his greatcoat closer around her and fingered the wool. When she met his eyes again, they had softened, and the corner of her mouth curled up in a tiny smile. She nodded. "You're right. I need to warm up. Thank you for the use of your coat. You must be cold, also."

He'd stand outside in the snow for days to have her look at him like that, with a light in her eyes. As if she trusted him to care for her. It made his heart give a solid thump.

Christian placed his hand on her lower back and guided her up the steps toward the door. He knocked, and moments later, Gabriel's butler answered.

"My Lord Hawthorne. It is good to see you," he said.

Bellamy's brows went up, and she glanced at him, no doubt wondering about the use of the Hawthorne name when he'd just told her he was an Albury. He cursed himself for not giving his title. This was why he avoided social interactions. He never said the right thing and always confused whomever he was speaking with.

Christian avoided her gaze and tipped his chin at the other man, then ushered her inside. The narrow entry hall had marble floors and a large, gilded mirror, with doors leading off to the drawing room and dining room. Gabriel's butler helped Bellamy out of the too-large great coat without a hint of surprise at her attire and took Christian's hat and gloves.

"Is Rothden in?" he asked.

"Yes, my lord," the butler replied.

"I consider it a special occasion when you drag yourself out of that bloody workshop to call upon me." Gabriel's voice rang out as he descended the stairs with a wide grin. Though he was a year younger than Christian, from the moment they met, Gabriel had felt like his older brother and often teased him like one as well.

Affection swelled in his chest. Gabriel would help him with the loss of his money. The man was brilliant when it came to finances. "It's good to see you, Rothden."

"It has been too long," he replied.

Beside him, Christian saw Bellamy stand straighter and offer a practiced smile that didn't reach her eyes. Most women offered him the same look at social events—polite, uncomfortable...*bored*. It made him want to see that soft light in her eyes again.

Rothden turned to her.

Christian hovered his hand over her back. He wanted to touch her again, and that surprised him. "Rothden, may I present *Bellamy Bennett*." He emphasized her name so that Gabriel would grasp the connection to Lily. "Bellamy, this is Lord Rothden. Or Rothden, if you prefer."

"Nice to meet you," she said.

Rothden's lips parted but nothing came out. He stilled at the introduction and stared at her.

Her cheeks flushed a little as the moment drew out longer than was comfortable. It occurred to Christian that it was rather nice not to be the one being socially inept for once.

He cleared his throat.

Rothden tore his gaze away and looked at him. "Bellamy?" he asked.

Christian nodded, answering Gabriel's unspoken question. This was his wife's sister.

"I don't want to trouble you," she said. "I can go." She turned to Christian. "Thank you for your help. I-I've warmed up." She made for the door.

Before Christian could stop her, Rothden spoke up.

"Miss Bennett, wait. Don't go. I think there is someone to whom you should speak."

Her eyebrows winged up. "Who?" she asked.

"My wife. Please, stay and join us for tea," Rothden said and gestured to the drawing room. He nodded to the butler who bowed and hurried up the stairs.

She looked uncertain.

"You're safe here," Christian murmured. It was the only reassurance he could think to give.

With only the briefest hesitation, Bellamy nodded and allowed them to escort her to the drawing room.

As usual, a fire crackled in the hearth, warming the elegant space. Christian guided her to one of the brocade chairs set close to the fireplace.

She let out the softest sigh and leaned a little closer to the heat.

He smiled, feeling as if he'd accomplished something monumental by gaining enough of her trust to assist her.

"Thank you for letting me warm up," she said to Rothden, who stood near the sofa. "You said I should speak to your wife?"

Gabriel's lips twitched.

Before anyone could reply, Gabriel's wife barreled into the room in a flash of green satin.

"Oh my God!" Lily cried.

Bellamy turned at the commotion. "Lily?" she whispered, rising to her feet. "Is that...*you*?"

Her older sister panted, no doubt from running down the

stairs, and launched herself into Bellamy's arms, nearly knocking her back into the chair.

"I think we should give them some time," Gabriel said.

Christian nodded, though he found himself loathe to leave Bellamy's side. He forced his attention to the reason he came. He clenched his teeth, thinking about Dale and his treachery. "I called today to get your advice. Finding Ms. Bennett at your door was quite the surprise."

"For all of us." The two men stepped into the hall.

"With Bellamy here, will you attend Lady Barlowe's ball this evening?"

Gabriel grinned. "Hoping to avoid it? Now that Bellamy has arrived, I imagine my wife might want to stay in. That is not to say that you must remain locked in your workshop for the evening. Why not go and dance with a few young ladies?"

He grimaced. "You're cruel."

Gabriel laughed and led Christian up the stairs to his study at the back of the townhouse.

He'd been in this room many times over the years and the dark wainscoting and light-yellow walls felt a bit like home.

He took the seat across the desk from Gabriel and considered what to tell his friend. In the end, only the truth would suffice. No matter how humiliating it was to admit that he'd allowed someone else to run his estate. That he didn't know enough to do so on his own.

"My steward, William Dale, has made a substantial effort to clean me out," he said.

Gabriel sat forward with a frown. "Pardon?"

Christian rubbed the back of his neck, then told his oldest friend of his meetings with the solicitors and banker. "I'm ashamed to say that I didn't pay attention to the accounts as I should. It was easier to let someone else bother with the whole business. I wanted to work on my projects." He ducked his head. "I thought the estate would be better off with someone who knew what they were doing."

"Your father did not teach you how to properly keep the Huntington estate sound. That is his failing, not yours."

"When the title fell to me, it was my responsibility to learn."

"You were a young man who'd gone through a traumatic experience." Gabriel's eyes narrowed. "If your father were any kind of a man, he would have been there to deal with the issue."

Christian looked away. He didn't want to think about that time.

"Regardless, what's done is done," Gabriel said. "I'll teach you what you need to know. I should have done so long ago."

"It wasn't your responsibility—"

"You're as close as a brother, Christian. I take care of what is mine. Let me help you. We'll go over your accounts and make some new investments."

Christian's heart warmed. Gabriel cast no judgment upon him for failing to properly manage his entitlement. Once again, he chose to stand beside him and help when Christian needed it most. He was so grateful to the man.

"What will you do about the money Dale has?" Gabriel asked.

Christian clenched his fist. "I intend to find him and shake every copper out of his pockets. Then send him to prison."

"What if he is no longer in London?"

Christian's stomach knotted with worry. "Then I shall hunt him down."

BELLAMY COULDN'T REMEMBER standing, but Lily was there, wearing a green satin dress straight out of a period movie, and wrapping her up in a tight hug. Nothing felt real, not even her sister's warm breaths that skated over her shoulder.

Lily was much shorter, with an hourglass figure that she envied. She was practical and thrifty, whereas Bellamy could be flighty and didn't hesitate to spend money on something she wanted. They couldn't be more different, and that had caused hundreds of arguments in their youth. Especially after the accident that left them orphaned.

How was Lily here? *Was* Lily here? Had she hit her head somewhere? Bellamy ran her fingers through her hair, feeling her scalp. It didn't hurt anywhere. "Is this real?"

Lily grinned up at her, eyes wet with unshed tears. "It's real. I can't believe you're here."

All the things she wanted to say, the fear she'd felt when she couldn't reach her sister, the worry and guilt as she stood in Lily's efficiency apartment, all froze on her tongue. Nothing made sense. "I don't understand." That was an understatement of enormous magnitude. She couldn't tear her eyes off Lily. Then Rothden's words from the hall rushed back. "Wait. His *wife*?"

Lily glanced over her shoulder as the men exited the room. She blushed, and a soft look entered her eyes. "I have so much to tell you, but yes, it's true. I'm married to Gabriel."

"He said his name was Rothden."

"That's his title. He's Gabriel Hawthorne, the Earl of Rothden."

Bellamy choked on a breath. "You married an earl?" She shook her head, unable to process that. "How are you married? How long have you known him? Why didn't you mention him the last time we talked? Why are you dressed like that? *And where the hell have you been, Lily?*"

"Maybe we should sit down."

"I don't want to sit down. I want answers."

Lily crossed her arms over her chest and tilted her chin up, an expression that never failed to rile Bellamy's anger. "Well, you're not getting answers until you stop yelling at me."

"Damn it, Lily. We've been worried. I flew to Goddamn *Kentucky* to try to find you when I couldn't reach you. *Archer* even tried to call you. The least you can do is tell me what the hell is going on."

Lily cocked an eyebrow and pressed her lips together.

Bellamy growled out a frustrated noise, stomped to the nearest chair, and sat. Absolutely nothing had changed since they were teenagers. As she stared at the stubborn look on her older sister's face, a mental playlist of all their worst arguments flashed in her mind. Leaving for college early because she couldn't wait to get away from Lily's stupid rules. Feeling like she was a bad sister anytime she didn't take Lily's calls after they fought, and finally taking responsibility for her part in those tumultuous years. She'd intended to try to restore their relationship. Right now, they'd never felt farther apart.

Lily uncrossed her arms and took the seat next to Bellamy, then reached over to squeeze her hand. "I'm sorry. I promise I'll tell you everything. I just…I didn't think I'd see you again, Bells. I can't believe you're here."

"Where is *here*? That man, Christian, said London. But that's not possible. I was standing in your apartment an hour ago." Wasn't she? She pressed a hand to her forehead. How the hell did she get from Kentucky to London? Was she really *in* London?

Lily smiled. "I'm surprised he said that much. It's true, though. We're in London. You were at my apartment?"

"Yes. God, I've been worried sick because I couldn't reach you. Why didn't you bring your phone with you? Why did you leave it and your purse in your apartment? I was starting to think you'd been kidnapped. Your creepy landlord said a man had been hanging out in the parking lot waiting for you."

Her sister wrinkled her nose. "I'm so glad I don't have to see either one of them ever again," she murmured. Then louder, "Leaving was…unexpected. I didn't have time to grab anything. Not that it would have made a difference."

"You could have at least called when you got here." Bellamy fumed. Lily sat there, looking unconcerned about the fact that she'd been going out of her mind with worry. "After all the times you've called me irresponsible, I can't believe you wouldn't reach out to me to at least tell me where you were going. Or invite me to your wedding." Her voice cracked. "I know that things have been strained between us. We're still family though. Are we on such bad terms that you don't bother to tell us that you're engaged and then married?"

"Uh… there's something you don't know—"

"It seems there are a lot of things I don't know," she snapped.

Lily stood and planted her hands on her hips. "If you would let me speak for a moment, I might be able to explain it to you. Although you're so stubborn that you probably won't listen anyway, no matter what I say." She stomped over to a writing desk, grabbed a newspaper, and marched back.

They glared at each other.

Bellamy looked away first. This wasn't how she wanted to reconcile with her sister. Bickering always made things worse. "Okay," she said after a few long seconds of tense silence. "I didn't come looking for you just to argue, Lily. I'm really relieved that you're okay. I'll listen."

Lily relaxed tense shoulders and nodded. She held out the newspaper.

Bellamy took it and scanned the front page. The stories and headlines looked like they were from another time, with small text in long columns along the page, but the paper itself didn't show any discoloration at all. It could have been printed yesterday. "What is this? It looks like a movie prop." With the antique furniture and everyone wearing period clothing, it was like she'd stumbled into one of those reenactment places. Nothing made any sense. Especially how she came to be here in the first place.

"Do you remember when Mom used to read us stories and fairytales at bedtime?" her sister asked.

Bellamy nodded.

"We've fallen down the rabbit hole, Bells."

"What does that mean?" Although, now that she thought about it, she was beginning to feel like she'd woken up in an unknown land full of people speaking in riddles.

Lily tapped her finger over the small print in the center just beneath the newspaper name. "That's today's date."

Friday, April 29, 1814. "Uh… okay." How was she supposed to respond to that? Lily said the words as if they were fact, but that was impossible. There had to be more to all of this. Whatever *this* was.

"Bells, as crazy as it sounds, we traveled through time. We're in London, yes, but not the London of *our* time."

"I don't—" She couldn't tear her eyes away from the date printed on the newspaper. It was impossible. Time travel only existed in fiction. Did that mean that she wasn't really here with Lily?

She tried to recall her last lucid moments. She'd been in Lily's shoebox of an apartment… holding… a little red egg that chimed. That's right, it was a decorative clock, and when she opened it, white light blinded her. Had she fallen and hit her head? Was she in a coma? God, she hoped not. She shuddered. Who knew what creepy Dennis might do if he found her unconscious? And Archer would never let her hear the end of it if he had to leave his house to visit her in the hospital because she'd tripped.

Lily put her hand on Bellamy's arm. She could feel the warmth of her sister's touch. "I can prove it. There are no cars. No power lines or cell towers. No airplanes. No electricity." She huffed a laugh. "No *toilets* as we know them."

Bellamy dragged her gaze from the newspaper and truly looked at Lily. Her sister wore a sage green satin dress with an empire waist and small puffed sleeves. Her hair was pinned up in soft curls.

And the men—Christian, and the earl Lily said was her husband—wore cravats. No one wore cravats anymore. All their clothing looked straight out of a movie.

She looked around at the room filled with antique furniture. She didn't spot a wall plug, lamp, or anything. Not even a USB cord. Out the window, she saw another horse and carriage rumble past. If this was a coma-induced dream, it was pretty vivid. But did coma patients dream?

"I know it sounds impossible," Lily said. "I didn't believe it at first either. I thought I was in a coma after hitting my head on the bookshelf. But I can smell the flowers in the garden and taste the food."

Bellamy remembered the brown stain on the side of the bookshelf in Lily's apartment. She'd been right—it was Lily's blood. As she considered what that might mean, she caught the scent of the burning logs. They smelled so real. She'd also felt Lily's hand on her arm moments ago and it felt the same as it had their entire lives. She'd dreamed plenty, but her dreams had never felt this realistic. "How?" How could this have happened? How could it be true?

And how did she get home if it were true?

"You must have found the little, red enamel clock. It looked a bit like a Fabergé egg."

Bellamy nodded.

"It was broken when I found it. I thought it belonged to my boss, so I tried to fix it for him." Lily chuckled. "Worked better than I expected. The next thing I knew, bright light spilled out of it. I tripped, and when I opened my eyes, I was here, in this time. Gabriel's sister, Violet, found me and brought me back to their house. Eventually, Gabriel and I fell in love."

Eventually? "You've only been missing for two weeks." Bellamy stared at her sister. This couldn't be true. Lily was crazy and somehow pulled her into the delusion as well.

Except...looking at her sister's face, she knew that Lily believed what she said. And that egg...the light *had* poured from it just like Lily described...

"Time travel," her sister replied. "I arrived in October last year. I've been here for six months."

Six months! Her head swam. She couldn't stay here that long. She had to be in France to start her new contract next week. Or rather, next week—plus a couple of centuries. She rubbed her temple, feeling a headache forming. "You couldn't find a way home?"

Lily pressed her lips together.

Bellamy froze as understanding dawned. "You had a way back home and you didn't take it?" Her words came out harsher than she'd intended, but dammit, she'd been worried about Lily. "What about me and Archer? If this hadn't happened—" she waved her arm around her—"we wouldn't know where you had gone. You *vanished*. I was going to file a missing persons report!"

"Bells, I couldn't risk it," Lily said softly. She placed a hand on her stomach. "If I returned to tell you, I might not have been able to get back to Gabriel and I couldn't leave him. You and Archer are doing fine without me. We barely talk. You...you would have moved on."

"I can't believe this." Bellamy rose and stalked to the window. She had no idea what to say. She *still* wasn't even entirely sure she believed her sister. The idea seemed too fantastical to be real. She crossed her arms over her chest, considering everything Lily told her. Outside, another horse-drawn carriage rattled by. Bellamy frowned, remembering what Lily said about proof.

"There are no cars. No power lines or cell towers. No airplanes."

She craned her head to look down both sides of the street, and then up to the cloudy gray sky. There were no cars parked by the curbs. No wires, or telephone poles. Nothing that resembled modern-day London. Even the people walking by the house were dressed in a similar fashion to Lily, Gabriel, and Christian... like extras out of a *Pride and Prejudice* movie.

And there was a haze of smog, as if many fires burned against the winter chill. Like the one blazing in the fireplace behind her, heating the room in which she stood.

A soft scratch at the door preceded the butler who entered with a tray laden with a tea service. Another man followed with a selection of sandwiches, breads, and jams. The fragrant smell of the tea and baked goods filled the room and her stomach growled.

Wait... she could smell everything. The things she heard and touched, all felt real. God, was this really happening?

"I know it's hard to understand," Lily said. "And I'm sorry that I chose not to return. I didn't want to worry you, but it was inevitable." Her sister blushed, and what Bellamy recognized as a lovesick smile spread over her face. "I-I've never been happier than I am with Gabriel."

Bellamy's heart sank when she heard the slight wobble in her sister's voice. "I'm glad you're happy, Lily. And I want you to be happy. You know that, right?"

"I do."

"I just...I don't even know what to think right now."

Her sister gave her another, smaller smile. "Come have tea with me, and we'll talk."

Bellamy returned to her seat and accepted a cup of tea and a sandwich. "I have a modeling contract starting in France soon. I must get back. I can't stay here."

Lily was silent a moment, then said, "You didn't bring the little egg clock with you when you came here, did you?"

"I-I don't think so." Her stomach tensed. "Should I have?"

"It would have been easier. The clock is what caused the time travel."

Bellamy's heart dropped to her toes. "If I left the clock at your apartment, how can I return?"

"There is a way. Christian made the clock."

Christian. Bellamy glanced at the door to the hall. "The handsome man from outside?"

"He's brilliant. The machines he makes are unlike anything you've ever seen. Honestly, that little clock, in all its intricate detail, looks like a wind-up toy compared to some of the other things he's created."

The panic Bellamy had felt when she'd suddenly found herself on an unknown street had consumed her until Christian arrived. His steady presence had settled her nerves, even though he hadn't spoken much. She remembered his flushed cheeks and the way he averted his eyes often. Living in Manhattan, she'd learned to be aware of the smallest details when unknown men approached and even kept pepper spray in her pocket. But Christian hadn't leered at her or made her uncomfortable. He'd shown concern when he offered his cloak and when he hesitantly took her into his arms when her world was spinning, and she'd needed a hug. He'd made her feel safe.

Her memory sharpened to focus on the details she'd not noticed initially. He'd been quite tall. Easily a few inches over six feet, which she found appealing. His blond hair curled slightly under his hat and his jaw had more than a five o'clock shadow. His cravat had been crooked, as if he'd tugged on it.

But it had been his eyes that had made her trust him. He had kind eyes, she decided. It was that and his care not to scare her when he slowly wrapped her in his coat that made her trust him that little bit. If she hadn't, she never would have found Lily.

"He made the clock?" *How intriguing.*

"He was constructing it when we first met. Can you imagine how strange it was to have used it to travel back in time, only to find that he hadn't even completed it when I arrived?" Lily gave a light laugh. "By the time I realized that he had the clock, I was already in love with Gabriel. I couldn't leave him." She looked at Bellamy. "I didn't want to."

"Christian has another clock?" This was getting confusing.

Lily laughed. "No. The clock he made a couple of months ago when I arrived is the same clock that brought us here. It was locked in the back of my boss's desk for at least a couple of decades if not nearly two centuries."

"Where is the clock that Christian made in… in *this* time?" If the clock was the reason for the time travel, then she needed it to get home. Presuming everything Lily said was true—and it was beginning to all seem very real, as crazy as that sounded—then she'd accidentally left her time travel ticket home in Lily's apartment. Her only chance to return was the clock in this time. God, if she didn't have a headache before, she did now.

Lily pursed her lips. "It might be here in London. Or it might be at Christian's country estate."

He has a country estate? She pushed the thought aside. *Don't get distracted, Bells. What matters is the clock.*

"Even if it isn't here in London, he should be able to retrieve it quickly. The roads are cleared of most of the snow. He could probably have it back within a week," Lily mused.

A week? That would be too long! Her panicked thoughts were interrupted by a male's voice.

"Have what back?" came from the doorway.

Bellamy looked up as Rothden—Gabriel—entered the room. She peered behind him, but Christian wasn't with him. Her sister rose and went into his arms, rising on her toes for a kiss.

Gabriel tucked a curl behind her ear and smiled softly down at her. He was very handsome, with his dark hair and hazel eyes. Not to mention the way his dark jacket accentuated his wide shoulders. But it was the look of love on his face that Bellamy noticed most. He clearly adored Lily and that settled a frisson of worry she'd been feeling for her sister.

"Where's Christian?" Lily asked.

"He departed and asked me to pass on his apologies to you ladies."

"Oh." Bellamy stood and cast a nervous glance at Lily. *Now what?*

"We wanted to ask him about the clock," her sister said. "Bellamy will need it to go home."

Gabriel gave a slow nod. "He has an urgent matter to tend to. I expect we shall see him at our dinner party in a few days. I'll send word to him about the clock. In the meantime, you should rest, love."

A few days! Her stomach dropped. She could only hope that however this time travel worked, she'd be able to get home before she had to be in France.

Lily rested her head on his shoulder and turned to Bellamy. "Maybe we can spend some time together since you're here?"

The hopeful note in her sister's voice tugged at the guilt

Bellamy carried over their relationship. "I would love that. I've missed you, Lily."

"I missed you too, Bellamy. I'm so glad that you're here."

Bellamy was glad too, in a way. If they were in the past, and Lily intended to stay here, then this would be her only opportunity to mend their relationship. She intended to make the most of it. And then, she would go home.

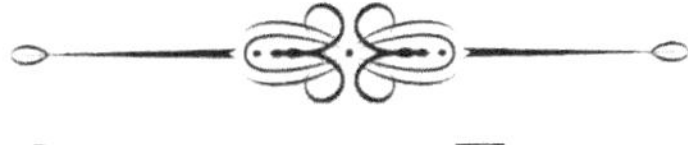

Chapter Four

"Forgive me, my lord." The maid's voice trembled. "I didna know he meant to steal from ya. If I had, ye know I'd never..."

Christian dragged his gaze away from the overturned tables and empty drawers in his workshop to see tears brimming in the young woman's eyes.

"Please don't dismiss me," she whispered.

"You went directly against his lordship's express orders," Malcolm said, yanking down on his waistcoat to straighten it as he glared at the girl. Despite his obvious irritation, the dark locks waving over his forehead hadn't budged. "You should be put out on your ear."

Christian gripped the bridge of his nose as his butler yelled at the girl. This was a disaster. He'd directed all staff to refuse Dale entry to his townhouse and for some reason, the chambermaid had allowed the man in. Christian returned from calling upon one of Dale's previous references to find his workshop in shambles. Worse, the man had stolen one of his inventions—the silver music box he meant to sell.

"My lord?" Malcolm said. His tone indicated that he'd called him at least once before.

Christian returned his attention to the maid. Tears stained her ruddy cheeks and turned her nose red. "What did he say that prompted you to ignore my orders?"

She darted a quick look at Malcolm, then ducked her head. "He…he gave me a guinea for it. Said there'd be no trouble. Please, my lord. My ma is sick. I-I ca-can't…" Fresh tears flooded her eyes and dripped off her chin.

Blast. He couldn't be responsible for putting a young woman out on the street when she had an ill mother. He waved a hand towards the door. "Go. Return to your duties."

Malcolm gaped at him, but Christian couldn't corral his rioting thoughts into something that might seem a reasonable explanation. Not that he needed to give one.

The maid swiped the tears from her cheeks, bobbed a curtsy, and scurried from the room.

All that remained now was to clean up the mess and verify nothing else was missing. He stared at the tools, gears, and books scattered across the floor. Christian grabbed the back of his desk chair and righted it. Beneath, he spotted one of the silver rose petals from his current project. It was the only one he could see. Not even the pedestal base or crystal vase was visible. "The bloody arse," he grumbled.

"Pardon, my lord?" Malcolm said.

He lifted the delicate petal. "He stole my current project as well."

Malcolm pursed his lips. "Silver sells for a fine price."

Christian squeezed the petal in his fist until the edges pressed into his skin. He scanned the room again. What could Dale have been after in here? He started to ask Malcolm for his thoughts when the half-empty shelf above his workbench caught his eye. He stilled, and it felt as if he couldn't draw air.

"What is it, my lord?" Malcolm asked.

The egg clock that somehow shifted time and brought Lily—and now Bellamy—here, was missing. A muscle throbbed in his jaw. It wasn't enough for Dale to steal almost eighty thousand pounds? He also had to steal his automatons? And the clock… the note he'd received from Gabriel yesterday indicated that Bellamy wanted it to return to her time. How could he face her after this?

"He stole my work, Malcolm. He stole money and my work. I'll see him hang for this." Christian focused on his butler, fists clenched. "It is unlikely that Dale will return, but in the event that he comes here again, inform the staff that anyone who allows him into this house will be dismissed immediately without references."

"Yes, my lord. Shall I have the maids tidy up?"

"Yes, but under your supervision. I also need a full inventory of what remains."

Malcolm agreed and Christian left him to it. In truth, he couldn't stand there another moment looking at what remained of his sanctuary. His stomach churned and his heart pounded as he took the stairs two at a time up to his bed chamber.

The visit to Lord Chamberlain earlier in the day had not delivered the results he'd expected. Had William Dale somehow known that Christian wouldn't check his references? How was that possible? Regardless, two of the letters of reference he'd given Christian were fraudulent. He hadn't worked for either man, and neither of them had any idea where Dale might be.

That left the last reference, a man Christian had no intention of speaking to, even in these circumstances.

He entered his bedchamber and undressed. Gabriel expected Christian to attend their small dinner party tonight. If he hurried to change his attire, he could meet with his friend before supper. Now more than ever, he needed Gabriel's financial expertise. He couldn't bear the idea of letting some of his staff go, despite his words to Malcolm moments ago. Many had been with his family since Christian was a lad. They shouldn't have to suffer for his failings.

Quentin would have made a better earl. His younger brother had shown an early aptitude for numbers and a keen interest in the estate. Christian had neither, but as the eldest, the title was meant for him. Much to his father's disappointment. Even if Quentin had lived, the duty would still be Christian's.

He vowed to do better in the future. To learn from Gabriel all that he could in order to improve the lives of the people dependent upon him. He would do it so Quentin would have been proud, even if their father would not.

Within the hour, Christian arrived at Gabriel's home in Mayfair.

"Lord Rothden is in the drawing room with the ladies," the butler said as he took Christian's hat and great coat.

He entered the drawing room and froze for only a second before Bellamy Bennett crashed into his arms.

She and Violet, Gabriel's younger sister, were dancing around as if they were at a grand ball, giggling like children. Violet spun Bellamy the moment he entered the drawing room, causing her to fall against him.

He sputtered in surprise and wrapped his arms around her to keep her upright.

She laughed as she found her footing and stood.

The delicate sound soothed the raw edge of his irritation over a wasted day of searching for Dale. Christian tried to steady his breath that suddenly felt too fast. "I do apologize, Ms. Bennett," he said.

And then he realized that his hands were on her back, holding her to his chest. He moved them, intending to release her, but instead slid them down her upper arms, feeling the satiny skin beneath. His heart pounded to match his breathing and his cock hardened, leaving him a bit light-headed.

"It's my fault," Bellamy said. Her smile was wide and carefree. "Violet was teaching me the Gallopade."

"Ah." How should he reply to that? Having her this close muddled his thoughts. She stood in the circle of his arms, not quite pressed against his chest, and every breath he drew smelled of her. Like lilacs and a deeper, more appealing scent he couldn't quite identify. Her glossy blonde hair was curled and pinned into fashionable ringlets, and she wore a gown as dark blue as her eyes. He couldn't help but stare.

Her lips parted as she stared back. Then she extracted herself from his arms and sunk into a curtsey for Violet. "Thank you for the dance, Violet."

Violet giggled and curtseyed back.

Gabriel appeared beside him and clapped him on the shoulder. "You're early. Supper doesn't begin for another hour."

Christian flushed when he realized that Bellamy hadn't moved away to sit with Lily. She remained standing close, looking at him expectantly. Damn, she was so beautiful that he forgot himself. He forced himself to look away and turned to Gabriel. He cleared his throat. "I...more has happened. With—with Dale."

He glanced at Bellamy and edged away the slightest bit. He didn't want to discuss his current misfortune in front of her. What if she laughed at him? Ridiculed him for not being able to manage his own affairs as any earl should? His stomach churned at the thought. Then he chastised himself for being a fool. Her opinion should not matter. He refused to examine why it did. "If we could adjourn to your office, I would like to speak to you before dinner."

"Of course. Ladies, if you will excuse us for a few minutes?" Gabriel crossed the room to press a kiss to Lily's cheek before he guided Christian to the stairs.

Christian looked back and saw Bellamy watching him from just inside the drawing room. His chest went tight, and he resisted the urge to adjust his trousers. It was disconcerting. He'd never reacted to a woman like this.

She won't want to stay. Even if she did, why would she want a man who couldn't form a coherent sentence around her? He sighed.

Gabriel shot him a concerned frown. "Are you well?"

No. "Oh yes. Quite."

They entered the office and Christian took his usual chair on the opposite side of Gabriel's carved wood desk. "What's happened? Did you find Dale?"

"No. But I did discover that two of his references were fraudulent."

"That's troubling. How many did he provide?"

"Three."

Gabriel nodded. "Planning to call upon the third?"

"Ah…no."

His friend sat forward. "You *do* intend to recover what money you can?"

"I do."

"Then why not call—"

"It's Shelby Wainsright."

Gabriel stared at him and then slowly sat back in his chair. "I thought Wainsright was abroad."

"Dale provided a letter indicating he'd worked for Wainsright as steward from 1803 to 1808. The others were dated more recently."

"Did you know he worked for Wainsright when you hired him?"

Christian looked away, unable to meet his eyes. His throat felt thick. "I confess that I didn't look at the letters. I saw Lord Chamberlain's name on the first and considered that enough of a reference. Although now, it seems that he never worked for the man." He felt so foolish. Pathetic. And ashamed.

Gabriel nodded. A heavy silence settled between them as memories of Eton returned in bloody detail. Neither of them would forget the harsh treatment they'd received at Wainsright's hand. Finally, Gabriel asked, "Would you like me to speak with Shelby?"

"No." The word came out sharper than Christian intended, edged with fear. "If I must speak with him, I will. First, I shall try another avenue. Besides, that is not the worst of the news. When I returned home today, I discovered that one of my maids allowed Dale into the house. He ransacked my *sanctuary*. My tools, my sketches…everything is in disarray."

His friend huffed a laugh. "It was not that orderly, to begin with."

Christian gave him a weak glare. "It is perfectly ordered to where I can find things."

Gabriel waved for him to continue, though looked to be holding back a grin.

"He stole a few of my inventions, Gabriel. The music box I meant to sell to the museum to increase my quid, the silver rose I am… *was* currently working on, and…" He rubbed the back of his neck. "The egg clock."

"Good Christ. The time travel clock?" Gabriel's dark eyebrows rose.

"The same."

His friend scrubbed a hand down his face, a concerned look entering his hazel eyes. "Bellamy needs the clock to return to her time."

Christian ducked his head, feeling the flush rise on his cheeks again. He looked down at his lap and smoothed a hand over his pant leg. "I will make every effort to retrieve it. However, I'm afraid that this more recent theft has put me in the uncomfortable position of possibly having to turn staff away. I could request a bank draft, but I must be assured there will be enough money coming in to pay it back." He returned his attention to his friend, who returned his gaze.

Gabriel traced his hand over the edge of the desk. "Before you told me you intended to sell the automaton, I had conceived of another idea, although I do not know how open you will be to it."

Christian sat forward. "Tell me, please. I can't bear the thought of losing my staff because of my own failings. People should not have to suffer because I'm not smart enough to be an earl."

"Christian, you're the smartest man I've ever known. The objects you create could rival the Renaissance men. You can apply yourself to a task and learn it faster than anyone."

"It may not be fast enough."

"It will be, my friend. Lease part of your townhome for the remainder of the Season. Twisden and Granville would love to get out of the Albany. While their lodgings are adequate, they can't carouse as they would prefer in the gentlemen's apartments."

He cringed. "I don't think I could live with them. Even my workshop wouldn't provide enough solace. Not two months ago, the pair were attempting to convince me to host a midnight supper for two dozen of their friends, after which, they intended to have a number of ladybirds visit for 'dessert.' I shudder to think of what those two will do once they have the run of the place."

Gabriel laughed. "Then stay here with us. We have plenty of room. You can lease your townhouse to Twisden and Granville, recoup some much-needed quid, and find Dale."

It was an ideal solution. The lease would bring in enough money to cover the estate's immediate expenses and allow him time to find Dale. If he couldn't get the funds returned, then with Gabriel's assistance, he would have a new investment or two to bring in additional quid.

His thoughts turned to the lovely Miss Bennett. He had trouble speaking to a woman at the best of times. Could he live under the same roof with her when being in her presence made his mind blank? What if she wanted to talk to him when they sat for tea in the drawing room or at breakfast in the mornings?

What if she demanded to know where the clock was?

He suddenly felt as if he couldn't draw a full breath, and his heart hammered in his ears.

As if Gabriel could read his thoughts, he said, "I will give you the two open rooms in the basement for those times when you need solitude. You can bring your tools with you and continue your projects here."

His chest went tight for an entirely different reason. Gabriel knew him better than anyone and accepted him like no other, not even his parents. "Thank you," he murmured.

He would make this work. He'd lease his family townhome,

find Dale, and have a place to retreat to when his brain crowded with ideas and the need to create the intricate mechanisms that made him happy. If Miss Bennett pestered him and he began to feel awkward, he would simply avoid her.

"DID YOU SEE the look on Christian's face when you fell into him?" Violet asked with a giggle the moment Gabriel and Christian left the room. She danced over to Bellamy's side and clung to her upper arm. "I don't think I've ever seen him turn quite that shade of red."

Bellamy's heart still pounded from the dance and the collision. When Christian had wrapped his arms around her to steady her, she'd felt solid chest muscles beneath her hands and in his arms. It surprised her. She hadn't really considered what might be hiding underneath his clothes before, but pressed to his body as she had been, she'd been intimately aware of him, and that quickened the desire to find out more. She'd felt as flustered as he seemed to be and had quickly turned her attention back to Violet until the men left.

"Maybe he likes you," Violet sing-songed.

She grinned down at the young woman. In the four days that she'd been in this time, she'd enjoyed coming to know Violet. Gabriel's little sister was striking, with her chocolate brown curls and amber eyes, but it was her excitement for life that made her sparkle. She radiated a vibrant energy that Bellamy envied, even if it leaned a little toward mischief. She wouldn't be at all surprised if Violet hadn't purposely twirled her into Christian just to see their reactions. There was a bit of a matchmaker in that girl; finding a husband was something she discussed often enough, anyway.

"You know how shy he is," Lily admonished. "He probably wanted to bolt for his carriage."

"I also know how lonely he must be. He needs a wife. He needs to be as happy as you and Gabriel," Violet said as she tugged Bellamy over to the sofa with her to sit across from Lily.

"Just because you want to find a match this Season, doesn't mean *everyone* wants to get married," Lily said.

"Whyever not?"

Bellamy laughed at Violet's bewilderment. As if she couldn't comprehend a person not wanting to marry. "Not all marriages are happy, Violet. If a person's parents were unhappy together, they often don't want to chance their heart on a relationship only to find the same heartache."

Violet leaned back to look at her. "Were your parents happy? I don't think I ever asked."

They had been. The words stuck in Bellamy's throat. She looked at Lily for help, but her sister had fixed her attention on the teacup in her hand as if it were the most important thing in the world. Maybe, at that moment, it was. For Bellamy, it was hard to think about her parents. She could only imagine it was harder for Lily.

Bellamy's memories of that time were probably skewed. She'd only been fifteen when they'd died on their way home from a charity event. That night changed all their lives and not for the better. So much had happened in eight years. It felt like a lifetime ago.

"I believe they were," Lily murmured, finally.

The familiar ache pressed against Bellamy's ribs. She couldn't linger on thoughts of their parents for long. It hurt too much. "Will any of your suitors be at dinner tonight?" she asked to change the subject.

Violet rolled her eyes. "No. If it were up to Gabriel, I wouldn't have a suitor until I was in my dotage."

"You know that's not true, Vi," Lily said. "He wants you to find the *right* man. Not the first man who comes calling."

"He gave the first man a bloody nose. How am I supposed to find suitors if they think they'll be assaulted by Gabriel for showing an interest?"

Lily gave Violet a pointed look. "Was that before or after you slapped the man and stomped on his foot? I forget."

"I have no idea what you're going on about," Violet sniffed.

Lily shook her head and turned to Bellamy. "Dinner tonight is more for us. To practice our etiquette and social skills before they throw us to the wolves at Lady Parling's ball in a couple of days."

"You'll both be charming," Violet declared.

"Only if we're prepared. The guests will be arriving soon. We should change for dinner." Lily set her cup down on the small table and led them upstairs to the bedrooms.

Bellamy wasn't concerned in the slightest. She'd spent years going to elite parties and could navigate the social strictures with ease. The hardest part for her would be adapting to a life without technology, even temporarily. How could these people survive?

Over the last several days, Lily and Violet had given her a crash course in society etiquette and dancing. They had also gone shopping for gowns and shoes and nightgowns and...all the things a woman would need to blend in with the Ton. She'd tried to protest that she wouldn't need more than one or two dresses. Once Christian brought the clock, she'd be going home. Neither woman would listen.

She was learning that women in this era changed their clothes up to four times a day, depending on the activity or what the clock read. There were dresses for the morning, dresses for walking, dresses for mealtimes, and dresses for balls. And all of them needed to be fitted properly. But Bellamy was several inches taller than both of the other women, not to mention thinner from modeling. The dress she'd borrowed the first day had hung on her frame like a short sack. Now, however, she had three new gowns—carefully created for her figure—and four more on the way.

The fashion lover in her was delighted. In some ways, modeling was like getting to play dress up as she had as a little girl. It was that aspect—and the travel—that drew her to the career.

Now, she got to wear gorgeous gowns from the past. The time she'd spent with Lily and her sister-in-law had been fun. Violet loved shopping as much as Bellamy, and that kept the mood lively.

Bellamy snuck a glance at her sister as they reached the third floor. She was happy that they would have that memory of going to the dressmaker in the years to come. But it still worried her that they hadn't spoken of anything too serious during the past four days. To be honest, Bellamy was afraid to broach the harder conversation that they needed to have. Bringing up memories of past arguments would ruin this fragile interlude of happiness they'd found. She had to at some point, though. She was leaving as soon as she had the clock.

Hopefully, Christian would bring it with him tonight. She hadn't had the opportunity to ask after colliding with him in the drawing room, and she had to admit, her thoughts had scattered a bit when she felt those hard muscles beneath his clothes and felt his arms close around her.

Through modeling, she knew hundreds of beautiful, muscled men. So why was this man different? They'd barely spoken and yet, he intrigued her. There was just...something about him besides his good looks and hard body.

"Come, dear Bellamy," Violet said. She linked their arms and pulled Bellamy into her bedroom. "We shall ready ourselves together. Every man at dinner will be in awe of our beauty and wish that they could court us."

She laughed and let Violet lead her to the wardrobe. If she secretly hoped that Christian would find her attractive, she wouldn't admit it aloud.

An hour later, she stood next to him as they waited to enter the dining room with the other guests. He looked mouthwateringly handsome in his dark-blue tailcoat and embroidered waistcoat. Even with a crooked cravat. Seeing it warmed her insides and made her smile. "Allow me?" She turned to him and reached up to indicate his carelessly tied cravat.

Christian gave a small nod and looked away.

She sensed he was embarrassed. "You look very handsome tonight," she said in a low voice meant for him only. This close, she could see his stormy-blue eyes and the little line between his blond eyebrows that seemed to betray a tendency for deep thought. He'd shaven, so his angular jaw was on display beneath nicely curved lips. What it would be like to kiss them? Of course, she wouldn't find out. So, she turned her attention back to his cravat and straightened it for him. He smelled good. Masculine, with the faintest trace of something else beneath, something citrus and spice.

A slight coloring of pink spread over his high cheekbones, and she realized his gaze had dropped to her mouth also. The sight made her heart skip a few beats. Was there more to his flush than shyness? "Thank you. In that crimson gown, you… are bewitching." He cleared his throat.

Her heart thumped harder at his compliment.

The corners of his mouth lifted in a tiny smile.

Before she could summon a reply, another man joined them.

"Come now, Christian. You cannot keep all of the beautiful women to yourself," he said.

Christian gave a soft groan and stepped back to gesture toward the man who'd spoken. "Zeph, may I present Miss Bennett, Lady Rothden's sister. Miss Bennett, this is Lord Zeph Lael."

She turned to him, frustrated with him for interrupting their moment, but found herself looking into eyes so light gray they were almost silver. The man was almost stunningly beautiful with his white hair and a spark of mischief on his face. He stood an inch taller than Christian, and his build was similar. He radiated a vibe of intensity and… something she couldn't quite name.

"Zeph, if you please." He offered his hand with a wink.

Bellamy laid her hand in his, and he brushed his mouth against her knuckles.

His eyes twinkled, then he side-eyed Christian. To make

certain he was looking? Oh, this one was trouble. She pulled her hand away but couldn't quite hide her grin.

"You're a menace," Christian murmured.

Zeph chuckled and then excused himself.

She turned her attention back to Christian. "You seem to know each other well."

"We schooled together." He nodded at the assembled group around them. "It brought us together as friends."

"I'm told you and Gabriel are quite close."

He nodded. "And Zeph, whom I'm…reconsidering."

She laughed.

Christian's gaze dropped to her mouth again.

She swallowed and her belly heated.

Once more, their moment was interrupted, this time by the dinner bell that announced they were to be ushered into the dining room. Bellamy wanted to tell him to forget dinner and follow her into a different room. If only they were in her time; she could easily find out what lay beneath that tailored dinner jacket and trousers. She sighed as he offered his arm and escorted her to dinner.

In addition to Gabriel, Lily, and Violet, five of Gabriel's friends were in attendance, as well as his Aunt Josephine. Bellamy had met her only once during the few days she'd been here. The older woman acted as Violet's chaperone for the Season, though it appeared she was usually either sleeping or calling upon friends. Tonight, she was sleeping.

At the dinner table.

The woman, with her unnaturally red ringlets, white rice-powdered face, and rouge circles on her cheeks, sat to Bellamy's left. Her chin rested on her chest, and she snored softly.

Gabriel sat at the head of the table, with Josephine to his right and Lily to his left. He turned his head at his aunt's snoring and shook his head. Violet, who sat across from Bellamy, gave her an impish grin, then turned to speak to the other woman in attendance, Patience Cradock.

Christian sat stiffly on Bellamy's right. He murmured several words to Zeph, who sat beside him, but otherwise hadn't said anything else to her.

She stirred her ham and leek soup and considered him from beneath her lashes. His hands looked strong, and his nails were neat. She'd always appreciated strong hands on a man. They made him seem...capable. Protective, maybe. Was he? He certainly had seemed that way in the street when she'd first arrived in this century, draping his coat, already warmed from his body, over her shoulders and making sure she was seated next to the fire when they'd gone into the house. It said a lot about his character.

Lily and Violet said he was one of Gabriel's closest friends and spoke often about his automatons. Apparently, her time travel clock was small, compared to some of his larger creations. If that were the case, she'd love to see more. The idea of moving machines created in this century was fascinating.

She waited until there was a lull in his conversation with Zeph, then said, "I never had a chance to thank you for helping me the other day, Mr. Albury. Or...should I call you Lord Huntington?"

The slight flush she'd become accustomed to tinted his cheeks; it was almost imperceptible in the candlelit dining room unless a person was paying close attention. Bellamy was. She noted the light coloring and the quick breath he drew when she said his name.

He turned those stormy eyes to her for only a moment before he looked at the bowl of soup in front of him. "Christian, if you please," he said quietly. "I...prefer not to use my title."

Warmth bloomed in her chest though she couldn't say why. "Call me Bellamy, then. With two 'Miss Bennetts' in the room, it will be simpler."

"Ah, but one Miss Bennett is now Lady Rothden."

Oh. She'd forgotten. Lily was married now. "It's so strange. It feels like I just talked to her a couple of weeks ago. Now she's married and I…" She stopped speaking when it occurred to her that he might not know about Lily and the time travel. It seemed likely that he would, but what if he didn't and thought she was crazy?

"Our world must seem quite different from what you know," he said. He looked at her once more, and she saw understanding in his eyes.

She almost breathed a sigh of relief. "It's amazing. I'm seeing something as it truly is, not what it's been represented to be. Does that make sense? Living in history instead of reading or hearing about it and finding that much is different…and much is the same."

"Quite philosophical."

She fell silent for a moment, afraid she'd insulted him in some way. When he didn't say more, she added, "Lily says that you are an inventor."

He shook his head. "I like to…tinker with things. To pass the time."

"It sounds like more than tinkering from what my sister has said." Bashful *and* humble? Bellamy never would have considered that a sexy combination, but on Christian, with his sweet, flushed cheeks and nervous smile, she found him *very* attractive.

"She's kind."

"What are you working on now?"

His eyebrows rose and he looked surprised that she'd asked. "It's a… a silver rose in a crystal vase. When the mechanism in the base turns, the petals will open, making the rose bloom."

A silver flower that bloomed? If it was anything like she imagined, she wanted one. "That sounds amazing."

"Sadly, it was stolen." He gave his soup a stir, frowning at it.

She'd heard a little about the thefts from Violet. It looked like they troubled him deeply. "You must be very talented," she said, hoping to steer the conversation back onto more pleasant subjects. "Lily said that you also made the clock."

"I…yes." Christian reached for his wine glass and his hand

trembled. Before she could ask if he was all right, he said, "Lily speaks often of you."

Across the table, she saw Lily laugh and place her hand over Gabriel's. A look of intense love filled her face as she gazed at her husband, and a pang of longing hit Bellamy so swiftly that it startled her. She turned back to the man beside her, unwilling to process that feeling just now.

"We haven't seen each other much in the last several years." How much had Lily shared of her life with him? She wanted to ask, but not here. "I've enjoyed spending time with her and Lady Violet."

He nodded and the conversation lapsed again.

Bellamy clasped her fingers together in her lap as her soup bowl was taken away by a maid. A different maid set a fresh China plate before her, and footmen carried in big platters of duck and fish, potatoes, and parsnips. Was it possible to gain ten pounds in a week? The amount of food and the frequency of the meals eaten during this time astounded her. She normally ate light, healthy meals, and of course, because of her modeling career, she was constantly conscious of her weight. Even now, though the food smelled delicious, she couldn't gain weight when she was about to start a new contract. With that in mind, she looked over the platters and decided on the fish and parsnips.

Aunt Josephine woke long enough to load her plate. She drained a glass of wine, demanded another, and began to shovel food into her mouth.

Bellamy met Violet's gaze again, to share her amusement at their sleepy chaperone's table manners before she smoothed her features and pushed the parsnips around her plate with her fork. They weren't appetizing. What *was* appetizing was the man seated stiffly beside her. She glanced at Christian again. Was he this uncomfortable around her or all women? Lily said he was shy, but *this* bordered on painful.

She wondered if he felt the same way. Was it as painful for him as it was for her?

"Lily says you have traveled extensively?" he asked suddenly.

Finally, he offered some conversation. Bellamy wanted to kiss him for his effort. And for other reasons. Instead, she offered what she hoped was an encouraging smile. "Yes, I've been to thirty-six countries so far."

He blinked. "Incredible."

"I loved the pyramids in Egypt and the temples in Cambodia. But my favorite places for… work—" she'd almost said "photo shoots"—"are beaches with white sand and crystal blue water." Tahiti had been amazing for the Luis Vuitton bathing suit collection. "I love when the water is warm enough for a swim."

"In summer, many journey to the shore for a swim."

"Do you?"

He shook his head. "Wearing wet trousers is unappealing."

Wet trousers? "What do the women wear?"

"Bathing costumes. Dresses are shorter, though no less fancy, I'm told. The women swim separately for propriety."

She tried to picture wearing a dress to swim in Tahiti and couldn't. "Women—and men—wear considerably less to swim in… where I'm from." She'd almost said, "in my time." She glanced around the table, unsure who knew about the unusual circumstances that brought her and her sister here.

Christian paused with the glass of wine halfway to his lips. His eyes slid over her body, then settled on her lips, and his cheeks flared a deep pink. He gulped some wine.

His little blushes were shooting arrows at her heart. Why were they so attractive? She'd always dated strong, confident men. Admittedly, they'd treated her like arm candy instead of a smart businesswoman. Perhaps that was the difference: Christian didn't look at her the same way.

"I had a brief look at the enamel clock before I… came here. It's beautiful."

"Thank you." He didn't look pleased.

"Did I say something wrong?"

His shoulders slumped. "No. I…I must beg your forgiveness,

Miss Bennett. I know you need the clock, but I am unable to provide it." Now it was his turn to push his food around with his fork.

She leaned toward him, unable to stop herself. "What do you mean? I need it to go home."

Christian lifted troubled eyes to hers. "I will do everything in my power to recover it."

"*Recover it*?" It took every ounce of her self-control not to shriek. She threw a quick prayer out to the universe. *Please don't let it have been stolen also…*"What do you mean?"

"I'm sorry," he murmured. "The clock has been stolen."

CHAPTER FIVE

"THIS MAY BE the first time that I didn't have to threaten you to attend a ball," Gabriel said in greeting as he joined Christian at the back of the Parlings' ballroom two days later. He held up two glasses of claret and offered one over.

Christian accepted and drank a healthy amount to soothe his nerves. He hated balls. Glittering chandeliers with dozens of candles shed light on the crush of people in attendance. Lady Parling prided herself on throwing one of the biggest events of the Season. This year, it seemed even more were in attendance. Hundreds of people in full evening dress packed into the ballroom, making the air overly warm and scented with too many perfumes.

"I wouldn't be here if it weren't vitally important," Christian said. The music changed to a lively tune and dancers gathered for a Scottish reel.

"Any luck finding Dale?" Gabriel scanned the crowd. He wore a black silk tailcoat with a gold waistcoat tonight, and his damned cravat was tied perfectly.

Christian tried to straighten his starched cravat with his free hand, though he feared he made it worse. "Not yet. I intend to talk to Major Waler tonight. He's been a family friend to the Wainsrights for years. He might know Dale well enough to have an idea of the places the man frequents while in Town."

"Hmm. If he doesn't?"

"Then it may be too late to find Dale. The money and my work could be lost forever." Christian's chest tightened at the thought. If he lost Dale now, he'd never be able to pay the people who had worked for his family for years, men like Malcolm who looked after him when he was so lost in his work that he forgot to eat. He couldn't let his personal failures harm those he cared for.

Gabriel shifted closer. "Including the clock?" he asked, his voice barely audible over the throngs of conversations around them.

Christian swallowed around a thick lump that settled in his throat. "Yes," he rasped. If he didn't find the little egg clock Dale had stolen, then Bellamy would be stuck in their time. Worse, what if Dale found a way to use the clock as a time travel device and disappeared before Christian found him? The thought made his stomach flip every time it occurred to him.

Gabriel gripped his shoulder with his free hand and gave it a gentle squeeze. "You'll find him. I know you well, old friend. You won't rest until you've taken back what belongs to you."

Christian looked down at the floor. He wasn't sure he held that same faith in himself.

"Lily and Violet are looking forward to you staying with us. Aunt Josephine assures me that it will be perfectly scandalous to have an unattached male living in a house full of marriageable ladies." Gabriel chuckled. "She makes it sound as if I have a harem. Only Violet and Bellamy are unattached, and both have proper chaperones."

Bellamy was unattached. His mind seized on that detail, answering one of many questions he had about the woman, even though he refused to admit to himself that he was interested. "I believe Josephine was counting herself in the ranks of the marriageable."

Gabriel choked on his claret. "Christ. I hadn't thought of that. Isn't it enough that Violet badgers me every week to find her a proper suitor? If I have to start looking for a suitor for Aunt

Josephine as well, I'll go mad. Where would I find a blind, deaf, and moderately foxed man, anyhow?"

Christian snorted. "Is that the type you would find suitable for Josephine?"

"It's the only type that would have her," Gabriel muttered. "Even now when she is supposed to be chaperoning Violet, the woman is tucked into a corner with all her dowager friends, getting well into their cups."

"I presume that is why you are here tonight?" Christian asked. "To chaperone Violet and find her a suitable match?"

Gabriel shifted and twirled the stem of the glass between his thumb and forefinger. "I am here to assure that my dear sister doesn't find herself in mischief that she cannot get out of. And to fend off men like that odious Musgrave."

Christian smiled. Musgrave had been infatuated with Violet at Gabriel's house party last year and pressed his suit. The man had found himself with a broken nose as a result.

"It seems that I must also fend off the fops around Bellamy. She's been surrounded by chaps begging her to dance since the moment we arrived." Gabriel finished off his claret in one gulp. "It's damned trying."

Christian swept his gaze over the dance floor then, through the groups of people. Tension tightened his shoulders as he searched the faces, until...*there*. He spotted Bellamy among a group of men. She stood in profile, giving him a glimpse of her delicate features and graceful neck. A strand of hair had come loose and brushed her collarbone. Somehow it added allure to a woman entirely too enticing for a man's peace of mind. She smiled as she spoke, but even at this distance, he could tell it was false. He'd received many similar looks from women when they found him tedious but were too polite to excuse themselves from his company.

Was she uncomfortable being surrounded by so many? Society functions could be overwhelming at the best of times, and she wasn't part of their world. Should he offer to take her out into the garden for a moment of fresh air? No, that was madness. Why would a beautiful woman like Bellamy want his assistance in escaping a crowd for a few moments? Especially, after the awkward way they ended supper the other night.

When he confessed that the enamel clock had been stolen, a range of emotions had crossed her face, from shock to disappointment to concern. But the ladies had withdrawn just after, and they hadn't spoken since.

"Christian?" Gabriel tilted his head, studying him.

He flushed, as if he'd been caught doing something he shouldn't. "Is she alone?" he found himself asking. *Blast.* He hadn't meant to voice that question.

"No. Lily and Violet are there with her." His friend studied him for a moment. "Tell me, my friend. Might I ask a favor of you?"

Christian nodded. Gabriel need not ask. Whatever he wanted, Christian would do. He raised his glass to finish off the claret.

"Will you dance with Bellamy? I think she could use a moment away from the wolves."

Christian froze with the glass halfway to his mouth.

"I know you don't care much for dancing. However, I think she would be more comfortable dancing with someone she knows, and I must keep track of Lily and Violet."

He lowered his glass. He couldn't read Gabriel's expression, but there seemed to be more to the request. "I..." His mouth went dry. Gabriel asked for so little. He should have immediately agreed.

Christian sought out Bellamy again. Could he ask her to dance? The thought of holding her in his arms again was both exhilarating and terrifying. He hadn't forgotten the soft press of her body to his when he found her in the street, or when she'd fallen into his arms during her dance instruction. The feeling had haunted him into his dreams.

He must have looked as panicked as he felt because Gabriel laid a hand on his arm. "I can ask Zeph to—"

"No." He said the word with more force than intended, startling them both. He cleared his throat. "No. I…I will dance with her."

One side of Gabriel's mouth twitched up. "Are you certain? Zeph would be more than happy to ask the lady…"

Christian glared at him. They'd been friends for so long that he knew the man's teasing tone well. Zeph had come into their circle years ago and simply inserted himself as if he'd always been there. He was one of the few men Christian considered a close friend. Though at that moment, he didn't want the man anywhere near Bellamy. With his nearly white hair, silver eyes, and a face and body that were the epitome of masculine perfection, he had an almost god-like beauty. Add in his mischievous charm, and women swooned at his feet. Christian couldn't compare to that.

Gabriel chuckled. "You may recall that she met Zeph at dinner two nights past?"

"She didn't dance with him," Christian muttered. Curse Gabriel's perceptiveness.

His friend tried to hide his smile, failed, and motioned to the women. "Shall we?"

They crossed the ballroom with relative ease. People moved out of the way when Gabriel walked. Christian accounted it to the strength in his movements more than his title. Gabriel moved with the boldness of a man who let nothing stand in the way of what he wanted. He envied that about his friend. Among many other things.

His steps slowed as he neared Bellamy, and his heart picked up speed. She wore a blue silk gown with fancy lace trim that made her skin glow. The low-cut bodice accentuated her lithe frame and small breasts, but it was that stray piece of golden hair brushing her collarbone that drew his attention. He wanted to twirl the strand around his finger to see if it felt as much like silk as it appeared, then trace the delicate skin beneath it.

Bellamy turned her head as they approached. She smiled at

Gabriel—a true smile, not the smile she saved for strangers—then turned her attention to him. Her lips parted on a breath and their eyes locked.

The ballroom faded. The music, the voices, the overly warm room, all disappeared as Christian slowly approached her. He couldn't look away. A slight flush spread across her cheeks as they stared at one another. For how long, he couldn't say. All the nervousness he normally felt in the company of a woman was strangely absent at that moment, replaced by an awareness of her.

"May I have the honor of this dance?" He extended his palm for her hand. The question rolled from him more easily than any question he'd ever asked.

With only the briefest hesitation, she placed her gloved hand in his.

Christian was vaguely aware of the knowing look Gabriel gave him as he guided her to the dance floor. The soft strains of music began to play as he drew her around to face him. He gave a brief bow, then took her hand in his. Incredibly, she floated over the dance floor with him, as if she'd danced with him a hundred times.

"You surprise me," she murmured. "Lily told me that you hate to dance."

"I confess that it is more the amount of people at these functions and...the young women on the marriage mart with their scheming mothers than the dancing itself."

She laughed. "I like your honesty." Then, "You don't plan to marry? I would think that having an heir to pass a title to would be important."

"It is. I must ensure that the people in Huntington are cared for." Not that he'd done so. "I suppose someday I shall have to take a wife." He swallowed hard. "Though I find the prospect of contracted marriage unappealing." He flinched internally. What was he saying? *Blast.* He couldn't even dance with a woman without making awkward conversation.

"You don't want to marry for love?"

He almost missed a step but recovered. "Ah. I don't expect…that is, it seems unlikely…" He closed his mouth to stop the tumble of words that he did *not* want to say in front of this beautiful woman.

Her face softened. "My mother used to say that love comes to us when we least expect it." She gazed at something over his shoulder for a moment, then looked up at him. "I think Lily and Gabriel would agree, don't you? They seem very much in love."

"Indeed." He focused on her delicate collarbone, which seemed a safe place to look that was unlikely to make him feel more awkward than he already did.

"I didn't realize love was something that I wanted until I saw them together. I think my parents had a love like that. I'm not sure. I can't remember them that clearly."

"Lily said that they died in an accident. Their carriage was hit by another?"

"Something like that. We were young." She shook her head as if to banish memories.

Christian recognized the movement. He'd made it often.

"Was your parents' marriage arranged? Is that the right term for it?" she asked. "I thought I read once that the nobility was particular about who their children married."

"Yes, it was arranged. I do not think they shared a deep love. Affection, perhaps. I'm not certain. Mother died shortly after my younger brother was born."

"I'm sorry. It's hard to lose a parent. Especially both of them."

The shadow of pain crossed her features, and he was loathe to speak of it more. He cast about for something else to ask, but the music was drawing to its conclusion. He would have to release her and escort her back to Gabriel and Lily. For once, Christian wasn't eager to be rid of a dance partner. Would it be improper to ask her to get some air on the balcony? The thought of taking Bellamy to a shadowed corner made his heart thud and his arousal flare, an unusual sensation that shocked him. Fortunately, the dance ended at that moment, and he could cover his embarrassment—and arousal—with a bow to her.

He took a breath to get himself under control, then asked, "Miss Bennett, would you care to…" Major Waler's booming laugh carried over the crowd, stopping the words. He spotted the portly man walking past with an older gentleman, heading toward the balcony. *At last.*

"About the clock…" she began.

"Your pardon, Miss Bennett," Christian said at the same time. He cast another look at Major Waler to keep him in sight. "Forgive me. I must go." He gave her a last, lingering look then followed them.

A moment later, her hand grabbed his and pulled him to a stop. "Who are you following?" Bellamy asked as she joined him.

He tried to untangle her fingers from his, but she held firm. "It's not your—"

"Does this have to do with the clock?"

"Yes. No. No, it doesn't."

Her sapphire blue eyes narrowed on him. "Which is it?"

He rubbed the back of his neck with his other hand. "Indirectly? There's a gentleman who may know the…the whereabouts of the man who stole it." *As well as almost eighty thousand pounds.*

"I'm coming with you," she said.

"No. That is improper." He didn't want her anywhere near these men.

"I need to find that clock. I can't stay here." She glanced around and then lowered her voice. "I *can't* stay in this time."

"I understand. But your reputation…"

Bellamy rolled her eyes. "That doesn't matter."

Christian fought the sudden smile that tried to form. She was like no other woman he'd met. Except perhaps Lily. But it wasn't Lily he wanted to pull into a shadowed corner and…He cleared his throat, feeling the damnable flush that always made his cheeks turn a light pink, and cursed. "I will seek you out after to let you know what was said. Is that agreeable?" He gently pulled his hand from hers.

"I suppose it must be." She gave him that fixed, false smile.

He lingered another moment, not sure if she really *was* in agreement. But he didn't have time to find out. In this mad crush, he might not be able to find Major Waler again. With a final look at Bellamy, he turned and followed the man onto the balcony.

Finding Dale took precedence over everything. The livelihood of hundreds of people depended upon Christian finding that stolen money as fast as possible. Whatever he was feeling when he was with Bellamy was of no consequence. It couldn't be.

BELLAMY WANTED TO stomp her foot in frustration as she watched Christian weave through the crowd of aristocrats toward the open balcony doors. The man planned on leaving her out of his search for the clock. Maybe he thought she wasn't capable.

She hadn't interacted much with the women of this time period, but maybe they weren't as *assertive* as a twenty-first-century woman. Regardless, she had no intention of waiting around for him to find the thief on his own.

She stepped off the dance floor and made her way past a group of giggling girls. A couple eyed her with open fascination, and others with disdain. She ignored them. *Two hundred years and women still act the same when they sense a rival in the room.* In truth, the ball felt no different than any of the hundreds of parties she'd attended in her modeling career. *The people are the same. Only the clothes and the dances are different.*

With a huff of annoyance, she squeezed past a few gentlemen discussing horse racing.

One of them spotted her and stepped into her path. He was about her height, with brown hair and eyes. Average looking but most women would find him handsome, she supposed. "What a foolish man to leave such an exquisite woman. Amid a dance no less."

"Always knew that Lord Huntington was stupid," another

said. "The man can barely finish a sentence." The men chuckled.

She sidestepped to pass them, but the first man pushed his way back into her path and took her upper arm. "What is the hurry, darling? I would like a dance." He leaned close to whisper in her ear. "I won't leave you standing alone out there."

She pulled her arm free and pasted on a fake smile. "That is a kind offer, but I must decline. There is somewhere that I—"

He took her arm again, and she felt the heat of the other men as they moved closer. "One dance, darling? Let me show you what a *real* dance partner is like. Not the clumsy stumbling of Lord Huntington."

Christian had been anything but clumsy. She found him quite graceful for a man who hated dancing. *The gall of these men to mock him for his shyness!* She yanked her arm free a second time and shoved past him. "Thank you. But I'd *much* rather dance with Lord Huntington."

With that, she quickly skirted an older couple and headed for the balcony. Before she could make it ten steps, another person stepped into her path. Bellamy barely withheld the frustrated sigh.

"You must be Miss Bennett that everyone is talking about," the woman said. "I'm Lady Montrose."

Bellamy gave a short nod. "Pleasure to meet you." The woman was beautiful, with her voluptuous curves barely held in by a sapphire gown. She held herself like a woman who knew she was attractive and used it to her benefit. Bellamy knew lots of women like her in the modeling industry, and a few of them were downright snakes. She had no doubt Lady Montrose was similar; something about this woman slithered.

"Is this your first ball? How *embarrassing* to be left standing there by the tongue-tied Earl of Huntington." Lady Montrose patted her arm. "Don't worry. I don't think the gossips will linger too long on that. I'm certain another scandal will turn their heads soon enough. A word of advice, my dear. If you want to make a good match, you would do well to stay away from the eccentric man. Lord Huntington is more an oddity than a good catch."

Her words wriggled their way under Bellamy's skin and raised her ire. Did *everyone* treat him this poorly? Christian wasn't an *oddity*. He was *shy*, that was all. Better that than some pompous ass—or the viper in front of her.

However, she knew better than to show her true feelings here. Any sign of weakness and the snake would strike. "Oh, I'm not the least concerned." She waved an airy hand. "But thank you for your thoughtful advice. If you'll excuse—"

"You *should* be concerned," Lady Montrose hissed. "Being the sister of Lady Rothden won't protect your reputation for long."

Bellamy smiled as pleasantly as she could at the woman. Her career in modeling had taught her how to mask her emotions under a veneer of calm civility. "Then it's a good thing I don't need her protection. Good evening."

She walked away as if she were unconcerned with the whole affair. Inside, her heart was fluttering like mad and she cursed these people for delaying her. What if she couldn't find Christian? She'd have to wait until he found her, either tonight or—hopefully—sometime tomorrow. Either way, she couldn't wait forever. The need to get home was riding her. She'd never broken a contract in her life, and this contract with Vivant would provide enough money for her to retire from modeling before she was considered too old and start something new. Her future depended upon it.

The balcony doors stood open for the guests to come and go. Cold air wafted in from the night beyond, making her shiver in the thin, silk gown as she stepped outside. She wished she had a coat or a cloak, but she'd left her wrap with a servant when they arrived. Large, candlelit lanterns lined the stone balustrade which overlooked a small mezzanine and the garden below.

A surprising number of people meandered through the shadows of the balcony and hints of whispered conversations floated on the breeze. She heard male voices to her right and followed them to find several men leaning against the balustrade, smoking.

Christian wasn't among them. She turned in the other direction and finally found him at the far end of the balcony. He faced away from her, speaking to someone. She admired the width of his shoulders in his corbeau tailcoat and his narrow waist as she approached, especially when compared to his companion, a shorter, older man, who was rotund even in his military uniform. He reminded her a bit of Humpty Dumpty from a book her mother had read to her when she was young.

"...because he thrashed you?" The older man's voice was laced with contempt.

Thrashed him? What did that mean?

"I...no." She saw Christian shift as if he were uncomfortable. "I heard you were close with the family and thought you might know where Dale was likely to be while in London."

"Even if I knew, I wouldn't tell the likes of you, Huntington. You caused Wainsright untold amounts of shame. Why, if the Ton knew how despicable you were, they'd cast you out of their good graces. I'd—"

Christian tensed and clenched his fists at his sides. "Tell them what you wish," he said in a low, harsh voice unlike any that she'd never heard from him before. "If I find that you know anything about Dale's whereabouts, I'll—"

The rotund man stepped forward and bumped his stomach into Christian. "You'll do what? Stumble over your sentences while putting me in my place?" He sputtered out some nonsensical words in a terrible impression of Christian and snorted. "You're a fool, Huntington, and everyone knows it. Get out of my sight."

Her gut clenched. The way people treated Christian infuriated her. As if his shyness were some horrible shortcoming. She hurried to his side, pasted on her best smile, and put her hand on Christian's arm, leaning into him. "I've been looking for you," she said, lowering her voice with a husky note she knew sounded sensual. His muscles bunched under her hand when he looked down at her. She couldn't read the look in his stormy gaze.

She then glanced at the older man and widened her eyes as if surprised he was there. "Oh, forgive me. I didn't mean to interrupt."

"Nonsense," the man said. "A beautiful woman like you is welcome to interrupt. I don't think we've been introduced."

Christian's voice was taut as he bit out, "Major Waler, may I present Miss Bennett, sister to Lady Rothden."

She held out her hand as Lily and Violet had instructed, and tried not to show the shiver of revulsion when the man bent over her hand and placed a kiss on her glove.

"A delight, Miss Bennett. All the Ton is talking about you. I confess I thought that their descriptions of your beauty were exaggerated. Now that I'm in your presence, I see it is quite the opposite. You are more beautiful than Aphrodite."

She extricated her hand from his. "Thank you, Major Waler. Oh! Are you *the* Major Waler? Lord Huntington said that you might be able to help me locate Mr. Dale. I'd be grateful if you could." Her teeth were going to ache tomorrow from all the sugar she was putting into her words.

Christian gave a slight cough.

She side-eyed him beneath her lashes and then turned her full attention back to the other man.

"Ah, yes. I…" Waler shot a glare at Christian. "Of course, I would be delighted to help you, Miss Bennett."

"Would you? I knew the moment I saw you that you would help." Was that a strangled groan from Christian? She bit back a laugh.

Waler wiped his brow and then ran his hands over his jacket, tugging at it to cover his rounded belly. "You may count on me. But if I may be so bold, why are you looking for him?"

Bellamy glanced up at Christian, not certain if he'd told the man why they were looking for Dale.

"Miss Bennett thinks he may be a relation," Christian said.

"Truly? How…how delightful." Waler sounded anything but delighted.

"On my mother's side," she added. "Can you imagine?"

The portly man cleared his throat. "I haven't seen him recently, mind you. But in the past, I know he frequented the gaming hells on King's Street in St. James."

She clasped her hands in front of her chest as if he'd fulfilled all her hopes and dreams. "Thank you, Major Waler," she said.

"Perhaps you can thank me by honoring me with a dance later this evening?" he asked, puffing his chest up.

Oh, gross. But she needed to play the role if she wanted to get out of this century. *One dance won't kill you, Bells, if it gets Christian the information he needs to find the time travel clock.* "I'd—"

The man's gaze moved to something behind her, and his eyes widened. "Excuse me, please. There is a pressing matter I must...excuse me." Waler strode quickly away.

She turned to see the major rush over to another man.

Christian took hold of her upper arm and steered her into the shadows. "Bellamy, why are you out here? Your reputation could be ruined." He crossed his arms over that wide chest and glared down at her.

She lifted her chin. "I'm helping you find Dale."

"I don't need help."

She waved at where Waler had been. "He planned to share the information with you?"

He pressed his lips into a thin line.

"I heard the terrible things he said to you," she added softly.

Christian looked away.

She laid her hand on his arm. "I don't understand their cruelty."

"It doesn't matter."

"It does if it hurts you." She cupped his cheek and made him look at her.

He sucked in a sharp breath at her touch. Whatever else she meant to say disappeared beneath his intense gaze.

The air changed between them. Grew charged in a way she couldn't describe. Every sensation was magnified. The coolness of his cheek from being out in the chilly air, beneath her gloved hand. The solid muscle she felt beneath her palm when she laid her other hand on his chest. She heard him swallow and watched his sensuous lips part.

Heat curled in her belly and her nipples pebbled. She inched closer.

Christian moved his hands to cup her waist. The warmth of his palms seared through her thin gown, warming her even more. His gaze dropped to her lips.

She pressed closer until their chests brushed.

"Bellamy." Her name was a soft sigh on his lips. It washed over her like a caress.

She wanted to kiss him, she realized. He was frustrating and shy, and at times achingly vulnerable, and she wanted to kiss him more than anyone she'd ever been with.

"Christian," she whispered as she slid her hands up to wrap behind his neck.

He startled at her touch, and she saw the desire-filled haze begin to clear from his eyes.

No. She wasn't letting this moment pass. She threaded her fingers into his hair, angled his head down, and kissed him.

He froze. Several seconds ticked by.

Did she read this wrong? Did he not want this? She pulled back, cheeks going hot as embarrassment swamped her. "I'm sor—"

Christian slanted his mouth over hers and kissed her back, hard. He let out a soft growl before maneuvering her farther into the shadows until she felt the cold stone wall against her back.

Yes. She licked his lower lip and clung tighter to him.

His mouth parted with a small gasp.

She gripped his hair and pulled him closer, opening her mouth to his.

He didn't immediately deepen the kiss.

Was this more shyness or was he unsure of what to do? Either way, she wasn't going to allow him to back away from this moment. Bellamy swept her tongue against his. Once. Twice. In response, Christian tentatively brushed his tongue over hers, the motions slow and hesitant. Had he never kissed anyone like this?

Somehow that made this interlude even more sexy. She pressed closer and took his lips with hers again.

Christian followed every swipe of her tongue until he grew more confident in his kiss. He wrapped his arms tightly around her, molding her to his body as their mouths fused.

Heat shot straight to her core. She slid her hands down his chest and under the bottom of his tailcoat, wrapping around his back, and when his hard thickness pressed into her belly, she moaned and pressed into it.

Christian pulled his mouth away. He panted against her lips.

Her body thrummed with delicious desire. Heat shot through her from every place his hands touched. She leaned forward for another kiss.

He jerked his head away, avoiding contact. "I…I'm sorry," he rasped before he released her and quickly stepped back. Cold air rushed between them, chilling her heated skin.

She stumbled a step toward him, brain still addled and her blood still pounding from the kiss. What was he sorry for?

"I sh-shouldn't have…" He took another step back and ran a shaking hand through his hair. "Forgive me, Miss Bennett."

Miss Bennett? The formality shocked her back to her senses. "Christian wait. I kissed…you."

He spun around and was gone before the last word was out.

Bellamy groaned in frustration. *Damn him.* She'd never had to chase a man for anything. And no one had run from her kiss before. She pressed her hands to her hot cheeks, then started back toward the ballroom.

She stopped when her neck prickled. Looking around, she spotted a man in the shadows not far from where she and Christian stood.

A burning red ember glowed from the end of his cheroot, lighting his face. Then, he stepped into the light, and she saw that he was tall, with pale skin, and thinning hair. It was the same man Major Waler had gone to speak with when he left them in such a hurry. He stared at her, as a slow smile crossed his face.

Bellamy suppressed a shiver of unease, but she wouldn't let him know he made her nervous. With all the grace she could muster, she turned as if unconcerned, and reentered the ballroom.

Lily, Gabriel, and a sulking Violet were just about to walk through the balcony doors.

"There you are," Lily said. "Did someone else ask you to dance after Lord Huntington? I thought he would have brought you back after."

Gabriel gave her a pointed look over Lily's head as if he knew what had happened on the darkened balcony.

Bellamy swallowed. "Uh, no. He spotted someone he thought might know about the theft, and I followed him because the stubborn man won't let me help him."

Violet coughed. She stood beside Lily with her arms crossed over her chest. "It's a trait he shares with Gab—"

Lily elbowed the young woman in the ribs.

Violet scowled but clamped her mouth shut.

"Huntington departed for the night," Gabriel said. "You will have plenty of time to wear down those defenses, Bellamy. He'll be staying with us for the next few months."

Butterflies erupted in her stomach. She pressed a hand over her belly to tamp down the feeling and focused on something else Gabriel said. *Months.* What if it took that long to find the clock? Lily had been here for over six months but only a few weeks had passed in their time. She tried to calculate how much time would pass in her century if she spent a month here, but math had never been her best subject and it only made her head hurt.

Lily took her arm. "Everything will work out, Bells. You'll see. You look tired. Let's get you and Violet home so you can rest. You can talk with Lord Huntington tomorrow."

Her patronizing tone made Bellamy's jaw clench. Coming on

the cusp of her frustration with Christian, and worry over her future, it pissed her off. Lily still didn't see her as an adult, even though she'd moved out to attend college six years ago. "I'm not a child anymore," she snapped. "You don't have to fuss over me."

"You've been through a lot recently, Bells. Sorry for trying to be supportive and care for you," Lily snapped back. She clenched her jaw and muttered, "Nothing's changed."

Bellamy's stomach sank. God, she wished she could take back the words. Lily was right. *Nothing* had changed. She needed to think before she spoke because otherwise, the result was always an argument. She pressed a hand to her temple.

"You're right. I don't want to be here anymore."

Violet linked their arms together. "That makes two of us," she whispered. "Boorish siblings are wearisome."

That made Bellamy smile a little. She put her hand over Violet's on her arm and gave a small squeeze. If she was stuck here for the time being, maybe she and Violet could learn how to deal with their siblings together. She had a feeling the young woman needed the lesson as much as she did.

Chapter Six

"THAT'S THE THIRD gaming hell we've tried," Zeph said, as the front door of the unassuming residence closed behind them. It was nearly three o'clock in the morning, but the streets were still full of carts and carriages, and people seeking the various entertainments to be found under the cover of darkness. "Are you certain Waler said St. James?"

Christian nodded. "He said King Street." Zeph had followed him out of Lady Parling's ball, claiming boredom. More likely, the man was trying to evade the grasping claws of Lady Montrose, who seemed to have taken a fancy to him after her humiliation at Gabriel's house party last year. Regardless, Zeph offered to assist him with finding Dale. Some of the gaming hells would not allow admittance without an introduction by a known member and Zeph had been to all of them.

Christian was not surprised.

"I hardly think that Dale is playing whist at Almack's, so it must be one of the taverns." Zeph adjusted his hat against the lightly falling rain that dampened their hair and great coats. "The Wooden Horse on Bury Street is a block away. It's possible he decided to move on and try his luck there."

"We may as well do the same," Christian said as they began to walk down King Street toward Almack's and Bury Street. "I hadn't realized you spent so much time at the hells."

Zeph remained silent for several moments. "Some nights, after a ball or dinner party, I feel…unsettled. Instead of returning to the townhouse alone, I find myself here." His lips curled. "There's nothing quite so entertaining as bluffing an arrogant man out of a bit of quid."

Christian chuckled. "For a man who adores mischief as much as you, I expect that is true. Although I imagine that Twisden would tell you that if you don't want to be alone, then you should find a mistress. Or at least some feminine company for a few hours." They'd met George Twisden at Eton years before. The man was infamous for his scandalous exploits when it came to female companions.

Zeph huffed. "Is there a woman in London he hasn't touched yet? I'm not after his cast-offs."

Christian pursed his lips to hold back his grin. "I believe Gabriel's Aunt Josephine hasn't shared his bed yet…"

His friend's loud bark of laughter made several people turn in their direction. Zeph's silver eyes glittered in the lamplight. "The next time I see Granville, I'm going to wager that Twisden won't be able to seduce the woman."

"I'm not certain whether I feel more pity for Twisden or Aunt Josephine."

"Speaking of dear Aunt Josephine, I noted that she was meant to chaperone Violet and Miss Bennett at tonight's ball." His tone turned sly. "I'm afraid she missed your dance with Bellamy. Do you think she would have approved?"

Christian gave a slight cough. "Gabriel insisted that I…"

Zeph raised an eyebrow in a way that told Christian he'd already known Gabriel intended to ask him to dance with Bellamy—if Christian declined.

He stuffed his hands in his pockets and dipped his chin, grateful that the night hid his embarrassment. He hadn't just danced with Miss Bennett, he'd kissed her on the darkened balcony. And, she'd kissed him, in a way that said she didn't think he was too awkward or shy. His face flamed, and he scrubbed a hand over it.

The way she'd looked up at him. The warmth of her body against his…His breath shuddered out of him. He didn't remember how it happened. All he knew was that one moment, he'd been wondering if her lips were as soft as they looked and if she would taste sweet or a little spicy, and the next, his lips had been on hers.

God, the taste of her. The satin of her skin, and her sweet scent as he'd nuzzled her cheek…the combination had almost overridden his nervousness.

He'd still felt terribly clumsy as their mouths moved together, and he'd feared that perhaps he wasn't kissing her properly. Had she known it was his very first kiss? Had his inexperience been obvious? He'd never kissed the one woman he'd been intimate with. Why would he? The entire experience had been humiliating enough without it.

He knew he shouldn't have run from Bellamy, but he'd been mortified that he'd stolen a kiss from her without her permission, and he'd been afraid he'd see disgust on her face because he didn't know how to kiss.

He huffed out a frustrated sigh. The memory of her kiss would be a single point of shining light in his memories. Meanwhile, he had no doubt she was trying to forget the matter entirely. *What a disaster.*

"Christian?"

He realized he'd been lost in his thoughts for an uncomfortably long time. What had they been speaking of? *The dance.* "I had no wish to disappoint her…or Gabriel."

"Mm." Zeph's tone said he found the explanation lacking.

He cast about for something to say that would draw the subject away from Miss Bennett. "Do you suppose Waler lied about Dale?"

"Let's find out."

A weathered sign depicting a trojan horse on wheels proclaimed the nearby establishment to be the Wooden Horse tavern. Bright light spilled between curtains in the bay window and loud voices sounded from within. Zeph reached for the door just as it opened, and a man staggered out with his arm wrapped around the shoulders of a plump doxy. He mumbled something, pressed a sloppy kiss to her cheek, and grinned widely. "A fine evening to ya," he said in an overly loud voice, leaning close to them. His breath reeked of spirits.

The woman hiccupped a laugh, and they staggered away.

"Interesting clientele," Christian murmured.

Zeph laughed and together, they entered the tavern. There was a long bar at the back of the room and a fireplace on the left wall, heating a room already too warm. Dozens of people sat around simple wooden tables, singing a bawdy song at the top of their lungs, led by one of the serving women standing on a chair in the center of the room.

They wove their way between the tables to the bar at the back. Zeph spoke a quick word to the bartender, and the man nodded at a dark passageway to the left.

Christian followed his friend into the dim hallway and up a flight of narrow stairs. The door at the top was locked with a small spyhole at eye level.

Zeph knocked, nodded to the man who answered and stepped into another hallway. Christian followed him as they went through two more doors, each guarded by large men who looked as if they lived in the pugilism rings when not standing guard. Each of the hells they'd visited had similar mazes of winding halls leading to discreet chambers. One never wanted to be in a hell that was raided and find themselves in prison as a result.

When they arrived at the gaming room, it was brighter and cleaner than Christian had expected. Chandeliers illuminated the green cloth tabletops where men were gathered around games of hazard, vingt-un, and faro, drinking an excess of ale and spirits. The windows were cracked open to let in fresh air against the cigar smoke curling overhead.

He scanned the groups for Dale, but his gaze snagged on a

familiar face.

"Granville is here," Zeph said from beside him.

"I suppose I am not surprised. The man can't go an hour without wagering on something."

Owen Granville was one of the half dozen men they'd met at Eton, which formed their small circle of friends—most of whom, with the exception of Gabriel and Zeph—Christian viewed more as acquaintances.

"I'll talk to him. Why don't you inquire after Dale with the director?" Zeph indicated a short man wearing spectacles standing behind a podium on the far side of the room.

Christian slowly made his way through the room, listening to the excited shouts and moans of frustration from gamblers at the various games. At a *vingt-un* table, the dealer passed out cards and gave an almost imperceptible nod at the player with the largest stack of chips. The man laid out a large wager, touting the bank's losses that night. The man beside him in a threadbare coat laughed, eyes too bright and eager. He sorted half of his dwindling stack of chips to wager. When the dealer turned the cards, the first man raked in more winnings. The other did not. He stuttered out something unintelligible, staring at the cards.

A cheat, Christian realized. The first player worked for the gaming hell to win and encourage others to gamble more in hopes of winning just as much. Little wonder so many men lost fortunes here each night. Had his father been one? Had Andrew Albury sat at one of these same tables, betting higher in the hopes of winning back what he'd lost?

He cursed under his breath and turned away. His father had died before he'd lost the family fortune. Whether he gambled here or not was of no consequence. Only Dale and the stolen money mattered.

The director looked up from a thick ledger when he approached. "Help ya?" He adjusted the spectacles on his bulbous nose.

"I'm searching for a…friend." He nearly choked on the word.

"He may have been in tonight."

The little man gave him a bland look. "We do not discuss our clientele. Especially with new faces."

"He may have lost quite a bit of money." If he had, Christian would be furious. That money meant a great deal to the Huntington estate.

An unpleasant smile crossed the man's face. "Then I can only hope he returns. To win some back, of course."

The man was vile. The glint in his eye said he cared more for money than the lives ruined here every night. Christian clenched a fist at his side. "His name is William Dale. He..."

"Not interested." The director picked up a quill and returned to the ledger.

He felt a throb in his temple as he stared at the man's bent head. For a fleeting moment, he thought of Miss Bennett. She no doubt would have charmed the information out of the man by now. However, she wasn't here. By design, he reminded himself. It was too dangerous for a woman like her to be in this place.

Greed motivated the director. A bribe might loosen his tongue, even though Christian was loathe to give the man a farthing. "How much—"

The man sighed and set the quill aside with care. He met Christian's gaze, then lifted a hand and flicked it in a side motion. A burly man stood from his lazy sprawl against the wall and started forward, hands flexing at his sides.

A thread of panic hit him. Not for the pain promised in the brute's eyes—he could attend himself well in a fight if required—but because of the fear of not finding Dale after scouring four gaming hells. What if Waler lied to get him to stop asking questions? What if Dale truly *had* left London? He forced his attention back on the small man. "I'll pay... for the information." He stumbled over his words in a rush to get them out before the guard arrived. "Please. This is important."

Dark, beady eyes assessed him from behind the spectacles, taking in the cut of his clothes and crooked cravat. The man smirked and gestured to the muscled man again. "I doubt you could afford my information." To his man, he said, "Ivan, please escort this gentleman to the door."

Ivan cocked a bushy brow, silently asking Christian if he intended to leave on his own or be forced out.

"I..." He couldn't leave without knowing if Dale had been here.

An elegant hand settled on his shoulder and gave it a small squeeze of reassurance. "Causing trouble, Huntington?" Zeph said. A smile teased his lips. "If I'd known that all it took was to get you in a gaming hell, I'd have brought you sooner."

"Lord Lael," the director said. His gaze flicked to Christian and back. "Is the gentleman with you?"

"He is."

"Then I advise you both to find a table and enjoy your evening or find other, more suitable entertainments *elsewhere*." Ivan stepped forward to emphasize the shorter man's words.

Zeph huffed a laugh. "A turn at the tables, Huntington?"

He'd be damned if he lost a farthing in this den of thieves. "Dale isn't here..."

"The hour does grow late. Shall we collect Granville and escort him home? I fear he's overextended himself for the night both in money *and* drink."

Christian followed numbly behind Zeph. He didn't know where to look next. No one had seen Dale, or if they had, wouldn't say. There was only one other man who may know. His gut curdled with the realization that he might not be able to avoid Wainsright in this.

"Your pardon," a man said as he stood from a nearby table, jostling Christian's elbow.

He spared the man only a cursory glance, realizing it was the man in the threadbare coat who'd been losing to the cheat. He gave a small nod out of habit.

"Huntington," Granville cried in a deafening tone from nearby.

Christian looked up to find him leaning heavily on Zeph as they came closer. His medium brown hair stuck up in tufts as if he'd tugged on it, and his waistcoat was misbuttoned.

Owen Granville usually took care with his appearance. His father was a baron, and Owen had often remarked in a lowered voice to mimic the baron, "What a man wears is his armor. Shield yourself as if you could take on any enemy, and you will be prepared for any situation."

Granville, it seemed, had lost the battle at the gaming table. He leaned forward to loudly whisper, "Hold onto your purse here. I think I've seen a cheat." He waved a glass of what looked like brandy as he spoke, sloshing it over the rim.

"I shall," Christian said, taking the drink out of the man's hands before it spilled on him. He sat it on the tray of a passing waiter and looked at Zeph over Granville's head.

Zeph smirked. "A night at the hells never lacks for entertainment."

Christian huffed in response. It was entertainment he didn't need or want; he'd much prefer to be in his quiet workshop, not here in this noisy, crowded place. "Need assistance with him?"

Zeph shook his head, and together, they left the room and descended the back stairs.

You were a fool to let someone else oversee the estate. Look what's become of it. Dale is gone with little hope of being found. And the enamel clock that Miss Bennett needs to get home is lost with him. It was bad enough that his failure was going to affect the lives of the people who counted on his estate for their income, now the thought of letting Bellamy down was inconceivable. It appeared that his only option was to face the man who tortured him for years at Eton.

He pushed his way through the tables of singing people in the tavern and opened the front door, holding it for Zeph and Granville.

"I love that song," Owen said.

"If you start singing in the carriage, I will tie you to the seat beside the driver," Zeph growled. "I might anyway. You stink of cigar smoke and cheap brandy."

Owen smiled at him, his eyes glazed. "I love you too. I've never had friends as good—no' as *great*—as you," he added, clutching Zeph's great coat and shaking him a little. "Do you love me?"

Despite his own frustrations, Christian chuckled. He clamped his lips together when Zeph glared at him, but the laugh escaped in a snort.

"If Twisden hears one word about this, I will match you in the boxing ring until you beg me for mercy. The man gossips more than half the women in the Ton." Zeph readjusted his arm around Granville and started for the carriage they'd left a couple of blocks over.

They hadn't often sparred in the boxing ring, but when they had, the matches were intense. Both had become skilled fighters in the days since Eton. Christian never wanted to be that vulnerable again. His thoughts went back to Wainsright and Dale.

His gut clenched. If he couldn't find Dale, either by his own search or through Wainsright, he was left with a single alternative, the thought of which sent shards of pain through him.

He would have to sell the musical songbird that he'd made in memory of his brother, Quentin, who'd loved birds. Even if he did, there was no guarantee that anyone would pay the amount he needed to make up his losses. The thought made him ill.

"Pardon, sir," someone said to his right.

He turned his head to find the man in the threadbare coat, clutching his hat in his hands.

The man shot a nervous look at Zeph, who'd half-turned their way, Granville still clinging to him and stumbling to find his footing.

He curled the rim of the hat in his fingers over and over. "I heard you asking after Dale," he said in a hushed voice.

Christian nodded. "Do you know him?"

"Only through the hells. He likes the faro more than the

vingt-un, so we don't often play the same tables. But sometimes when we're both down…" he shrugged. "Spent a lot of time commiserating, is all."

"Did you see him tonight?" Zeph asked.

"No," Granville answered in a conspiratorial whisper, then laughed until he wheezed.

Zeph rolled his eyes and motioned to the man to continue.

"Left before you gents arrived. Said he'd lost enough for one night."

Christian ground his teeth together. He barely held himself back from snarling that it was *his* money Dale gambled and lost. "Do you know where he was going? Or where he might stay?"

The man looked down at his hat and twisted the rim tighter. "I know where he'll be."

When he didn't add anything more, Christian asked, "Where?"

"You offered to pay the other gent that runs the hell…" He seemed to realize what he'd inferred and looked up with wide eyes. "I don't want much. Really. I'm down on my luck is all…" The words rushed out of him. "Five guineas. Five, and I'll tell you everything I know."

Christian and Zeph exchanged a look. Zeph gave a small shake of his head, saying without words that he didn't think it wise to give the man money for the information. But Christian knew that he had to take a chance, even if the man was only trying to gain a few farthings by lying. Who knew how long it would take to find Dale?

He studied the man for a moment, noting the hole in the side of his shoe and the misshapen hat that went with the threadbare coat. He reached for his purse. "Tell me about Dale."

"I overheard him say he'd come by money. The more he drank and talked, the more it seemed the money weren't his. Then he started going on about one of those machines that are on display in Spring Gardens. Said he could get even more if he could sell it to the right man." He squeezed the rim of his hat tight. "He plans to meet someone to sell it. I overheard where."

"Tell me and the money is yours," Christian said.

"Vauxhall Gardens, two nights from now," the man said quickly. "He's meeting someone who buys things that aren't supposed to be bought. Means to use the dark paths for the exchange."

Zeph cursed under his breath.

Christian handed over the money. "Did he say anything else?"

"Only that he hoped his employer would give him a raise for the hardship."

Blood rushed in his ears and his heart thudded hard. His employer. Someone else was paying Dale. Did that mean they were paying Dale to steal from him? To what end? Was it Christian's machines he wanted? Or the money? An icy chill spread through his veins until he felt numb.

"Are you well?" Zeph asked.

"I..." Was he? He turned to thank the man, but he'd already returned to the tavern, pulling the door open and disappearing inside. Those five guineas would be gone before the sun rose. Christian felt a moment of pity for him, then looked to Zeph and Granville, whose eyes were drooping.

"Shall we get him home?" he asked.

Zeph nodded and they began the short walk back to the carriage. "Will you go to Vauxhall in two nights?"

"I must."

"I shall join you. We don't know who Dale is meeting with. But any man who buys stolen goods will be prepared for the worst. We must be suitably armed."

Christian nodded. He just hoped that Dale wasn't meeting with Wainsright.

SHE SHOULDN'T HAVE kissed him last night.

Bellamy sat in the drawing room, staring out the bay window at the carriages that rumbled by. Lily, Violet, and Lady Patience Cradock were there having tea and gossiping about the ball. She should have been using this time to work on her relationship with Lily. Instead, all she could think about was that kiss. That passionate, delicious kiss in the darkness.

It had been both a surprise and a revelation. She hadn't realized that she wanted to kiss him until the moment before their mouths had touched. His lips had been firm and unmoving at first, and she worried that she'd overstepped. How embarrassing would it be to throw herself at Gabriel's best friend, only to find that he hadn't the slightest interest? And what was she thinking anyway? She was supposed to be focused on going home, not kissing a man she'd be leaving behind soon.

But oh, when he'd returned the kiss and pressed her up against the wall…that little bit of domination had sent a shot of heat south, lighting up everything along the way. He hadn't been rough. Not at all. In fact, he seemed unsure of his kiss. She remembered how he was slow to stroke his tongue with hers, how his hands barely held her waist, but his mouth was eager for hers. Christian Albury was an interesting mix of contradictions, and she found herself quite intrigued.

When he'd broken the kiss, he'd looked panicked. That was the only word she could think of to describe the look in his eyes. Then he'd bolted, as if he'd done something he shouldn't and was wary of getting caught. She hadn't expected that reaction. And, she was a bit ashamed that her ego took a hit because of it.

The thing was, Bellamy knew she was beautiful. She'd built a career on it. When it came to dating, it was usually a matter of not having the time versus a lack of options. Men loved the idea of dating an underwear model though often, that meant she didn't live up to their ideals, and most of her relationships were short as a result. She'd never had to work for a man's initial interest though. In a way, it presented a challenge that she found exciting. Yet the rational, sensible part of her brain continually reminded her that she couldn't explore a relationship with him. Since she was going to leave this time, it wasn't fair to either of them. What if one of them became emotionally attached?

Bellamy bit her thumbnail, seeing his sweet smile just before the panic set in and he fled. She wanted to kiss Christian again. Kissing him felt different from every other kiss she'd ever had, and she didn't know why. Worse, he'd been avoiding her. The man had moved into Gabriel's townhome earlier in the day and then, disappeared. She didn't even know *why* he'd moved in. Didn't he have his own home here in London?

She set her cup of cold tea aside, feeling the throb of a headache begin in her temple. Sleep had eluded her most of the night. When she did sleep, she woke from the nightmare that had plagued her for years. Those horrible, grasping hands pulling at her hair and clothes. She shuddered and locked the memory of it as far down as possible.

She looked at the other ladies. Maybe she should try to get answers about Christian out of Lily and Violet. Women tended to be better at sharing details than men.

"What about Felton Seabright?" Lady Patience asked Violet. She was pretty and plump, with brown hair and twinkling gray eyes.

Violet shook her head, chocolate curls dancing. "Gabriel said he didn't consider his friends to be suitable matches for me. Besides, Felton shot Musgrave at Gabriel's hunting party in October. How can I marry someone who can't even teach me to shoot?"

Lily choked on her tea. "Violet, please do not say such things around Gabriel. If he hears that you want to learn to shoot for sport, he won't let any man be a suitor."

Violet's eyebrows shot up. "Whyever not? He promised."

Patience pressed her lips together and stared into her teacup, while Lily searched for words. Bellamy wanted to laugh. She adored Violet. The young woman had an unmatched spirit of adventure. Violet simply couldn't fathom why anyone wouldn't want her to learn to shoot.

"Is Christian a good shot?" Patience asked. "He seems to be a man of utmost character."

Bellamy's stomach clenched. Christian was a good man. Would Gabriel consider a marriage between Violet and his best friend? The thought sent a bolt of something she couldn't identify straight to her heart until she had trouble drawing a breath.

"He's a better fencer," Violet said and waved away Patience's suggestion with an airy hand. "I couldn't marry Christian. He is too much like a brother to me."

The tight knot in her chest let loose so quickly that it made her lightheaded. *God, pull yourself together Bells. You're leaving, remember?* She forced her thoughts away from kissing him and took the opening that the conversation provided. "Speaking of Christian, I thought he had his own home here in London?"

Lily nodded. "He does. He's decided to lease it for the remainder of the Season to Lord Twisden and Lord Granville. I believe they normally stay at the Albany, which is a gentlemen's boarding house, so they were more than happy to lease the townhouse from him." She poured more tea for them all.

When no one elaborated further, Bellamy pressed the question. "But why does he need to lease it? Surely having his own house would be more comfortable. Even if he allowed the other gentlemen to let rooms, he could stay there. Why move here?"

Patience stared back into her teacup as if contained the mysteries of the universe.

Lily looked uncomfortable. "I shouldn't really say..."

Violet leaned forward as if imparting a great secret. "His steward stole money from him. Until he can get the money back, he's in need of additional income so that he can pay his staff. Twisden and Granville can be insufferable, and Christian prefers quiet."

The man that stole the clock also stole money? No wonder Christian was so desperate to find him. *I want to help him even more.*

"Did you hear that Vauxhall Gardens has opened for the Season?" Patience asked, in an obvious attempt to change the subject.

Violet's eyes lit up. "Have they? I love the fireworks." She turned to Lily. "We should go tomorrow. They have dinner and dancing, fireworks, and the most beautiful gardens. Plus, all the Ton go for the grand walk."

"I've heard of them," Lily said. "I never imagined that I'd see them." She glanced over to Bellamy. "Would you like to go?"

She nodded.

Violet clapped. "Wonderful! We shall have Gabriel take us tomorrow evening then."

"Take you where, darling?" Gabriel strolled into the drawing room and leaned down to press a lingering kiss on Lily's cheek.

"To Vauxhall Gardens," Lily answered. "Patience said it is open for the Season. I've heard so much about it. I'd love to see it."

"Then we shall go." He lifted her hand and kissed it. "Enjoying your tea, ladies?"

"We're plotting the route to Gretna Green, should you not approve of my next suitor," Violet said, with a sweet smile.

He looked at the ceiling and released a put-upon sigh. "Do consider a conveyance other than the mail coach, at the least. I could outrun it with my slowest horse."

Lily coughed to cover her laugh.

"I shall add that to the list of desirable qualities: 'Must come with own coach and fast horse,'" Violet replied.

"Who was the gentleman I saw you speaking with last night?" Gabriel asked.

"Perhaps you should have inquired his name before you growled in his face like a bear and—"

A sense of something like homesickness hit Bellamy as the two continued to bicker. She missed those days when the fights hadn't been painful. She still had much to say to Lily, but every time the opportunity presented itself, the words dried up because she feared arguing during their limited time together, and then she couldn't think of anything to say. She wished Archer were here to talk to, although she couldn't picture Archer wearing the elegant fashions and sitting politely for tea.

Her brother was consciously closing himself off from everyone who cared about him. She knew he did it to shield himself from hurt, but all it did was hurt those around him. Soon, he'd lock himself away in his house, like Christian.

The moment the thought crossed her mind, she realized that was *exactly* what Christian was doing, and why. Someone had hurt him deeply. He was protecting himself with actual walls. She rose and excused herself from the drawing room. She couldn't help Archer right now, but maybe she could help Christian.

Though it was probably considered improper, she went to his bedroom on the upper floor, next to Gabriel and Lily's room. She and Violet had bedchambers one floor up for additional propriety. Anticipation curled in her chest as she knocked. It was silly. She hardly knew the man. But she couldn't ignore the desire to talk to him more.

When he didn't answer, she went to the library, the drawing room, and even Gabriel's office. Had he left?

"Looking for Christian?" Gabriel said as he entered the hall.

"I…yes. I think he might be avoiding me." She twined her fingers together.

Gabriel smiled. "He's in the basement. I made room for a workshop for him."

"Thanks," she said and moved toward the staircase.

"Don't hurt him," Gabriel said.

She stopped on the top step and looked at him. He watched her with a steady gaze.

"Pardon?"

"Do not hurt him," he repeated. "If it is your intention to leave this time, do not take his heart with you."

His words hit their mark. Her throat felt thick, and she swallowed over the painful knot. Gabriel was right. She couldn't kiss

Christian again. She needed to stay far away from him, in fact. Bellamy didn't know if she could or even would take his heart when she left, but she didn't want to leave hers behind.

She nodded at Gabriel, then descended the stairs to the basement. The kitchen and stores were down here, as well as a couple of the servants' chambers. The scent of baking bread drifted in the air and a maid hurried past with an armful of linens. The workshop turned out to be a small chamber at the back of the basement. The door was open a few inches, so she pressed a palm to open it more. Light spilled in from the windows higher up on the walls, illuminating the room. "Christian?"

He turned on his heel and froze when he saw her.

Bellamy stopped in the doorway, equally shocked. He'd divested his shirt, cravat, and waistcoat and stood in just his pants and boots, with a sword of some type in his hand. She took in his wide shoulders and narrow waist and the light hair on his chest that arrowed down below the waist of his pants. The muscles beneath his skin were strong and defined, much like his arms. He panted softly and glistened with a sheen of sweat that covered his body.

Heat curled in her belly. She wanted to touch all that beautiful, pale skin on display.

He backed up a step when she drifted closer and bumped into the table behind him.

It pulled her out of the fog of desire. She met his wide, almost panicked eyes.

"Wh-what are you doing here?"

"I wanted to talk to you about last night." He seemed nervous today. Did he regret their kiss? "Were you fencing?" she asked.

He looked down at the foil in his hand as if he'd forgotten that he had it. "Practicing," he said quickly, and set it down on the table. "Forgive me. This is hardly appropriate." He fumbled for his shirt which he'd tossed over a chair. It slipped from his fingers and landed on the ground.

He leaned over to retrieve it, which exposed his back. She sucked in a breath. Thick scars covered his skin. It looked like he'd been whipped.

She moved before she thought better of it, crossing to him and reaching out her fingers to touch the raised welts. The silvery scars were rough beneath her fingers, though faded with age. *This happened some time ago.*

Christian jerked away from her touch and tugged his shirt over his head until the linen covered the marks.

"What happened?" she whispered.

He shrugged his waistcoat on, buttoning it up like armor. "How may I be of service, Miss Bennett?" His voice was stiff, formal, and the usual, faint flush darkened his cheeks.

He was embarrassed, she realized. He hadn't wanted anyone to see the marks. Who had hurt him so terribly? Was whipping as corporal punishment something they still did in this time? Christian didn't seem like a criminal, so it didn't make sense.

Worse, she realized, these physical marks were the external sign of the emotional scars he tried so hard to hide from view. Her heart wept for him, and she wanted to pull him into her arms with every fiber of her being. But she wasn't sure he wanted her touch. He'd fled from her at every opportunity.

"I wanted to ask you about last night," she said, hoping the change in topic would put him more at ease.

It was the wrong thing to say. He backed farther away as he slipped his jacket on. Soon, all the empty space in the room stood between them.

The distance felt far greater. She felt like a tiger backing its prey into a corner. It was terrible and she hated it. But she didn't know how to gain his trust. Instead, she said, "Thank you for the dance. I was nervous about dancing in front of others when I'd just learned the steps. You made me feel graceful."

He nodded his head and gripped the back of the chair behind him.

Bellamy tried again with a different subject. "Was the information that the Major provided helpful?"

He sighed and raked a hand through his hair, making it stand on end as if he'd just climbed out of bed. It didn't make him less attractive. She wanted to run her fingers through the silken strands again and press a kiss to his lips. "We didn't find Dale. Or the clock. I'm sorry."

She nodded. "So, what's next?"

"He may be at Vauxhall Gardens tomorrow evening. To meet with…someone who might buy one of my automatons." He looked away as he spoke.

Her gut clenched. "The clock?"

"I don't know. He also stole a music box, and the silver rose I was working on."

"And money," she said.

He stared at her. "How did you…?" He appeared to compose himself. "I will go tomorrow night and put an end to this. If it is not the clock he means to sell, then I'll make him take me to it. You…you should be able to return to your time soon."

"I'm coming with you," she said.

"No," he snapped, his voice harsh. But then he swallowed and lowered his voice. "No. That would be improper."

"But—"

He held up a hand to stop her objection. "It will also be dangerous. I don't know who he is meeting, or how many men will be there. I won't risk your safety."

She crossed her arms over her chest and stared at him. "As it so happens, I will be at Vauxhall Gardens tomorrow night anyway. Since the gardens are now open for the Season, Gabriel wants to take Lily to see them. Violet and I are going as well."

He paled. "It's dangerous. You must always stay on the lit paths. The pleasure gardens are known for their abundance of finery, but also their more…unsavory nature. Do not leave Gabriel's side. I beg of you."

"If they are so dangerous, who will protect you?"

He looked away.

"Will you let me help you, Christian?"

"No," he said, meeting her gaze once more. "In good conscious, I can't."

She stared at his handsome face, her eyes locked with his. Neither looked away for long moments. She wanted to cross to him and put her arms around him. She wanted to tug his head down to kiss him. But Gabriel's words from earlier rang in her head.

Don't hurt him.

She turned and left the room.

CHAPTER SEVEN

VAUXHALL PLEASURE GARDENS were magical under the bright moon on a clear spring night. Hundreds of people visited the dinner boxes and danced to the music or strolled along the Grand Walk in their best finery. Thousands of lamps lit the pathways and bouquets of sweet flowers scented the air.

Christian strolled along the path under the sycamore and elm trees. Miss Bennett walked beside him. Lily held Gabriel's arm as they walked in front, and Violet and Aunt Josephine meandered behind. They'd supped at one of the extravagant dinner boxes, paying an exorbitant sum for ham sliced so thin, it was nearly invisible, and a couple of small chickens. One could hardly complain, however, as the look of delight on Lily and Bellamy's faces at the wonders of the garden made the evening worth every farthing.

"I've never seen anything more beautiful," Bellamy said softly, obviously enchanted.

He could only see her. She wore a shawl over a lavender dress cut low to emphasize her lovely bosom and tiny waist. She was thinner than most ladies he was acquainted with, probably due to how little she seemed to eat at the meals they'd shared. Tonight, her hair was pinned in the ringlets fashionable among women, and decorated with a small feather comb. She was the most beautiful woman he'd ever seen.

"I quite agree," he murmured.

She glanced up at him from beneath her long lashes and a small smile curled the edges of her pretty, pink lips.

His gaze locked on them. He remembered how they felt against his, and how sweet they'd tasted. He wanted to kiss her more than he wanted his next breath. With effort, he looked away and as they walked, he began to wonder. Should he offer her his arm? They were not courting, and he had no wish to spark any rumors that might adversely affect her. But would she accept it if he did?

They hadn't spoken much today, and he was certain that was because their conversation yesterday eve had not pleased her. She'd shocked him when she walked in during his fencing drills and the humiliation he felt, knowing she'd seen his scars, had unnerved him. He also couldn't knowingly put her in danger and his refusal to allow her to help made her walk away from him. The pain he'd felt at the disappointed look on her face before she left lingered in his heart throughout the day, and he found he didn't know what to say.

Under normal circumstances, he would be happy to let the silence continue but with Bellamy…the silence between them felt uncomfortable. He considered and discarded a number of things to say but eventually decided on, "The gardens cannot compare to your beauty, Miss Bennett." He winced. Did that sound as dreadful as it seemed?

Her mouth opened and he heard her breath catch. She stopped and turned to face him, her eyes searching his. "Thank you, Lord Huntington," she said softly. "You are very handsome as well." She reached out and smoothed her hand slowly down his waistcoat.

Her touch left a trail of heat he could feel through his clothes. He didn't know how to respond to her words or her touch. Had anyone called him handsome before? "You're as lovely as you are kind," he said. That, too, sounded wretched. Curse his awkwardness.

Bellamy gave him a soft smile, then she turned and tucked her palm into the bend in his elbow and they began walking again.

All the tension and awkwardness drained out of his body at that simple touch. He smiled and pressed his gloved hand over the top of hers, holding her to him. Emboldened, he said, "Lily has told me some about your time. That most women are employed. That you are what's called a 'model,' and that you earn a living…displaying clothing for others?"

She nodded and swayed closer to him as they walked. Her delicate lilac scent teased him and his heart began to pound harder.

"It's like…if the modistes were to present all their latest designs to the *haute ton*, but instead of using fashion plates, they had models, like me, wearing the gowns so that women could see what they look like on a real person. How the fabric moves. That way women can decide whether the gown might flatter their own figures."

"What a marvelous idea. Have you worked in this manner long?"

She nodded. "Five years."

"There are that many modistes?"

She laughed. "Thousands. But I've been lucky to be chosen by some of the most famous, which in turn, has made me well-known."

"It is something that you enjoy, then."

"Hmm. At first, I loved it."

Her answer surprised him. "Why not now? I thought that was the main reason that you were eager to return to your time."

"Oh, it is. But I'm not sure the work is making me happy like it used to. In my time, a woman can't model for long. Not one of the top models like I am, anyway. Soon I'll be considered too old to be what they call 'a fresh face.' Because of that, I recently signed a contract that would give me work for a few more years and provide enough money for me to start something new."

His eyebrows shot up. "Old? Are you considered 'on the shelf' at a certain age?"

She grinned. "Something like that."

He considered her comments, turning them over in his mind. "You have signed a contract for this work, but you do not enjoy it any longer. Why not?"

"It's a difficult business to be in. Models close to my level of success will often do anything to get there. Not all of them, of course. But there is no shortage of rivalry, sabotage, or sleeping with whomever they need to in order to get the good contracts."

Anything? Sleeping with...He must have looked aghast because she ducked her head. "There is also an extreme emphasis on body image. I dare not eat too much. Three extra pounds can make the difference between keeping and losing a contract for being too fat."

"Why in heavens would you..." He trailed off when he realized how insensitive it might sound to ask why she would choose such a terrible vocation.

She squeezed his arm. "At first, it was the excitement of travel and the glamour. I could travel the entire world and be paid to splash in the ocean for a few hours. I didn't realize the darker side of the business until much later. Lily tried to warn me. To get me to stay in college, but I didn't listen. I thought she was trying to hold me back, so I took as many jobs as I could, just to spite her."

He glanced at Lily, who rested her head against Gabriel's shoulder as they walked a little bit ahead. "She seems the type of woman who cares for everyone she considers friend or family. She wouldn't want anyone to come to harm."

"She is. But we'd been fighting for years by that point. I couldn't see her concern, only the restrictions she was trying to place on me."

"I suspect Violet is experiencing much the same in her relationship with Gabriel."

She smiled faintly. "Maybe we can help each other before I go."

That she wanted to help Violet, someone whom she'd just met, during the short time that she was here, said much for her character. Christian rubbed his thumb over her gloved knuckles and tightened his elbow to his side to keep her close. He wasn't ready to lose even the slightest contact with her. He wasn't ready for Bellamy to leave at all.

What would it be like to wander down this grand avenue with her on his arm if they were courting, instead of looking for a thief? To slip to the edge of the dark walks, and steal another kiss?

What if she decided not to leave?

His heart thudded hard at the thought. What a fool he was, to hope for something that would never be…

"You said that the man you're looking for stole something other than the clock and rose. What was it?" she asked.

"A music box. It…well it has a mechanism in it that moves a picture throughout the day. In the morning, the picture is of the sunrise with birds nesting in the trees, and as the day continues, the picture changes. The birds take flight, the clouds cross the sky. In the evening, the sun sets, and the stars and moon come out." He rubbed the back of his neck. "Nonsensical, I know. No one would want it."

Bellamy tugged him to a stop, ignoring the grumble of Aunt Josephine and Violet's giggle when they were forced to walk around them. "Christian, that sounds *incredible!* What do you mean 'no one would want it'? I bet half the women here tonight would clamor to own something so unusual."

Could that be true? He'd never really thought anyone would find his inventions that interesting. "Would you?" he asked.

"Yes. I confess I didn't get a good look at the clock, but from what I remember, the detail was amazing. I can't imagine the talent it takes to create something so unique."

The glow of pride he felt at her words made him feel capable of accomplishing anything, and his heart felt full. He smiled down at her. "My newest project, the silver rose that Dale also stole—"

"Ah, Huntington. I feared I wouldn't find you in this crush.

But I heard a couple talking about clocks and silver roses and—here you are!" Zeph pushed through the crowd and sauntered over to join them. "I should have known I would find you in the company of the most beautiful woman in London." He stood in front of them, blocking their progress as he smiled at Bellamy and bowed over her hand. His silver eyes twinkled when he glanced at Christian. "Were you aware, Miss Bennett, that Lord Huntington is regarded as one of the finest clockmakers of our day? I would wager that his clocks could remain intact for centuries."

"I…" She looked at Christian with wide eyes and seemed to struggle with a response.

"Zeph…" he began, feeling terribly on display.

"You will have to show her some of your inventions," his friend continued. Then he turned to Bellamy and added, "I think you would find them all quite…*magical*."

Christian stilled. *He* knew the clock was somehow responsible for time travel, as did Bellamy, Lily, Violet, and even Gabriel. Did Zeph know? Had Lily told him? He opened his mouth to ask, then, remembering where they were, closed it. There would be time to ask later.

In all the years they'd known one another, Christian had often thought of Zeph as an enigma. He refused to speak of his family or where he came from. He had a slight accent that Christian had yet to identify. At times, he seemed to know things that no one should know while often, he swore he knew nothing at all. Which was the truth? Even though they were close friends, Christian wasn't certain that he'd ever know.

"I'm certain I will," Bellamy replied. "I hope to see some more of his creations for myself."

Christian gave her a small smile, then turned back to Zeph. "You were looking for me?"

"I believe I spotted your man. He went down Druids Walk, going deeper into the shadows of the gardens."

Dale was here. Christian's muscles tensed with the need to find him. He glanced down at Bellamy, who looked at him expectantly.

"Lead the way," she said.

He frowned. "I think not. As I said before, Miss Bennett. Those dark paths are dangerous. I do not know how many men will be there."

"I can take care of myself," she said. "I took some self-defense classes."

Classes, to defend oneself? How dangerous was her time that she'd felt she needed instruction to defend herself against an attacker? He'd learned defense at the boxing saloon under the tutelage of Gentleman Jackson and others, spending hours taking heavy blows. At times, his body had ached for days, and he often came away with large bruises. The thought of Bellamy doing something similar was incomprehensible. Perhaps her training hadn't been anywhere near as physical as his, but he found himself shying away from the very thought of her sustaining any injuries. Regardless of what training she had, he couldn't allow her to get hurt.

Zeph cocked a single, white eyebrow and gave him his usual enigmatic grin, but remained silent.

Christian took her elbow and guided her through the crowd toward Gabriel and the other ladies in their party. "I won't risk your safety," he said.

She tugged her elbow from his grasp and glared at him. "Then I'll follow you once you leave. I need to know what's happened to the clock. Let me help."

He shook his head, biting back a curse. "I did not take you for a fool, Miss Bennett. Those darkened paths are often full of libertines of the worst sort. Allowing a young woman to walk them alone would be like parading a virgin sacrifice through the streets." Good God, what was he saying? He sucked in a breath and searched for words that wouldn't be so shameful to speak of in front of a lady. "Please," he begged in a low voice, "nothing is more important to me than your safety. Stay with Gabriel. I won't be able to focus on Dale for fear of you getting hurt. But I promise, the moment I have news, I will share it."

She glanced at Zeph. When he offered her no assistance, she huffed and crossed her arms over her chest. "Then, by all means, lead me to wherever helpless damsels are supposed to wait while the gallant knight battles the dragon." With that, she turned and stomped toward Gabriel and Lily.

Christian's lips twitched, though whether in frustration or humor, he couldn't be certain. At the moment, he keenly felt both.

He felt Zeph's gaze boring into the side of his face and turned to look at his friend. As usual, his friend smirked in amusement.

"You're certain she's the one that you want?" Zeph asked.

"What? I don't...I can't..." Christian let his words trail off as he watched Bellamy to make sure she rejoined her sister and the others safely. Whenever he thought of her, indeed whenever he was *around* her, his emotions were heightened. She made him feel things that he couldn't even name, and as a result, he felt off balance. That Zeph could read it in his countenance was disconcerting.

Zeph squeezed his shoulder. "Let's find Dale and finish this business. Then you can worry about how to make the lady yours."

They stepped off the main avenue onto the center walk and then made their way to Druids Walk. Here, with the lanterns spaced much farther apart, all manner of meetings and trysts could be found and as they continued on, the sounds of music and laughter faded.

Did he want Bellamy to be his? His heart thumped hard, and his stomach flipped with excitement. He'd never felt as comfortable or spoken so much with a woman. Not even Lily. It was exhilarating, in a way. And with every conversation with her, he felt more confident. She'd never once shown disdain for him—not even when she'd seen his scars. Her only reaction had been concern and instead of disgust, she'd touched his back as if she could heal his skin and make the marks disappear. His thoughts stalled. What if those were the only reasons he found her fascinating?

Voices ahead broke into his thoughts. He and Zeph slowed their pace until several men came into view. Christian's heart jumped. Though he only had the light of the moon and a couple of dim lanterns spaced too far to be of much use, he immediately recognized one of the men—William Dale had come to meet the buyer.

As they watched, a wiry man wearing what appeared to be gold satin breeches and a red velvet great coat emerged from the other darkened path. He looked like many of the dandies known to frequent the social events of the Season.

Zeph cocked his head. "He is not what I expected."

Christian agreed. He scanned the five men who surrounded the buyer, each with a pistol pointed at Dale. "They are."

"What 'bout us?" a male voice said from behind them.

Something hard and cold pressed into Christian's back with the man's words. A pistol. He glanced left to see a second man with his weapon pointed at Zeph. "Most unexpected," Christian replied.

BELLAMY GLOWERED AT Christian's back as he and Zeph melted into the throngs of people on the Avenue. Frustration burned in her gut because he'd insisted on leaving her behind again. Despite his warnings, she considered following him anyway as remnants of a teenage rebellious streak—perfected during the years that it was just her and Lily—reared up to protest. But the adult in her acknowledged that he was right. She didn't know the garden paths or even how big the garden was and wandering around could be akin to walking through Central Park at night. Was she really willing to risk a terrible fate just to prove a point?

She ground her teeth and turned her back on their retreating figures. *Dammit.*

"A little more of that rack punch, I think," Aunt Josephine was saying. She blinked slowly and swayed. "It's delightful."

"What a grand idea, Aunt Josephine," Violet said. "Allow me to escort you."

"Violet…" Gabriel began with a sigh.

"The gardens are perfectly safe on the Grand Avenue, aren't they, Aunt Josephine?" Violet said, drowning out his protests.

Josephine laughed. "Quite right. Er…right." She patted her bodice, and Bellamy's eyebrows rose as the woman's entire hand disappeared down the front of her gown. She dug deep between her breasts and then pulled out a quizzing glass to peer through. "I say, is that the Dowager Parling? I should like to speak with her."

Bellamy blinked. Where, exactly, did the elderly woman keep that magnifier?

Gabriel coughed and turned his head away.

"What about the rack punch?" Violet asked.

"Oh. Yes. Perhaps we should have some punch before engaging in conversation with her. Gird our loins, eh?"

"Oh, Aunt Josephine," Lily said and started to giggle.

Gabriel pinched the bridge of his nose. "Aunt Josephine, I really don't think it's necessary for anyone in our party to gird anything. Now if I may suggest—"

"Pardon the interruption," a cultured male voice said. The gentleman emerged from the throng to stop beside Aunt Josephine. He scanned their small party, eyes lingering on Lily, and then Bellamy. "I understand that congratulations are in order, Rothden."

Bellamy recognized him. It was the man that Major Waler had spoken with after telling them where to find Dale. The man who'd spied upon her and Christian when they'd kissed.

"Wainsright," Gabriel bit out and Bellamy shivered. The air turned frosty at his tone.

"At first, I thought it gauche that you would marry a foreigner without a title. But now that I see the enchanting lady for myself, I quite understand." Wainsright extended his hand for Lily's.

She hesitated, glancing at Gabriel, then placed her fingertips in his. He bent over her hand politely. He greeted Violet and Aunt Josephine in a similar fashion, then extended his hand toward Bellamy.

"And *this* must be Miss Bennett that all the Ton is talking about."

The etiquette that Lily and Violet had drilled into her during her first few days in London dictated that she should put her hand in his for a proper greeting, but the smoldering look he gave her beneath his pale lashes was anything but proper.

Lily cleared her throat. "My sister, Miss Bellamy Bennett."

Bellamy pasted on her customary smile and placed her hand in his. "A pleasure…Mister Wainsright, is it?"

"It's Lord Wainsright," he corrected in the same obnoxious manner a doctor corrected you of his title when you accidentally called him, "Mister."

What a pompous ass. She smiled brighter.

He bowed over her gloved hand, lips coming alarmingly close.

"You've had your introductions. Be on your way, Wainsright," Gabriel growled.

"Good gracious, Gabriel. Your manners," Aunt Josephine tutted. She swayed toward Lord Wainsright. "You'll have to excuse my nephew. He didn't learn social niceties at Eton." Her laugh ended in a hum as she looked Wainsright over with her quizzing glass. "I say, you are a fine fellow, aren't you?"

Violet broke into a coughing fit and turned away.

Wainsright's eyes turned flinty. "Quite right you are, Lady Bancroft. As your nephew's prefect for a time, I was disappointed that he didn't learn a great deal more."

Something frigid and hostile passed between the two men as they stared at each other for long moments.

"William Dale was your steward for a time, wasn't he?" Gabriel asked, suddenly. "Tell me, why did he leave your employ to work for Huntington?"

Wainsright smiled slowly. "He expressed an interest in moving on. I could not, in good conscience, hold him back."

The temperature dropped another degree. Gabriel appeared on the verge of violence.

"I say, have you had that rack punch yet, Lord Wainsright? I was just remarking to..." Aunt Josephine squinted at Bellamy—"Miss...Bennett. Yes, *Miss Bennett*, that the rack punch was not to be missed."

"I have not sampled it this eve," he replied, his gaze still on Gabriel. "Might I escort you and Miss Bennett to the Promenade for a glass?" He flicked a glance at Bellamy from beneath his lashes.

"That would be lovely, yes," Josephine tittered.

"No," Gabriel snarled. Lily put a hand on his arm.

Bellamy had no desire to go anywhere with the man. But he presented an opportunity that she couldn't pass up: a way that she could help Christian. Wainsright knew Dale. He might know more about the theft and where Dale might keep his money or items of importance.

He wouldn't give the information to Gabriel, that was clear. But years spent going to the parties of the rich and famous had taught Bellamy how to talk to people. Or more accurately, how to get them talking about themselves. And that experience made it obvious to her that Wainsright was just the type to enjoy boasting about his accomplishments.

"I'd love to join you," she replied.

Violet sucked in a breath beside her and tugged on the back of her gown.

When Bellamy glanced at her, the young woman shook her head, verbally telling her not to go. But she ignored the warning.

"Excellent. Rothden and his lady wife can enjoy the gardens and then join us," Wainsright said with a slick smile. He offered his arm to Aunt Josephine, who latched on and leaned into him.

Lily leaned over to Bellamy and whispered, "Are you sure? Gabriel doesn't like this man for some reason."

"I can handle him," Bellamy whispered back. "I'm used to swimming with the sharks." With that, she raised her voice. "We'll be waiting for you at the Promenade. Enjoy your walk."

Lily looked uncertain, but she nodded.

Gabriel, however, looked murderous.

She gave Gabriel a small nod, trying to convey that she knew what she was doing, and then accepted Wainsright's other arm, and the three of them turned around to meander back toward the Promenade.

Aunt Josephine chattered drunkenly about one thing or another as they walked. Wainsright provided non-verbal cues at the appropriate moments to keep her talking but otherwise remained quiet.

Out of the corners of her eye, Bellamy studied the man beside her. Aside from his height—he was probably an inch taller than Christian—and his thinning blond hair, he was fairly unremarkable, and he spoke with the hint of an accent she couldn't quite place.

"Are you from England, Lord Wainsright?" she asked when there was a lull in Josephine's prattle.

He smiled down at her. "I am. Though, I've spent the last few years in India."

She vaguely remembered that India had been important to Britain during this time period, but history was not her best subject. "Fascinating. What did you do there?"

"I helped a bit with the tea trade and other exports. Nothing a woman such as yourself would find interesting, I'm certain."

If he pats me on the head and calls me "little lady," I will deck him right here. It might cause a scandal, but Lily will understand.

She faked a smile.

"Ah, I believe they are selling rack punch just there," Wainsright said. They'd reached the edge of the supper boxes.

Hundreds of people milled about the area, talking loudly over the music being played by a small orchestra on a platform.

Bellamy didn't see anyone selling rack punch.

Wainsright crouched down to ask Aunt Josephine, "Is that Lady Somersby?" He pointed to a plump woman stuffed into a peacock green dress that appeared two sizes smaller than her figure.

"Why yes. Good eye, young man." She tapped his arm with her quizzing glass. "I should like to go speak to her."

"Allow me." Wainsright led Aunt Josephine over to the woman, who looked to be as in her cups as Josephine. "Here you are."

Aunt Josephine tittered again, then leaned close to Bellamy. "You should flirt with that one," she whispered loudly. "He's a fine catch. Quite affluent." She winked, then patted Wainsright on the arm. "Thank you for the escort. You'll see to Miss…*er*…Bennett, won't you?"

"Indeed, I shall," he said.

The look he shot Bellamy gave her pause. But Josephine had turned away to join her friend and left the two of them unchaperoned.

Wainsright offered his arm. "Shall we stroll the gardens, Miss Bennett?"

She hesitated. She didn't want to be alone with the man, but she needed to get him to talk. Squaring her shoulders, she took his arm. She didn't have her pepper spray, but hopefully, she wouldn't need it *or* the self-defense techniques she'd learned. "Certainly," she replied. "You seem to know Ga—I mean—Lord Rothden. Does that mean you also know Lord Huntington? I understand he also went to Eton."

The man smirked. "I do, though I daresay I do not know him as well as you, Miss Bennett."

Ice slid down her spine at his implication. "I don't know what you mean. I only met him a few days ago when I came to visit my sister."

He tightened his arm, capturing her hand in the crook of her elbow, and pulled her a little closer. "Oh? Do you always kiss men you've just met? Is that the sort of woman you are, Miss Bennett?"

She tried to release his arm to put distance between them, but he clamped his other hand down onto hers and held her to him.

"Let me go," she said between gritted teeth.

The few people surrounding them gave them cursory looks but continued on their way without stopping.

"Answer the question," he replied, his tone pleasant.

She glared at him.

He chuckled. "Come now, Miss Bennett. I'd hoped that this would be an enjoyable walk. I would hate for it to devolve into something uncomfortable. Wouldn't you?"

The veiled threat was clear. "No. I don't kiss every man I meet," she bit out.

"I cannot fathom why you would kiss the tongue-tied earl." His eyes glittered when he looked down at her. "Perhaps you don't know better. Perhaps you would like a lesson in a real kiss."

She opened her mouth to respond when the silence surrounding them pressed in on her. It was too quiet. There was no one on the path. She looked around frantically and discovered that he'd guided her onto a darkened walk while she was focused on the hold he had on her arm.

That was stupid, Bellamy!

She shuddered as a different fear took over. Wainsright was taller, stronger, and suddenly seemed far more dangerous than she'd first thought. She'd practiced the self-defense techniques for a few months. But now, standing in the face of a dangerous situation, her mind blanked, and her feet felt rooted to the ground. Should she call for help? Go along with him and still try to get the information? Fight?

Wainsright pulled her closer. "Don't look so frightened, kitten. I won't hurt you," he cooed.

"Stay away from me."

She tried to pull away, but he grabbed her arms and yanked

her against his chest. His warm breath brushed her ear. "Scream now, and I'll make certain that anyone who comes running knows that you were in the throes of pleasure."

She flinched away. "Let…let me go."

"Not yet, kitten. Come along quietly. Huntington is waiting for us."

What? Why would he take her to Christian? How would he even know where he was? He had to be lying. "You expect me to believe that you're taking me to him?" She struggled to free her arms. He tightened his hands in a harder grip and pulled her closer.

No. She wasn't going anywhere with this creep. Heat rushed through her. She tried to stomp on his instep, but Wainsright grinned and easily avoided her boot. Then he spun her around in a lightning-quick move and yanked one arm up high behind her back.

She reached back, trying to grab his hair, but only succeeded in knocking his hat loose.

Wainsright grabbed her wrist with his free hand and wrestled it down to her side. He tugged on her other arm, forcing it higher on her back. Bellamy cried out as pain flared into her shoulder and through her wrist. She arched back, pressing her shoulders to his chest to try to alleviate the pain and awkward angle.

"Mm, I bet you make the most delicious sounds in bed. Perhaps you'll be more amenable to that later." He forced her to walk down the dark path.

Now that she was in motion, the veil of terror was beginning to lift. She ran through every self-defense move she knew but couldn't remember any that would help her slip out of this bone-wrenching grip. Even the slightest movement made him yank her wrist higher up her back until her shoulder felt like it was on fire.

He marched her forward until the path met with another. Then they turned a corner and Bellamy found herself staring down the muzzle of several pistols. No less than eight men stood in a huddle, all of them armed. Kneeling in the middle of them, with their hands behind their heads, were Christian and Zeph.

Chapter Eight

Dale's whimper of pain gave Christian some satisfaction, where there was generally none to be had.

"I ting you brog my noz, Hundingdon," Dale whined. Blood seeped between his fingers as he clutched his nose.

Christian bared his teeth at him. The two men who'd snuck up on them had prodded them onto the path to join Dale, the dandy, and the five other, rough-looking men accompanying him. The moment Christian was close to Dale, he'd stepped forward and punched the man. His knuckles stung, but the pain seemed a small consequence for the gratification he felt as a result. At this point, however, he and Zeph had been forced to their knees and surrounded at pistol point.

The dandy pushed Dale aside with a brief look of contempt as he approached. "I thought perhaps Dale ignored my instructions to come alone. His broken nose indicates otherwise. Who are you?"

Zeph spoke up. "Lael. That's Huntington."

"Lael. Why do I know that name?"

A corner of Zeph's lips turned up.

The dandy studied Zeph, then dragged his gaze to Christian. "Huntington. An earl if I recall? What business do you have here? Or was it simply happy circumstance that brought your fist to Dale's nose on this particular path?"

"Bathdard," Dale muttered.

"Dale worked as his steward," a man said.

Christian's muscles tensed. He'd heard that voice in his nightmares. He turned his head to see Shelby Wainsright approach, holding Bellamy in front of him.

The chilly night air froze in his lungs.

Both of her arms were behind her back, her body arched against the man. Lines of pain bracketed her wide eyes, and trembling breaths escaped her parted lips.

He lunged to his feet. One of the brutes kicked the back of his knee, sending him crashing back down. Gravel bit into his kneecaps. Christian gritted his teeth but kept his gaze locked on her.

"My, my," the dandy replied. "Lord Wainsright with a pretty filly in tow. Is there no end to the delights of this garden?"

"Carter." Wainsright nodded to the dandy in greeting. His gaze flicked over the armed men, then to Dale, Christian, and Zeph. "I would ask what brings you out this night, but it seems my enterprising former steward has found something to pique your interest."

"As have you," Carter replied, taking a step towards Bellamy. "Perhaps more than one agreement can be reached tonight."

White-hot fury burst in Christian's chest but before he could act, a hard, gloved hand came down on his shoulder and pinched the muscle to keep him in place.

Bellamy's eyes blazed at Carter. "Lay one hand on me and you'll wish you looked as good as the guy with the broken nose," she snapped.

"A beautiful woman with fight." Carter grinned. "A rarity. You know of my affinity for the exotic, Wainsright."

Bellamy struggled against Wainsright's hold and kicked his shin.

He grunted and pulled her arms high until she cried out. "Do that again, and I'll gladly hand you over."

Christian struggled forward, but the man holding him

pinched harder.

"Move again and I'll slit your throat," the gruff man murmured in his ear.

Carter chuckled. "I love spirit." He slanted a look at Dale. "In women. Should I find it concerning that two of your employers have decided to join us on this lovely evening? No? Let's see about our business then, and everyone can be on their way. The music box, if you please."

Bellamy met Christian's gaze. The light of the moon shone down on her pale hair and delicate form. In the relative darkness of the path, her cheeks looked flushed with indignation. She was gorgeous, even in her anger. Christian refused to let this dandy or Wainsright mar an inch of her perfection. The thought of the harm these men could do to her made his chest tight.

He had to get her free of Wainsright. The man possessed the volatility of a madman.

I swear they won't harm you, he tried to impart as they stared at one another. Christian was not a man of violence, but if she was hurt in any way, he would show no mercy.

He felt Zeph shift beside him. His friend gave the tiniest nod, an affirmation of support in the face of so many pistols. It would be ten men against two. While he and Zeph both spent time at Gentleman Jackson's boxing saloon and were adept with swords, neither form of defense seemed in their favor in this situation.

They needed a distraction.

Dale wiped his bloody hands on his jacket and removed the silver music box Christian had spent weeks crafting. " 'ere," he said with a snuffle. He handed it to Carter, who eyed it eagerly.

"How does it—" Laughter rang out. Carter whipped his head to the right, staring hard down the darkened walk. A man and at least two ladies were nearby. Their voices grew louder as they drew closer.

Several of the men with Carter lowered their pistols, attempting to conceal them in the folds of their coats. It was the distraction they'd needed. Christian shot to his feet, ramming an elbow into the face of the man behind him. He heard a crunch and a muffled groan of pain. Something heavy hit the gravel. He dropped to a crouch as another man rushed him, avoiding his punch. Christian hammered the man's ribs with a hard punch that sent the brute staggering back. The few seconds of reprieve allowed him to swipe the ground and his fingers brushed the cool metal of a pistol. He grabbed it and turned on one knee, looking for Wainsright.

In his peripheral vision, Zeph punched one man and kicked another. The remaining men jumped forward into the fight, one raising his gun. Carter and Dale stumbled out of the way.

"Who goes there?" someone called out.

"Is there a fight?" a woman asked. They sounded close. Too close.

Christian heard a muffled thump and a hoarse wheeze. Wainsright swore. He followed the man's voice and found him hunched over, one arm wrapped around his waist. The other hand pressed between his legs.

Bellamy stood beside him, panting. But then she gripped the skirts of her silk gown, hiked them higher, and kicked Wainsright with enough force to send him stumbling back. He snapped his head up and bared his teeth at her, then regained his footing and charged.

A gunshot rang out, and a woman screamed.

Christian's heart stopped.

Bellamy staggered as Wainsright caught her around the waist.

Christian couldn't tell if she'd been shot. It was too dark on the path, and there were too many people. He surged toward her, heart pounding hard in his chest.

Just before he reached her, all hell broke loose. Three men surged out of the darkness to grapple with Carter and his men. Christian spotted Gabriel, and behind him, the lanky frames of Twisden and Granville.

Where was Bellamy?

Another shot rang out.

"Stop Dale," Zeph growled. "Don't let the dandy disappear with that silver box."

Blast! Dale lurched in one direction as Wainsright and Bellamy went in the other. If Dale escaped now, Christian knew that he'd never locate the man. His steward now knew that he was searching for him. He would take the money and disappear. With the music box in Carter's hands, any hope of getting enough funds to pay his staff lay with Dale. He couldn't let the man disappear.

But then, Bellamy cried out, her voice pained.

Christian shifted his focus back to her. Her face looked ashen. She fought Wainsright with whatever hits and kicks she could get but she was constricted by her gown. Wainsright deflected most of her strikes until finally, he grabbed her around the waist, hoisted her over his shoulder, and ran for the woods.

No! Ice-cold fear spread through Christian's limbs. Visions of finding her broken and bloody filled his head. He knew what Wainsright was capable of, and it petrified him.

He had to choose. Bellamy or people who'd worked for him for years.

His stomach churned, and he couldn't breathe. Memories of pain assailed him. Wainsright had nearly killed him once. He couldn't let that same fate befall Bellamy.

"CEASE YOUR STRUGGLES," Lord Wainsright barked as he jogged down the edge of the dark walk, sticking even closer to the shadows.

"Like hell," Bellamy spat. She was slung over his shoulder like a wayward child. She bucked against his shoulder, trying to force him to set her down.

Instead, he wrapped a second arm around her thighs to pin her in place.

Bellamy balled her hand into a fist and slammed it against his back.

"Ow. Damn you. I am not in the habit of hurting women. Unless you wish to be the first, I insist that you *calm yourself.*" The snarl in his voice said he was losing patience.

Was he being honest about not hurting women? Could she afford to trust that he was?

"I am taking you to safety," he grumbled.

"Safety? *You* are the one who put me in danger," she snapped. "Let me down!" Bellamy pushed at his back and shoulders, kicking at anything she could reach. The tip of her foot hit something soft.

He gasped and suddenly, she was falling. Gravel bit into her hip and shoulder when she landed hard on her side. *Oh God, that hurt.* She scrambled to her feet as fast as her aching body would allow.

Lord Wainsright was doubled over, groaning. He glared at her. "Damnation, woman. You are a menace. I'll—"

"Stay where you are." Christian came out of the darkness. Moonlight glinted off the pistol in his hand.

Wainsright slowly straightened, unable to hide his wince. Or his burning hatred when he looked at Christian.

Bellamy took one step toward Christian, unable to tear her gaze from the mottled red fury on Wainsright's face. Two steps. Then she rushed to Christian's side. He reached for her hand and tugged her behind him.

She sucked in a jittery breath. The clean, masculine smell of him hit her senses. Somehow it soothed her, and her muscles began to relax so that the wild trembling that wracked her began to abate. She tangled her fingers with his and held tightly.

Wainsright held his palms out at his sides. "I'm unarmed. Though that hardly matters to a man like you."

Christian tensed beside her, and his grip tightened. "What is your business with Miss Bennett?" he ground out.

The smile that stretched across Wainsright's face sent icy fear down Bellamy's spine. He stepped backward toward the woods.

She realized why a moment later when a familiar voice pierced the darkness.

"Find them," Carter said. "They can't have gone too far." Then, "No one makes a fool of me!"

Wainsright gave a husky chuckle. "They're here!" he called.

Christian swore. He cocked the pistol. But heavy footsteps were growing louder, coming closer.

"Shall we wait to see what Carter will do?" Lord Wainsright's voice was far too smug.

Bellamy tugged on Christian's hand. "Let's go," she whispered.

He didn't move for several long moments. The thundering of footsteps matched the frantic pace of her heart.

The hell with this. Bellamy knew that even if armed, Christian would be no match for several of the big thugs she'd seen earlier. She gripped his hand and tugged him away.

At last, he lowered his gun and together, they ran from Wainsright. She could hear men shouting and Wainsright directing, "Follow them!"

She glanced over her shoulder to see him pointing toward them as four men sprinted in their direction.

Bellamy gripped her gown in one hand, pulling the hem up so she could run faster. Thank God she'd spent time on the treadmill as part of her daily exercise routine, but the next time she saw her self-defense coach, she was going to challenge him to try those moves while wearing a gown. Beside her, Christian ran, never letting go of her hand.

Clouds shifted above, blocking out the stars and part of the moon's bright glow. Christian cast a glance over his shoulder before he pulled her off the gravel path toward the trees until the darkness obscured them.

He stopped and cocked his head as if listening to their pursuers. Their gazes met. She could just make out his outline.

Christian cupped her cheek for a moment, and the warmth of

his palm sent a wave of calm over her. Then he took her hand and silently guided her a little farther away, to a group of elms clustered together. He settled between them and pulled her close.

"Quiet," he whispered, his lips brushing her ear.

Bellamy tensed when she heard their pursuers stop only a few feet away. She held her breath, heart pounding, and pressed closer to Christian. He wrapped a strong arm around her waist and held her against her body.

The scent of him enveloped her. He felt so warm, so strong. He'd come for her. Dale had been there with the knowledge of the money and the music box Christian had said he was trying to get back, and yet he'd come for her instead of going after the man. He'd put her first.

His protection and sacrifice were something she'd never had before from a man. Bellamy rested her hands on his chest. He was solid. Strong. And his heart thundered under her fingertips.

She remembered his muscled chest glistening with a sheen of perspiration the day before when she found him in the basement. Beneath the fine clothes was a beautiful male body. She tilted her head back to look up at his face. His jaw was stubbled with whiskers, and his lips looked firm. She wanted to kiss him, even at this dangerous moment. His warm breath caressed her ear as he breathed, making her shiver for an entirely different reason.

"I think they've moved on," he whispered. Christian tipped his head down when he spoke and jumped beneath her fingers when he realized how close their heads were.

So close that if she leaned up the slightest bit, their mouths would brush.

The air grew heated.

"You came for me," she whispered, lips tracing his with each word.

He swallowed and she could feel his thrumming heart begin to pound even harder. "I will always come for you."

"I know you will." Bellamy raised on her toes to close the last bit of distance between their lips.

Christian sucked in a sharp breath and stepped away so suddenly that she toppled forward before catching her balance.

"I…forgive me, Miss Bennett." He reached out his hands to stop her from faceplanting on the forest floor but let her go as soon as she was steady.

Miss Bennett. They were back to that again. She knew him well enough now to know that he "Miss Bennetted" her any time he was uncomfortable and wanted to retreat behind the safety of etiquette. She glowered at him.

Christian looked away. "Let's cut through to the other walk." He reached for her hand, hesitated, then stepped away without touching her. "This way."

It took everything in her to keep her steps quiet and not stomp after him in a huff. Was he nervous or just not attracted to her? Was she throwing herself at a man who didn't want her? The mixed signals he was giving her were confusing.

She thought back over every awkward interaction they'd had, including that heady kiss on the balcony at her first ball. The way he'd backed her into the wall and devoured her. Bellamy had been kissed plenty of times but none of them affected her the way Christian's had. And the way he looked at her spoke volumes of how much he wanted her. *He just refuses to act on it.* She narrowed her eyes at his back in the darkness. What was it going to take to break through that wall he'd built up? Was there a way to go around it?

She was so focused on the thought that she wasn't minding where she stepped, not that she could see much with the moon behind the clouds and the trees blocking what little light broke through. She tripped over a root and stumbled into his back.

Christian let out a quiet huff and half-turned to grab her, keeping her upright. "Are you all right?" he asked.

She righted herself and brushed at her skirt, as heat washed over her. "Fine." In the darkness surrounding them, she sensed him staring down at her.

This time, he took her hand. "Come on. Not far now."

Several seconds later, he guided her out of the woods onto a dark walk that ran parallel to the one they'd been on. Two men were approaching them, their faces difficult to discern in the dim lamplight. Christian tightened his grip on her hand and took a step back toward the woods.

The clouds above cleared, letting the bright moon shine down. Bellamy whooshed out a breath of relief when she realized that it was Gabriel and Zeph. Christian immediately released her hand as if she were too hot to touch and stepped forward to meet them.

She tried not to feel disappointed that he didn't want to be seen holding her hand by the two men who were his best friends. Bellamy crossed her arms over her waist and followed.

"What happened?" Gabriel demanded. "Are you both all right?"

"We are," Christian said. "Wainsright took Bellamy. When I caught up to him, she'd managed to get free. Then Carter and a few of his men came, and we ran."

Zeph clenched his fists. "That's why we lost them. They doubled back to go after you."

"What about Dale?" Christian asked.

"Twisden and Granville followed him. I think he was injured, but it was too dark to tell," Gabriel said. He turned to look her over. "Are you certain you're okay, Bellamy? Lily would have my head if anything happened to you."

"I'm fine." She refused to look at Christian. "But I think I've enjoyed all the entertainment that the Pleasure Gardens have to offer this evening. I'm ready to go home." Her stomach swooped when she realized that she was calling Gabriel's townhouse *home*. Shouldn't she be wanting to go back to her time?

Whatever. She was too tired to think about it all at that moment.

"I have to find Lily and Violet immediately," Gabriel said. "I need to be certain that Wainsright didn't return to them, knowing that I wasn't with them."

"Bellamy, I'll take you and Lady Josephine home," Zeph said. "Christian, why don't—"

"No. I'll take her home," Christian interjected. He cleared his throat. "Zeph, you would be better at protecting Lily, Violet, and Aunt Josephine, should there be further trouble."

Zeph's eyes twinkled and his throaty voice turned wry. "Of course. Should there be trouble."

Standing there, listening to the men decide how to proceed, Bellamy felt a chilly wind brush over her exposed arms. In the intense moments of the last hour, she hadn't noticed the cold, or that at some point, she'd lost her wrap. She wrapped her arms around herself tighter and tried not to shiver.

Christian looked down at her, then slid off his great coat, and wrapped it around her shoulders. Enveloped in his lingering heat and scent, Bellamy nearly moaned.

Gabriel pinched the bridge of his nose in a gesture she was beginning to recognize as his reaction to anything stressful. "Huntington, it is improper. You should have a chaperone…maybe Aunt Josephine…"

"I don't need a chaperone. I'm not used to having one anyway. Please go make sure Lily and Violet are okay. I'll be fine. Aunt Josephine was at the pavilion drinking punch with Lady Somersby."

Zeph snorted. "She'll be quite all right if that is the case, though there may be no rack left for the rest of the crush."

Gabriel nodded before he moved close to squeeze her shoulder, then nodded at Christian. "I'll collect the ladies and see you back at the townhouse. Thank you for taking care of Bellamy. Let's hurry, Zeph. I don't trust Wainsright."

The two men hurried off, melting into the darkness.

Christian fidgeted beside her. "Shall we go, Miss Bennett? I'll have my carriage brought around. You'll be warm…and safe."

Bellamy nodded. She knew that Christian would make certain that both were true. He was honorable to the core. If only he wanted more from her. Right now, she just wanted the comfort of his arms—and his body—to drive away the fear lingering from her fight with Wainsright. Maybe that wasn't fair to him, since she wasn't planning to stay, but it wasn't likely to happen anyway. Christian might protect her, but he was too afraid to touch her.

CHAPTER NINE

CHRISTIAN USHERED BELLAMY into his carriage, directing the driver to return them to Gabriel's townhouse. He climbed in and shut the door, then took the seat across from her. Several people had been waiting nearby for their carriages, and he had been terribly aware of their stares as he assisted her inside without a chaperone. Why hadn't he followed Gabriel's suggestion and retrieved Aunt Josephine to travel with them?

Bellamy tucked her knees up to her chest and wrapped her arms around them, huddling in the corner under his large great coat. She looked so thin and frail in the dim interior. It made his heart ache. Foolishly, of course. He didn't know how to comfort her. Or even what to say.

"Thank you," she whispered into the silence. "For coming for me. I'm sorry that you lost the chance to find your steward and retrieve your music box and the money. I should never have gone with Wainsright when he offered to escort Aunt Josephine and me to the pavilion. I was trying to help… I thought I could get information out of him. But he distracted her and then, before I knew what was happening, he'd ushered me onto a dark path. I feel like some dense heroine with no sense of danger who is too stupid to get out of the way." She shivered and pressed her head to the glass window.

"You couldn't have known of his treachery," he replied. She

was clearly upset with herself and he wanted to soothe her.

"I knew that Gabriel had some sort of bad history with him. I just...I thought maybe I could find out something for you. Maybe learn what Dale had done with the money."

For me? His chest clenched as he fought with warring emotions, unsure if he was angry with her for putting herself in danger to help him or in love with her for being so selfless. On the other hand, he'd made clear that he didn't want her assistance. A muscle in his jaw ticked.

"I'm sorry," she said, huddling deeper into his jacket. The sorrow in her voice made his heart hurt, and the need to comfort her overrode his irritation.

"You were brave," he said. It was true, and she needed to know it. "You managed to free yourself from Wainsright, twice. Few women of my acquaintance would have fought him, never mind escaped his grasp." He gave her a small smile. "Most would have fainted in fear."

"Probably not Violet." She smiled back at him, the corners of her mouth just barely lifting.

His lips twitched. "Not Violet. I daresay she put the last man who tried to take liberties with her in his place."

Her smile widened. "Good for her. I hope Gabriel is looking for a man strong enough to put up with her mischievous ways but who will allow her to be herself."

"Does such a man exist?" he teased.

Bellamy looked out the window. "Archer put up with both Lily and me and still managed to love us. Someone like him would be perfect."

"Your brother?" Lily had mentioned the man a few times. From what he gathered, Archer Bennett was in the military and the sisters didn't see or talk to him often.

She nodded and the look in her eyes turned sad. For her brother? Or someone else?

"Do you...have someone? Waiting for you?" He hadn't meant to ask. Now that he had, he couldn't breathe, waiting for her reply. Gabriel said she was unattached. Not married. But what if she had a beau, eager for her return? He didn't want to know.

But he *needed* to know.

She plucked at the sleeve of his coat. "No. I wouldn't have kissed you if I did."

Christian swallowed around the sudden lump in his throat. She'd almost kissed him again in the forest when they'd been pressed together, hiding among the elms. He'd panicked and backed away. The disappointment on her face after that had made him feel like the worst sort of man. "Bellamy…I…"

"It's okay. I'm sorry that I made you uncomfortable. I won't try to kiss you again." She looked back out the window.

Bellamy *had* made him uncomfortable, but not in the way she believed. Did this smart, brave woman truly desire him? It was madness to even consider. After all, when he found the clock, she would leave. Nothing good would come from forming an attachment.

Added to that, she was Gabriel's family. His sister-in-law. Wouldn't that intrude on their friendship?

Bellamy pressed her temple to the window and looked down at her hands in her lap where she twisted her fingers together. She looked lost. Embarrassed. And so beautiful, she stole the breath from his lungs.

This is madness. The risk is too great. It will only bring me pain…

But to not know, not have her, will also bring me pain. And therein rode a single desire. To finally feel a connection that went beyond friendship. Deep within his heart, he knew he wouldn't find that connection with anyone other than Bellamy.

He needed only the courage to move beyond his fears.

Christian removed his gloves, then he slowly leaned forward and took her gloved hand in his. He drew her to him as he sat back against the cushion.

Her lips parted in surprise, yet she came to him.

He wrapped an arm around her waist and settled her across

his lap. Her hands rested on his chest, the heat of them warming something inside him, something that had felt cold for far too long. He could feel that icy coldness thawing and melting.

Christian traced her temple with his fingertips. The skin beneath felt as soft as down feathers. He tucked a stray curl behind the delicate shell of her ear, then continued the exploration of her cheek, down to her chin. His thumb brushed her full lower lip, and he felt the warmth of her breath on his skin.

Christian's entire body tightened with want. The sensation was new, and a little frightening in its intensity. Much of his life had been devoid of any intimacy, even from his parents. He was ashamed to admit that he didn't know how to express it.

"Christian?"

He heard the hesitant hopefulness in her tone. Her dark blue eyes shone in the lamplight, glittering as she searched his face. For what, he couldn't fathom.

"Do you still desire to kiss me?" He cupped her cheek and tilted her face up.

"Yes," she breathed against his lips. Her hands skimmed up his chest, over his shoulders, and circled behind his neck. She winced.

Her arms must hurt from the way Wainsright held her. He wanted to hunt the man down and make him feel every ounce of pain he inflicted on Bellamy. "Are your arms okay?" He gently ran his hand over one.

She nodded. "A little sore but they'll be okay tomorrow."

"Perhaps we should—"

"No! Kiss me, Christian. Please."

She never needed to beg. Christian lowered his head and pressed a light, lingering kiss to her mouth. Her sharp intake of breath poured fuel on his need for her. He cupped her neck in one hand and pulled her closer with the other. Then he slanted his lips over hers and deepened the kiss. He hesitantly stroked her tongue with his, remembering what she'd taught him at the ball.

Bellamy met him eagerly, pressing her breasts against his

chest and twining her fingers in his hair to pull his mouth closer. Heat spiraled through his body, lighting up areas he hadn't known were sensitive. The way her body moved against his. How her bottom felt in his lap, pressing over his rapidly swelling cock. He moaned against her lips, awash in sensation. She was intoxicating. What man would want a bottle of port when he could drink from her lips?

They kissed for long moments. Christian quickly grew more confident in his kiss, paying attention to what made her sigh and moan.

She wriggled on his lap, rubbing against his hard cock until he thought he might go mad. He broke the kiss as sensation overwhelmed him.

"Christian," she breathed against his lips.

He stroked gentle fingertips over her temple, admiring the graceful curve of her cheek. But not for long. He needed to kiss her again, deeply and with an intensity with which he'd never thought himself capable.

The carriage hit a nasty pothole in the road, banging their teeth together with a painful click and making them lean apart.

"Ouch!" Bellamy laughed, holding her fingers to her lips. "Next time, we should tell them to drive on better streets. Even if it takes much longer to reach home."

Next time.

Yes. He wanted more of this. More of her.

Bellamy tugged his head back down to hers. "Kiss me, Christian. Touch me," she whispered. "I need to feel you."

His breath caught.

She must have seen the uncertainty on his face because she reached for one of his hands, where it rested on her hip, and dragged it slowly up her side. Bellamy bit her lower lip, eyes locked with his, and placed his palm over her breast. She squeezed their hands over that small mound until he felt her tight nipple through the silk of her gown and her stays. He wanted to stay like that forever, with the hot, hard little nub boring into the center of his palm while his fingers filled with the firm flesh of her breast.

"Like that," she said. "Touch me."

He barely refrained from asking if she was certain. She wouldn't have put his hand on her if she wasn't.

"Please."

Christian tightened his hand around her breast, squeezing gently, wanting to—no, needing to—do more. Especially when she shifted, rubbing her bottom over his lap. When she let out a little sigh of pleasure, he was emboldened to explore her more. He traced the edge of her hard nipple with his thumb, drawing a circle around the bud. Bellamy arched into his hand.

"Yes. More."

He moved his thumb over her nipple, and then pressed it between his finger and thumb, relishing the feel of it beneath the fabric of her gown. She rocked her hips against his, arching into him over and over. And then, Bellamy sat up straighter and grasped his hand.

He froze. Was she…did she want to stop making love?

In response, she slipped his hand inside her bodice to cover her bare breast, then kissed him again, stroking his tongue with hers.

His every sense focused on the heat and hardness of her nipple against his palm. He rubbed his thumb over it and felt her shiver. What would it be like to press his lips to her breast? How would she taste? What would that hard bud feel like against his tongue?

Christian kissed his way across her jaw and down her throat. Everywhere he touched felt like silk. Bellamy eased his access to her body, tilting her head back to give him more room and pressing harder into his hand. He skimmed his mouth over her collarbone and pressed kisses to the soft skin above her breasts then moved lower.

She clutched at his hair, urging him down.

He smiled against her skin. Good God, she was beautiful and

passionate. He never dreamed that kissing a woman would feel so good. To gain pleasure by giving it. How had he not known? He traced his lips along the edge of her bodice, savoring the satin skin of her upper breast.

Bellamy shifted her hips, rubbing against his arousal even harder. He sucked in a breath. Did she know what she was doing to him?

Her half-lidded gaze with a sultry smile said she did.

Christian responded by dipping his tongue inside her gown to trace the top edge of her nipple. Bellamy moaned and scrambled to yank the fabric down to give him access to one perfect, creamy breast with a dark pink nipple. It tantalized him. He closed his lips over the firm bud and sucked lightly.

"Oh God," she whispered, arching her back.

He took the invitation and drew the hardened nub more deeply into his mouth, then flicked his tongue over it. She gasped. Emboldened, he began alternating, sucking and flicking at her sensitive peak. She writhed beneath his mouth, panting out little moans and begging for more. Christian palmed her other breast, gripping her hip with his free hand, and grinding into her bottom, reveling in the feel of her softness against his hard cock. He gave himself over to instinct, learning what made her moan and writhe.

A fine tremble began in her limbs and her eyes widened. She released his hair to tug on her skirt and petticoats, pulling them up over her bare legs to pool in her lap.

"I need..." She shivered. "Christian, I..." Bellamy took his hand and moved it again. Right between her thighs.

He almost choked on a breath as his fingers slid through her damp folds at her urging. His entire body clenched with need. Instinct made his hips buck against her bottom.

She guided his hand through her wetness and shifted his thumb to the little nub he felt. "Like that. Rub..." she moaned and pressed her forehead to his as he followed her guidance. "I...I..." Tremors wracked her.

He stroked her with his fingers, drowning in the sensations her body gave him.

Bellamy crushed her mouth to his and cried out against his lips.

He felt her release as it painted his fingers and his palm, proof that he'd brought her pleasure. Christian stared at her in wonder. Surely this angel belonged back in the heavens, not down here. With him.

Her breathing slowly returned to normal, and a smile graced those plump pink lips.

Christian reluctantly removed his hand from between her thighs then tugged his handkerchief from the inner pocket of his coat that she still wore and wiped his fingers clean. Then he slid the linen between her thighs to clean her as well.

Her smile faded and her look changed to one of intensity.

Had he done something wrong? Was it inappropriate to have…have cleaned her? He removed his handkerchief quickly and tugged her skirts down. The back of his neck heated.

"Forgive me. I only meant to…to take care of…"

Bellamy pressed her mouth to his in a lingering kiss. When she pulled back, she stroked his cheek. "No one's ever taken care of me after," she said. "Thank you." She paused. "When Lily told me that ladies didn't wear panties during this era, I thought she was kidding. But I can see the appeal."

The pleasure that he'd pleased her warred with the knowledge that she'd done this before. He couldn't think about her with another man. His hands trembled as he readjusted her bodice, covering up that beautiful breast.

At the same time, he felt her hands at the buttons of his trousers. His hips bucked as the lightest touch of fabric over his cock sent tingles of pleasure down his spine. A few more touches like that and he'd spill.

She seemed to sense his need and opened another button.

Christian caught her hand in his. "Bellamy, I…"

The coach hit a small bump and seconds later drew to a halt.

It tilted as the driver climbed down from the seat. A quick glance out the window showed the red brick of Gabriel's townhome, with the windows lit in welcome.

"Over to your side," he said, ushering her off his lap and hastily trying to close the fall of his trousers. He managed to get the buttons done up as the carriage door opened.

A servant reached a gloved hand in to help Bellamy from the vehicle. Christian followed, the cold, April air welcome against his overheated skin.

"Shall we?" he asked as he gestured toward the front door as if he hadn't made her climax only moments before.

Bellamy gave him an inscrutable look, then climbed the stairs to the house.

Christian swallowed. He felt as if he were a different man from the one that set out for Vauxhall Gardens a few hours before. It was a thought as exciting as it was unsettling.

HEAVY FOOTSTEPS POUNDED the ground behind her in the darkness. Too close. Cold, clammy fingers touched her shoulder. They gripped tight. Squeezed. She felt claws pierce her skin and cried out for anyone.

Anyone.

Bellamy bolted upright in bed, the scream still lodged in her throat. She felt the cold hand on her and flailed to push it away. She scrambled out of bed and hit the floor hard on her knees. A dream. Only a dream. She clutched the blanket in her fists and let out a small sob, her heart still racing from her flight through the darkness.

God, she hated her nightmare. The same cold, grasping fingers, the same chase. Only this time she wasn't searching for her parents before the thing tried to grab her. This time, she'd been alone.

Bellamy pressed her cheek to the side of the bed. Her chin quivered and she scrubbed at a tear with a shaky hand. She could still feel the fear, the helplessness. Her heart hammered in her chest and every breath felt like a battle to get enough air into her lungs. Every tear a fight to get herself under control.

"Why now?" she whispered. The answer was obvious. Lily's disappearance, and a few hours ago, her fight with Lord Wainsright in the darkness of the wood had triggered her fears of not being safe. Of having no one to run to for help.

She gave a soft snort. She'd prided herself on being an independent woman, not needing anyone to hold her hand or fight her battles. Facing the very real possibility of being hurt—or worse—ground that pride to dust. Huddled on the floor beside the bed, still shaking in fear, she admitted to herself that she needed a hug.

Lily would be in bed with Gabriel at this hour. She wouldn't wake her. Besides, things were stilted between them, and a hug would be...awkward. Yet she knew she wouldn't be able to go back to sleep. Not until she'd thoroughly banished the dream.

She rose and slipped her silken wrapper on, hoping it would fortify her against the shadows in the hallways. Maybe she could find a book to read. She lit the candle on the table by the bed and slipped out into the hallway.

The corridor was silent. Thick shadows clung to every corner, sending a fresh shudder down her back. Bellamy scurried to the stairs. They too descended into the penetrating darkness. Her breath hitched.

This is stupid, Bells. Go back to your room and pull the covers over your head. Try to go back to sleep.

It wouldn't banish the dream, though. She squinted, trying to see the landing on the floor below. The drawing room had several books she could read until she fell asleep. If she went down there, she could be back in bed in minutes.

Something creaked behind her. Bellamy jumped, heart pounding, and hissed when candle wax splattered on her hand. Nothing moved in the shadows.

Just the house settling. It's old. It makes noise. Like Aunt Josephine's knees every time she stands up.

Pulse thumping madly, Bellamy eased down the steps as quietly as she could. As if staying quiet would keep the other noises at bay.

The next landing seemed a little brighter. She tilted her head to look at the hall beyond and spotted a light under one of the doors. Not Lily and Gabriel's at the end of the corridor, but the other guest room.

Christian's awake.

She stood before his door before she'd consciously decided to leave the staircase. Heart in her throat, she knocked quietly so as not to wake the sleeping house.

Especially Lily and Gabriel.

Things had been awkward after they'd returned to the house. She and Christian hadn't had time to discuss what happened in the carriage because Gabriel and Zeph brought Lily, Violet, and Aunt Josephine home moments after the two of them had arrived back at the townhouse. Gabriel had pulled Christian away to report that there'd been no further sighting of Lord Wainsright, which she was immensely grateful for. She'd never forgive herself if he'd harmed one of them. She should never have gone with him in the first place. Never have let him get her alone in the dark and then try to use her against Christian.

Then she'd plastered herself against Christian in the carriage and kissed him senseless, practically forcing the man's hand down her dress. Now she was standing in front of his door in the middle of the night.

She rubbed her temple. God, was there no end to her bad decisions? *Yes. Yes, there was, starting now.* Bellamy turned and hurried back toward the stairs, hoping he hadn't heard her rap on his bedchamber door.

But then it swung open behind her, light spilling in a wide arc into the hallway.

"Bellamy?"

She froze. He'd called her Bellamy. Not Miss Bennett. She

turned slowly to face him.

"Are you well?" Christian stepped into the hallway. His shirt was open almost to his navel, exposing that muscled chest and his sleeves were rolled up to his elbows. Oh God, even his forearms were muscled and sinewy, demanding to be touched and stroked. She lowered her eyes over his trousered legs…to his feet bare feet. Bellamy had never found feet attractive. Until now. She felt herself flush and dragged her gaze back to his handsome face. He looked…more comfortable than she'd ever seen him.

He frowned. "Bellamy?"

She cleared her throat. "I'm sorry. I shouldn't have…I'll go."

He left the doorway, moving to gently grasp her arm above the elbow. "You look frightened. You're trembling. What is it, love?"

The warmth of his palm seeped through her thin wrapper, soothing when she felt like she'd never stop shaking. Her need for comfort overrode her embarrassment and thoughts of bad decisions.

Because right now, staying with Christian felt like the right decision. *Just for a moment. Then I'll go back to my room.* Bellamy wrapped her trembling arms around his waist and burrowed into the warmth of his arms. She felt his breath hitch under her cheek pressed to his chest, but the closeness to him felt too good to apologize for.

Christian slowly wrapped her in his embrace and held her close. The stubble on his chin snagged in her hair, connecting them in a different way that somehow felt just as intimate as the hug. "You're safe," he said in a low voice. "I won't let any harm come to you."

She pressed her nose into his neck between his jaw and shoulder and breathed in his masculine scent. It settled her as nothing else ever had.

"Take what you need from me," Christian whispered. He stroked a finger along her cheek and tucked a strand of hair behind her ear, then hesitantly pressed a kiss to her temple.

Bellamy's heart melted. This man, who sometimes seemed like he didn't know what to do with her, was offering her comfort in the middle of the night. He felt strong. Safe. The fear from her nightmare slowly lost its hold, and the anxiety it gave her began to fade. She was reluctant to release him, half afraid that the shadows would press in on her the moment she let him go.

"Saving the damsel in distress twice in one night. That must be a record for any knight. Once the gossips hear, you won't be safe from anyone on the marriage mart." She tried to keep her tone light. The stab of jealousy she felt upon saying the words was unexpected.

He huffed a laugh. "Then we best not tell anyone of my heroic deeds. Else I may have to flee to the country to get away from them."

She smiled at the mental image of Christian running from a pack of women in ballgowns, their eager mothers trailing behind. "What would it take to win the heart of the Earl of Huntington?" She'd meant it in a teasing tone, but he tensed beneath her hands.

"Sorry, I shouldn't have asked," she said.

"No. No, of course, you may. It is simply that…I do not know. Speaking with people is often difficult for me, as I'm sure you've surmised. It is rare to find a woman that I can converse with. Lily and Violet seem to be the exceptions. And…and you."

Bellamy's throat went tight. She rested her forehead on his shoulder. Something about standing in the shadowed hall in the middle of the night made it seem like she could say anything. Do anything. "I like you." Damn. She meant to say that she liked talking to him. She bit her lip and waited for his reaction. Would he push her away? Force her to return to her room?

Christian was quiet for so long, that she wondered if he'd heard her. If he hadn't, she'd be relieved. Right?

No. Not at all. She wanted him to know how she felt about him. God, she was such a jumbled mess inside. Though she wanted to blame it on the nightmare, she'd been feeling this way—anxious and emotionally heightened—for days, anytime she was in his company.

"I like you too, Bellamy," he whispered.

She looked up in surprise.

He gave her a small smile and traced her cheek. "What scared you?"

"A nightmare," she said as she tucked back into the curve of his neck. "I…didn't want to be alone. I came down to see if Lily was awake and saw the light under your door. I probably should have woken Lily, but I…I'm sorry if I disturbed you."

"No. I'm glad you sought me out, Bellamy." His arms tightened until she was completely pressed against the length of his body.

Her breath shuddered out of her on a sigh of pleasure.

"Was it because of what happened? Tonight, with Wains—?"

She covered his lips with her hand. "Don't. Don't say his name right now. But no, not because of him. Not really. It's just…After my parents died, I had nightmares for months. The same one every night. Something was trying to catch me as I ran after my parents, trying to get them back. The faster I ran, the farther away they were. Tonight, they weren't there. Just me. Running as fast as I could but not getting anywhere with the thing getting closer…When I woke, I felt like I couldn't breathe. Couldn't get warm."

"Still cold?" he murmured.

"A little."

"Will you allow me to care for you tonight? I promise, nothing untoward will—"

Bellamy pressed a soft kiss to his neck, which stopped the rushed flow of his words. "Yes."

Christian lifted her into his arms and carried her into his bedchamber. She had a sense of comfortable furniture fashioned with red fabrics and matching curtains over the windows. Against the wall, the writing desk was cluttered with scraps of metal, gears, and tools. Seeing it made her smile and chased the shadows a little farther away.

"Let's warm you by the fire." Christian leaned forward to set her in a chair near the fireplace, but she tightened her arms around his neck and held on.

"Can I sit with you?" she asked. *Please don't say no.*

His stormy blue eyes met hers. A long moment later, he nodded.

Christian sat in one of the red brocade chairs and settled her across his lap. He wound an arm around her waist, tucking her close. His other hand settled over her knee.

She felt the heat of his touch through the silk wrapper. It warmed her more than the dying flame in the hearth. She kept her arms around his neck and rested her head on his shoulder, feeling his chest rise with his steady breathing. His heart beat, strong and steady, where their bodies connected.

They sat in silence for long moments. She had never felt more comfortable, more cared for, than she did sitting in Christian's lap. The world faded around them, as it had in the carriage, until only they remained. She'd tucked her nose back into the spot where his neck and shoulder met to breathe him in. He smelled so good.

He tipped his head and brushed another kiss to her temple.

She pressed a kiss to his neck, letting her lips linger there. Gradually, she became aware of his heart pounding a little harder and the stiffness of his muscles. His eyes were closed. As she watched, he swallowed hard.

Christian's hand trembled as it slid over her thigh and back to her knee.

She wanted him. Wanted the shy man who avoided people, but who hadn't hesitated to come for her when she'd been in trouble. He'd been affected by their kisses in the carriage. He'd kissed her with matching passion. She'd felt his arousal beneath her when she'd been pressed against him.

Feeling bold, Bellamy pressed another kiss higher, beneath his ear. Another at the junction of his jaw where the stubble brushed her lips.

His breath hitched. "I…Miss Be—"

Bellamy cut his words off with a kiss. "Not tonight. Please don't put up a wall between us tonight."

Christian pulled back, searching her eyes.

"I want this. I want you, Christian." She yearned to touch him. To feel his skin beneath hers and explore his big, beautiful body and the scars she'd seen on his back. If he'd let her, she'd kiss every one.

He pressed his forehead to hers and she felt his internal battle in his tense muscles.

God, she'd never had to beg a man to sleep with her, but she was moments away from doing it. Why couldn't he want her the way she wanted him? Even if it was only for momentary pleasure. Although, she was starting to want more. She liked Christian. He was so smart, and he never made her feel like arm candy, like a beautiful woman to be seen and not heard.

He'd kissed her so passionately earlier; there had been no doubt that he desired her. And his touch lit her body on fire. She wanted to feel that again now, here in the safety of his arms. Here where the rest of the world was shut out and it was just the two of them. She wanted to give him pleasure too. To give him something instead of only taking.

His lips feathered slowly over her temple. "Are you certain?" he whispered.

She heard the trepidation in his voice, and her heart melted a little more for him. She cupped his cheek so he could see her earnestness in the dim candlelight. "I've never been more certain. Let me touch you, Christian. Please."

The "please" snapped him out of his hesitation. He cupped her cheeks in his hands and pressed a kiss to her lips, even giving her lower lip a light lick, as she'd done to him at the ball, and then opened her mouth with his.

Instead of hot, frantic kisses, he kissed her slowly and deeply, as if he were savoring every brush of their mouths. His confidence in taking control of the kiss was so sexy. Bellamy moaned against his lips. Only when she was boneless in his arms, panting, lips swollen, did he release her mouth and kiss his way down her neck.

Christian pressed soft kisses along the opening of her wrapper. "May I remove it?" he asked.

She shivered. "Yes." Their hands bumped as they tugged the ties open. Then the wrapper was slid off her shoulders.

His eyes flared. "Your chemise?"

She shrugged. "It's more comfortable to sleep in than the night rail. I'm not used to sleeping in a gown that tangles around my legs or with a high neck. Even this is more than I wear at home."

His throat bobbed as he stared hungrily at her body. "What do you wear?"

"My underwear and a tank top." At his curious look, she said, "The top fits tight to the bodice with thin straps and ends at the waist." She drew a line just above her hips that he followed with his eyes. "And my underwear is also close-fitting and uh…have even less fabric."

"Less?"

He hadn't looked up once. His gaze was glued between her thighs and his hard length pressed into her hip. His expression was equal parts intrigued and scandalized. She'd worn only a thong bikini bottom on her last photo shoot. Probably best not to mention that just yet. He'd be flabbergasted.

"Christian?"

"Hmm?" His hand clenched on her knee as he ran his gaze from her breasts down to her bare calves and back.

"Will you kiss me again?"

"With pleasure," he murmured, dragging his eyes back up to meet hers.

She grinned and pressed a hot kiss to his mouth. Then his arms were back around her and the heat in her core began to build. Bellamy squirmed on his lap, then shifted so she could straddle him. Her knees sank into the chair cushion on either side of him. She hiked up the chemise and settled right over the hard length that was pressing against his trousers.

His breath caught as he broke the kiss. He gripped her hips, holding her in place. "I can feel the heat of you," he panted.

Bellamy slid her hands beneath his shirt while he adjusted to the sensation. His skin was warm and firm. She had to see his beautiful chest again. She pushed his shirt up.

Christian let her slip it over his head, then sat, tense, to let her look.

His chest and arms were strong and well-defined with muscles. She trailed her fingers through the light hair on his chest and down his taut stomach. "You're beautiful."

He huffed a laugh.

"You are!" She cupped his cheek and rubbed her thumb along the stubble on his chin. "You're strong. You take care of your body. You're kind, caring, and so smart. Plus, this jaw is a work of art."

He ducked his head. God, she loved his shyness. It was adorable and sexy at the same time. She kissed him again.

Christian relaxed and ran his hands up and down her back. "You're the one who is beautiful, love." He twined a lock of her hair around his fingers and used it to tug her forward to capture her hips in another deep kiss.

She ran her hands over his shoulders and down his chest. Over his flat stomach to the waist of his trousers. Lower, feeling the hard length of him.

Christian grabbed her wrist to hold her hand in place and broke the kiss. He pressed his forehead against hers and took a steadying breath. "Bellamy."

She froze. Was he going to stop this again?

"I want you, Christian," she said quickly, in case he was unsure of her feelings. "I want to make love to you."

He closed his eyes. "We don't have to."

Yes, we do, she wanted to shout. But deep down, she knew that was being *slightly* irrational. She pulled her hands away from his body and clasped them behind her back. "O-of course." She tried to hide her disappointment. And her confusion. One moment he was kissing her senseless, and the next, when she wanted to take it further, he turned to stone.

He frowned. "It's not that I don't want you. I do."

"Right. No, I understand." She didn't understand any of it, but she couldn't sit here a moment longer. She slid back to stand.

Christian wrapped a strong arm around her waist and pulled her back down to his lap. "Bellamy, listen to me."

She looked at her hands, feeling her heart in her throat and her stomach at her feet. She felt sick. God, what was wrong with her? Why couldn't she stop throwing herself at this man who clearly didn't feel the same way about her as she felt about him? He was attracted to her but not enough to *want* her the way she wanted him. Having the nightmare was less painful than this.

CHAPTER TEN

BLAST! HE WAS mucking this entire thing up. His beautiful Bellamy had offered herself to him—again—and now she felt rejected. He read it clearly on her face when she'd struggled to flee him. She wouldn't even look at him now.

He felt as if someone had stabbed him in the chest.

Christian sighed and pulled her closer. "I'm sorry, Bellamy."

"It's fine. Just—"

He brushed a finger over her lips to hush her. "I've never told anyone this before."

She stopped trying to flee his arms and stilled, but she didn't look up.

He felt flushed from head to toe, mortified to even have this conversation. But he didn't want to hurt her anymore. If that meant exposing one of the worst moments of his life to her, he would. "I've only been with one woman." His mouth was suddenly dry, and his voice sounded raspy even to his ears. "It was...quite humiliating."

When she finally looked at him, her brows drew together.

Christian swallowed past the lump in his throat, suddenly feeling exposed and on display. "When Gabriel and some of my other mates at school found out that I hadn't...had relations with a woman yet—" he winced at the words—"together, they hired some barmaid to...service me. Of course, I hadn't known. They took me to a tavern under the guise of a celebration of something." He couldn't remember what. "Then proceeded to ply me with liquor and push the woman at me."

Bellamy cupped his face and stroked one of his cheeks with her thumb. She stayed silent.

"I…hadn't the faintest idea what to do with her. She laughed and promised to guide me through it. But I didn't want to be there. I didn't want her. Nor did I want to disappoint my friends." The upstairs room she'd taken him to had been dirty and clearly used for such intimacies often, judging by the odor alone. "It took a while to…ready myself. I remember she began to get impatient and asked if I was too stupid to use my cock."

Bellamy sucked in a breath. Then she crushed her mouth to his.

He welcomed the kiss. It offered comfort, and time to gather his courage to say the rest.

When she pulled away, she wrapped her arms around his neck and buried her head against his neck. "Go on," she whispered.

"I managed to make myself hard enough for her. She climbed on my cock and rode me until I came. Then she thanked me for a good time and left. I never kissed her. I didn't see to her pleasure. I didn't even know how." He closed his eyes. "But I put a smile on my face and thanked my friends, even though it was the most humiliating moment of my life. It felt dirty and sordid. I've never wished for a repeat."

Christian felt Bellamy's eyelashes against his skin as she blinked. Then something wet hit his shoulder. He threaded his hand in her hair and tilted her head back. Her eyes were as vibrant as sapphire and sparkling with unshed tears. His heart clenched.

"They meant well," she said. "But it's not supposed to be like that."

He nodded. "I know. I don't blame them. The failing was mine. It would have been better if I'd known what to do."

Christian took a deep breath. It felt like he couldn't drag enough air into his lungs. "I didn't have friends growing up, people to talk to about things like…that. Other children my age didn't understand me. So, I spent a lot of time by myself, reading anything I could."

Another tear slipped down Bellamy's cheek. Christian brushed it away with his thumb. "I should have studied some before finding myself in that situation."

She huffed. "There's not supposed to be a written test, Christian. No required reading with an essay due to the professor."

His lips twitched and a little of the weight lifted from his soul. "Perhaps not. However, I *did* study afterward."

She gave a watery laugh. "Of course, you did." Then, "I understand why you want to avoid that intimacy. Thank you for telling me. I can't imagine how hard that must have been to bare your soul to a stranger."

Christian drew her back down to his chest and wrapped his arms around her. "You are not a stranger, Bellamy. You're the only woman I would consider taking to bed. I meant it when I said I wanted you." He kissed her temple, letting his lips linger. "I'm just afraid you will be disappointed. Or impatient."

She shook her head. "I won't. It's okay if you want to wait—"

"*No*. No, I…I'm afraid if you leave this room, I will never have another chance to experience true lovemaking. You will return to your time, and I know that I will never find another like you."

Bellamy slowly sat up. She searched his eyes.

He gave her a small smile.

Then she whipped her chemise over her head, dropped it behind her, and kissed him.

Christian nearly choked in surprise. His hands met warm, bare skin and silky hair. He smoothed his palms up and down her back, returning her kiss. Their tongues tangled. Bellamy was a woman who boldly went after what she wanted. And, she encouraged him to do the same even in intimate moments like this.

He nuzzled her cheek. Placed a kiss on her jaw, the spot beneath her ear. She shivered when he placed an open-mouthed kiss on her neck, sucking slightly.

"It feels so good," she breathed. "Touch me, Christian. Please."

He threaded the fingers of one hand in her hair and gently tugged back to expose more of her neck to his mouth. Bellamy let out a breathy moan and clutched his shoulders.

"More," she said.

He explored the fine bone at the base of her neck with his lips, down toward her heart. Christian pressed a kiss over that precious part of her. He looked up her body at her face and found her lips parted, her eyes focused on him.

She ran her fingers through his hair, making his skin pebble and flush as her soft touch caused tingles to flow over his body, and cupped the back of his head, urging him on.

He smiled against her skin. But he needed to see her. He eased her body back to look his fill at the exquisite woman on his lap.

Bellamy was slender. Slimmer than any woman he knew. She picked at her food and often passed up entire dishes and he knew it was because of the modeling. Her breasts were small, with rosy dark nipples on fair, perfect, silky skin. He smoothed his hand down her side, marveling at her toned stomach and slim hips and at the way her long blond curls fell around her body. She looked like Botticelli's Venus come to life. Better than any illustration, any dream.

Between her legs, he found a small strip of hair instead of the triangle of curls he'd expected. He brushed the back of his fingers over it.

Bellamy ran a finger over the strip. "I had the extra hair permanently removed. For when I wear more revealing clothes or underwear for modeling."

Curious. He wanted to know more. *Later*. He stroked back up her sides until his thumbs brushed the undersides of her breasts. They fit his palms perfectly. Her rosy nipples beaded, growing harder when he circled each with his thumbs. Each brush of his fingers deepened the flush spreading over her chest and made her hips rock against his.

What surprised him most was the physical sensations he felt by touching her. Every kiss sent heat through his veins, causing his cock to pulse and thicken as it pressed against the flap of his trousers. Eager to explore more, he lowered his head and sucked a firm nipple into his mouth.

Bellamy gasped and tightened her grip on his hair.

He flicked his tongue over her, then sucked, aware of her every move. Hearing her soft sighs and discovering what she liked best. When he kissed his way to her other breast, she guided his hand back to the first, urging him to cup her.

Christian explored her breasts for long moments. He couldn't get enough of the way she moved against him, grinding her hips on his lap when he sucked hard, or the way she gasped when he circled a nipple with his thumb.

Bellamy slid her hands down his chest and stomach to hover at the waist of his trousers. "May I?" she whispered.

He felt the slightest flutter of nerves but ignored them. Making love to Bellamy would be different than the rough coupling he'd endured in the past. And her impatience was born of eagerness, not frustration. She *wanted* to touch him because she *liked* him. Not because she'd been paid to.

Christian nodded.

She beamed at him and then began to fumble with the buttons in her hasty desire to free his cock.

Her radiant smile settled something in his chest, then sparked something new. He wanted her. Now, in his bed, and in the future. He wanted her to be *his*. Christian's heart skipped a beat. Then it started to pound.

Bellamy opened the fall of his trousers, slipped her hand inside his drawers, and freed his cock. Her touch was gentle, not impatient, and in her hand, his arousal felt heavy. It felt divine. She stroked him in just the right way, in all the right places, while watching his face.

He tipped his head back against the chair, unable to muffle his groan of pure pleasure. Any thoughts he'd had disappeared under her touch. "B-Bellamy," he gasped.

"I want to make you feel good," she whispered in his ear.

"Then don't stop. Good God." His hips arched of their own volition, his body completely under her power.

She gave a throaty chuckle, then slid off his lap.

Christian blinked at the sudden loss of her sleight weight. Then he choked out a groan when hot, wet heat slid over his cock, and he saw Bellamy kneeling between his thighs. She'd taken the head of his cock into her mouth and proceeded to do something with her tongue that had his eyes nearly rolling back in his head.

"Enough. Enough," he panted when tingles shot down his spine. He surged to his feet, swayed, then steadied himself and swept her up into his arms. Bellamy giggled against his neck. He strode to the bed and lay her down, then stripped off the rest of his clothes.

He hesitated at the side of the bed. *Can I give her pleasure? Will I remember what to do?* Christian cursed his insecurities. A lifetime of them seemed difficult to overcome.

Bellamy rolled onto her side to face him and patted the bed. "Time to show me what you learned in those books, handsome."

The invitation gave him the boldness he needed. He climbed into the bed and pulled her flush against his side. The feel of all that silky skin pressed against his naked body felt extraordinary. She kissed him, reigniting his desire. He trailed kisses down her neck to her breasts, then lower. He ran his nose over her navel. Her skin was so soft, and she smelled divine.

Bellamy parted her thighs, letting him settle between them.

He stroked her legs, cupped her bottom, and pressed kisses to her stomach. Feminine heat beckoned him lower. He touched her folds, finding them slick as they had been in the carriage. Only now he could see her pink skin. A woman's body was wondrous. The books he read couldn't convey what it felt like to touch Bellamy, or how much satisfaction it gave him to see her shiver in pleasure from his ministrations.

She arched her hips as he stroked and gripped his hair.

Christian smiled. His Bellamy liked his hair. She tugged on it to move him, or when the pleasure became overwhelming, as it did now. She moaned and writhed as he learned her body. He stroked his thumb over her nub, and she jolted beneath him.

"You are so beautiful," he whispered. Candlelight played over her skin. She didn't hide from him. Perhaps that was the difference between women of this time and those of the future. But he wanted to believe that, in part, it was because she was comfortable with him. That she wanted him as much as he wanted her.

As if reading his thoughts, she said, "I need you, Christian. I want your mouth everywhere and I want to put mine on you, but right now, I need to feel you inside of me."

Her words sent shards of pleasure through his body, straight to his cock. He was painfully hard. He slid up her body to catch her lips in a deep kiss and moved his cock through her folds.

She stroked him again and he bucked in her hand.

God help him, he wasn't going to last.

Bellamy wrapped her long legs around his hips, drawing him closer. "Don't make me wait," she said.

Christian pressed the head of his cock to her entrance and slowly pushed inside. Her tight channel clenched as he rocked his hips, sliding in deeper. This was heaven. Nothing could have prepared him for the sensation of being sheathed in her body. He pushed in to the hilt and kissed her to give her time to adjust.

She didn't hesitate. Instead, she rolled her hips, tilting her pelvis to press him in even deeper, urging him on.

Christian slowly pulled back and then sank back in. Any faster and he'd come. He had to see to her pleasure first. He skimmed his fingers over her breast and down her side. Goosebumps rose in their wake. She shivered and tightened her legs around him.

"Faster," she breathed.

Instead, he moved his hand between their bodies and found that small nub, circling it with his thumb. She trembled in his arms. Christian thrust into her in steady strokes, feeling her clench around him with every brush of his thumb. It was agony. It was heaven.

"Oh God," she whispered, throwing her head back in pleasure. "Don't stop. I-I'm a-almost…"

A second later, her channel pulsed around him, and a rush of heat coated his cock. She trembled wildly in his arms, little moans of pleasure escaping her lips. Christian thrust into her hard. Then his body took over and all he could do was grip the sheets in his fists as he pounded into her.

Bellamy wrapped herself around him, clinging tight. He gathered her in his arms and brought her up with him as he sat. With her body locked to his, he thrust harder, deeper, faster. Tingles shot down his spine, making him gasp. His cock grew impossibly hard. His testicles tightened and fire flared in his veins. With a groan, he pulsed inside her, emptying himself.

Long moments later, when he could breathe again, he wrapped his arms tightly around her and hugged her to his chest. He buried his nose in her hair and breathed deeply, taking in the scent of her lilac bath and the sweetness underneath, the scent he'd come to recognize as all her own. "Bellamy," he whispered. Meeting her had changed everything. How would he ever be whole when she left?

She cupped his cheek and kissed him tenderly. Her eyes were soft as she traced his face.

Christian lay her down on the bed and pulled the blanket and sheets over them. He tucked her into his body, unwilling to part from her. She would have to return to her bed before dawn. But for now, Bellamy was his, and he could pretend that she belonged at his side, now and always.

⋙⋘

THE HEAVY, GRAY clouds outside the mullioned windows promised rain. To Bellamy, the world was all sunshine as she swept downstairs for breakfast.

She'd awakened at dawn in Christian's arms, more content than she could ever remember being. Last night, he'd opened himself up to her emotionally and physically. He'd trusted her with a memory that helped shape him into the man he'd become, and then he'd given her his body. Making love with him had been exquisite, greater than it had been with any other partner. Christian's touch brought her deeper pleasure than she'd ever experienced from any other man's touch. He'd given her a glimpse of what love with the right person could be like.

When they couldn't avoid her leaving any longer, he'd walked her to his bedroom door and kissed her so sweetly she'd wanted to push him back onto the bed and make love to him again. Christian had shown her his heart, and it was the most beautiful thing she'd ever seen.

Despite a few aches and pains from the run-in with the ruffians the night before, and some delicious tenderness from her time with Christian, she felt a lightness in her heart that she couldn't remember ever feeling. He stirred things in her heart that she couldn't describe, and she found she wasn't ready to let go of that heady warmth just yet. She hadn't felt this happy in a very long time.

Bellamy reached the ground floor where more windows let in the weak morning light. A fat raindrop splattered against one. In seconds, the clouds let loose. Watching the rain fall reminded her of the hours she'd spent sitting in a chair in her apartment, reading while it rained. She'd loved those peaceful moments.

And now, here, that old life seemed so far away. Almost like it happened to someone else. Would she feel the same way about her time here when she made it home? The thought made her stomach swoop in an unpleasant way. After everything that had happened last night, even the scary moments in the Gardens, leaving was going to be so much harder.

She was still thinking about Christian when she arrived at the dining room for breakfast, wondering if the glow she felt would make it obvious that she'd spent the night with him. Lily, Gabriel, and Aunt Josephine were there already, filling their plates.

"A note arrived for him earlier," Gabriel said as he sipped his coffee. "Twisden found Dale and sent for a doctor. Christian left immediately."

"I hope he can get everything back," Lily replied, pressing a hand over her stomach.

Bellamy's mouth went dry. He was alone? Those men last night had seemed huge. What if they found him? What if they hurt him? She fought with herself and wanted to demand that Gabriel go after him. But Christian was his best friend. If he thought he would be in danger, Gabriel would have gone with him.

So she steadied herself, pasted on a smile, and greeted everyone.

Gabriel and Aunt Josephine smiled at her.

"You look lovely this morning, Bellamy. That dress is quite becoming," Gabriel said.

"Yes. Though I can't understand why all the young ladies want to wear white in the morning," Josephine said. Her unnaturally bright red curls danced when she shook her head. "Makes for a damned nuisance when you spill your tea on your bosom." She waved a fork at Bellamy. "Do remember that in the future."

"I will." Was that wine in the woman's cup? It was too dark for tea.

Bellamy selected some fruit and toast, then took the seat across from Lily. Her sister was studying her plate.

"Everything okay, Lily?" she asked.

Lily stabbed her eggs with her fork.

Gabriel put down his coffee. "Aunt Josephine, would you join me in the drawing room? I think Lily and her sister would like a moment of privacy."

"Then maybe they should have thought of that before breakfast, hmm? Oh, all right." The elderly woman rose and took Gabriel's arm so he could escort her from the room.

The moment they cleared the door, Lily glared at her. "Several nights ago, you accused me of still treating you as a child. Do you remember?"

"Yes, I remember." Bellamy stirred her tea and whacked the spoon against the china a couple of times before dropping it on the saucer. She knew that look. Lily had stewed all night about something and wanted to argue about it.

"How do you expect me to do that when you act as recklessly as you did when you were a teen, Bellamy? Ignoring Gabriel's signs that the man was not to be trusted. Dumping Aunt Josephine at the line for booze and then disappearing into the dark with a man you don't know? Gabriel told me what he and the others came upon last night when they found you. What if Christian hadn't rescued you?" Her voice rose with each sentence.

Bellamy bristled. "Wainsright hadn't quite tied me to the train tracks. I had just escaped him."

"You shouldn't have had to escape him in the first place, because you shouldn't have been there! It's just like that time when you snuck out the window to go to Jer—"

"I'm not sixteen anymore, Lily. I can make my own choices. I was trying to do something to help Christian, and it backfired."

"It always backfires because you don't think things through," Lily shot back. "When will you stop acting like a child?"

"When you stop trying to replace Mom!" Bellamy gulped the moment the words left her mouth.

Lily looked stricken. "I'm not trying to replace her. No one can," she said, her voice rough. "I was afraid for you last night. If you don't want me to be, then it would be best if you return to your time as soon as possible."

"Lily," Bellamy began, wishing she could take those hurtful words back.

Her sister stood and set her napkin on the table. "Aunt Josephine and I are going calling today. Perhaps it would be best if you stayed behind with Violet."

Bellamy watched her walk out of the room. She wanted to call Lily back, but she didn't know what to say to her. She knew it had been a bad decision to go with Wainsright, even though she'd only wanted to help Christian. And confessing that she recognized her error in judgment hadn't helped in the past, so it wouldn't help now.

She spent the next couple of hours in the drawing room trying to distract herself with several issues of Ackermann's Repository. The fashion plates especially were fascinating. She was trying to picture modeling them when Patience Cradock arrived. She rose and went to the hall.

Violet bounded down the stairs to drag Patience into a hug. "I didn't know you'd call today."

"Mother insisted on visiting with Lady Parling as part of her rounds. It was *quite* unfortunate that you were expecting me so that we could discuss designs for the next masked ball, so it was impossible to join her." She widened her grey eyes at Violet.

Violet gave a soft snort. "We've used a similar story for the last two Seasons. Do you truly think that she hasn't discovered the ruse, or is she happy to visit Lady Parling without you so that they might delve a little harder into the spirits without your knowledge?"

"Either way suits me well," Patience said. She spotted Bellamy in the doorway to the drawing room and hugged her in greeting.

Bellamy masked her surprise. She remembered the woman from her first dinner here, though they hadn't spoken much. She seemed more reserved compared to Violet's exuberant nature. Perhaps that was why she and Violet were such good friends.

They balanced one another out.

"I'll have tea brought in," Violet said. "Please join us, Bellamy."

"Yes, do join us," Patience said. "We can enjoy a few hours together without husbands—and brothers—to frown upon our conversations."

Bellamy considered the invitation while Violet asked the butler to bring a tray of tea. Visiting with them would help take her mind off her troubles with Lily and the uncertainty of her relationship with Christian. But they might enjoy themselves more without her brooding company. She bit her thumbnail. When she realized what she was doing, she clasped her hands together.

"Come sit with us," Violet sing-songed. "We can plot a siege campaign against our siblings."

"Oh heavens," Patience muttered. "Perhaps we shouldn't have donated that suit of armor to the museum last month."

Bellamy laughed. The tension drained from her shoulders. She followed them into the drawing room and sat on the sofa next to Patience.

"That's why one should never throw anything out. One never knows if it could be useful later," Violet said.

"Has it come to full-scale war, then?" Patience asked. "I thought your brother had agreed to find you a suitor."

"He did. But that is the issue. I forgot that with Gabriel, I must be specific in my wording. He agreed to find me a suitor. He did not agree to let me choose my own."

"That does make a difference," Patience agreed.

"He is only just beginning to see me as an adult," Violet huffed.

Her words hit Bellamy like a punch. She sat up in her seat and leaned toward the women. "Do you suppose that is normal for all siblings? That the older ones *never* see their younger siblings as adults?"

Violet's face scrunched. "I heard your argument with Lily this morning. I had just come down to breakfast when Gabriel suggested that perhaps I ought to take a tray in my room."

Patience pretended to study a bow on her cuff.

Wonderful. They'd kept poor Violet from having breakfast with her family. As if Bellamy could feel any worse about things. "It's an old argument. I'm not certain how much Lily has told you, but after our parents died, she raised me. I was fifteen and thought I knew everything. She tried to look out for me as a parent would, but I just wanted her to be my sister. We've never been able to break that cycle. Last night brought it all back."

"What happened last night?" Patience asked.

"Lord Wainsright asked Bellamy and Aunt Josephine to stroll with him through Vauxhall Gardens. Gabriel was quite against it but *of course*, he wouldn't tell me why." Violet rolled her eyes. "He was furious. Then the next we know, Lord Wainsright is trying to compromise Bellamy, while Gabriel and Christian are fighting off thieves."

"How marvelous! Er… dreadful. Marvelously dreadful." Patience shifted in her seat and cleared her throat. "What happened?"

Bellamy reassessed her original impression of Patience and decided she and Violet were a lot more alike than she realized. "Christian helped me get away from Wainsright while Gabriel and Lord Lael fought with the other men." She didn't want to gossip about why Christian had been there; fortunately, neither woman pressed for additional details. "Lily thinks I acted recklessly. She's right. I could have thought things through a little better."

But then again, if she had, would that have made any difference in their relationship? Probably not. She and Lily *both* needed to change in order to truly make things better between them. "Still, the decisions I make about what I do are my own, and whatever comes of them is mine to deal with. I understand that. I wish *she* did."

Violet nodded. "Gabriel is much the same. He's afraid that I can't make a good choice for a husband. While he says he will let me marry for love as he has, he seems to be blocking my every attempt at it. He's so insufferable."

"I think your siblings care very much for you," Patience said. "You're lucky to have them. I don't have any siblings and my husband's only brother refuses to speak to him since he inherited the title."

"I know Lily cares," Bellamy said. She looked at Violet. "As does Gabriel."

Violet nodded. "Perhaps a little too much."

"Oh, pish." Patience waved the words away. "Telling them that you're an adult is not enough. When I had the same problem with Mother, it wasn't resolved until I showed her. Violet, you must show Gabriel that the matches you are considering are up to his standards." She turned to Bellamy. "And you must show Lily that you've thought through your decisions. She may not like them, but she'll at least be able to understand that you reasoned them out. That's probably all either of them needs." Patience smiled at them. "Oh look, there's tea."

Bellamy slumped against the sofa back while the butler set the tea tray down on the table between them. Could she truly prove to Lily that she thought through her decisions? Would it be enough to change them both? She had to try.

She looked up to find Violet equally lost in thought. When the young woman met her gaze, a silent understanding passed between them. They would *both* try.

"Thank you, dear Patience," Violet said. "You are an excellent siege strategist."

Her friend giggled. "I am ever at your service, my liege."

Bellamy accepted a cup of tea, feeling better already. Her thoughts turned back to Christian. Was he with Dale now? She hoped he hurried back so she could share with him everything that had happened with Lily and hear about his time with Dale. It surprised her that she wanted to share with him. She hadn't felt that need with past boyfriends. With Christian, she wanted to open up to him, the way he'd trusted her last night.

Should I though? What happens when I leave?

CHAPTER ELEVEN

RETURNING TO HIS townhouse should have felt like coming home after a long journey. Instead, after spending so much time at Gabriel's home, it felt like stepping into someone else's hall. Only Malcolm, his butler, felt familiar. Christian removed his hat and handed it to Malcolm, then his drenched great coat. The rain started shortly after he'd left Gabriel's and continued to pour in heavy sheets. He and his horse had been soaked through in seconds.

"Good to have you back, my lord." Malcolm shook out the coat and hung it up to dry. Not a speck of lint showed on his black suit and the dark hair that waved across his forehead looked as if it wouldn't move in a stiff wind.

"How is it that you look respectable at any moment, while I merely have to walk through the house to have a crooked cravat and untidy hair?" Christian asked. He was stalling, taking the time in conversation with Malcolm to prepare himself to face the man who'd worked for him for years and stolen so much.

"It is one of the great mysteries of life, is it not, my lord?" Malcolm's lips twitched.

"How have things been in my absence? Are Lords Twisden and Granville..." Christian trailed off, unsure how to inquire if they'd subdued themselves or opened his home to wild parties. He removed his gloves and handed them to Malcolm.

"My lords have conducted themselves as gentlemen of leisure should."

Christian's eyebrows rose at the vague reply. "Is anything broken?"

"Nothing valuable."

He ran a hand down his face. "Send word to Rothden's if they become overly boisterous. I shall have a word with them."

"At once, my lord. You will find both men upstairs in one of the guest rooms with Mr. Dale." The man's name rolled off Malcolm's tongue like an insult. "The doctor left moments before you arrived."

He fought off a feeling of satisfaction. Even though he was not a man of violence, he couldn't help the small surge of pleasure knowing Dale received a bit of due reward.

Christian straightened his waistcoat and started up the stairs. He heard Malcolm following behind. Voices drifted down from the second floor, among them, William Dale's. He would demand to know why Dale, a man he trusted for years, would steal from him and where both the moncy and the automatons were. If his former steward refused to share, he would have to determine more persuasive methods.

When Christian entered the room, Dale lay propped up against the pillows with a thick bandage wrapped around his waist. His nose and lips were swollen, and both eyes were blackened.

Twisden and Granville stood on either side of the bed.

Twisden noticed him first. "Ah, there you are, Hunt. Dale here was telling us that you are the one responsible for the new shape of his nose."

"The gunshot wound was Carter's doing," Granville added.

Christian narrowed his eyes at the man in the bed. Days of worry for his people and his estate, of searching for this man, and wondering what offense he'd made that would make his steward embezzle from him, roiled in his chest until he felt he might thrash the man again. Were he not lying in a bed already wounded, Christian might not have restrained himself.

He stared hard at Dale.

The man paled and shrunk in on himself. "Lord H-Huntington."

Christian stalked forward to the foot of the bed. "You have a single opportunity to confess. Tell me where the money and my inventions are. Tell me why you did this."

Dale swallowed. "If I don't?"

Granville leaned in. "Then I would bet against you leaving this room in as fine a state of health as you are currently enjoying."

The man's throat bobbed. "If…if I tell you, you have to protect me."

"What reason have we to do so?" Twisden asked, crossing his arms over his chest. "By all rights, we could see you hanged for theft from a peer of the realm."

Dale pushed himself up. "You won't do that, Huntington. I know you. You won't want the scandal."

Christian nodded slowly. "I *do* wish to avoid scandal."

"I rather enjoy it." Twisden smiled at Dale. "Shall we say you stole from me instead?"

The man trembled, looking between the three, no doubt attempting to determine if they would lie in order to see him hang. "I'll tell you. I swear. When I do, you won't need to concern yourselves with my hanging. He'll kill me himself."

Christian stiffened. "Who will?"

Dale lifted a shaky hand to brush the hair out of his face. "W-Wainsright."

Ice slid down Christian's spine at the name.

Twisden frowned. "Lord Shelby Wainsright?"

"Wasn't it Lady Wainsright you seduced three weeks ago at the British Museum?" Granville asked Twisden.

"No, that was Lady Winville." His eyes took on a faraway look. "Quite a delightful interlude."

"That's right. I wagered he would challenge you to a duel

over the affair." Granville stuffed his hands in his pockets.

Twisden grinned. "How much did you lose?"

"Fifty quid. I'm astonished the man didn't call you out."

Christian stared at the ceiling, grasping for patience. Malcolm gave a slight cough from where he stood near the door.

"If we could return to the matter at hand," Christian said, then pinned Dale beneath a hard stare. "Leave no detail out, or Wainsright shall be the least of your concerns."

Dale slumped back and lifted his shaking hands in acquiescence. "Fine. Fine. May I at least have something to drink for the pain? A brandy? Anything?"

Christian looked over his shoulder to Malcolm.

"At once, my lord," he said.

Before he could leave, Granville stopped him. "Malcolm," he called in a cheerful voice. "Best make that four glasses."

"Of course, my lord." The butler met Christian's gaze with a resigned expression, then left.

Christian sighed and gripped the back of his neck, fervently wishing the Season was already over so he could return to his country estate to live in peace. "What happened to my money?" he asked Dale.

The man plucked at the blanket, avoiding the scrutiny. "I worked for Wainsright's family after he finished his schooling at Eton and returned home shamed. The elder Lord Wainsright wasn't happy that his son was disgraced." His gaze darted to Christian, then away. "His lordship threatened to disinherit Shelby. The boy was right mad about it. He...he still blames you."

Granville shifted on his feet. Across from him, Twisden's brow furrowed.

Christian clenched his fists. "Continue," he ground out.

"Don't know what happened at Eton between you," Dale said. "But the man weren't the same after. He convinced the elder lord to let him stay with the family and spent the next years doing everything the lord said. Part of it was sitting with me, learning the estate books. When he heard you'd inherited the earldom, his plan started to form. Oi, the hours he spent asking me about investments. How I decided what to invest the lord's money in. What were good investments and what were bad." Dale scrubbed a shaky hand through his hair. "Then one day he stopped, and I thought he were done. Instead, he moved on to creating fake investments. Buying land for cheap and creating opportunities for people to invest in something that weren't even real. Then his father ordered him to India to manage the family trade. He couldn't continue his schemes from there. That's when he came to me."

Dale lowered his chin to his chest and fell silent.

"Tell us the rest," Granville urged.

"He knew about my gambling. He worked with one of the club owners to rig the cards, until I was desperate. Then he told me of his dealings. Said if I ran them while he was in India, he'd clear my debts. He offered to double my wages. All I had to do was get you to invest." He smoothed his hands over the blankets, making them as flat as possible. "It were that, or debtors' prison. He helped me with the recommendations so I could replace your last steward. When I realized that you preferred to let me handle the estate books, it was easy. I thought I could invest maybe a thousand guinea that you wouldn't miss. But that weren't enough for Wainsright. He—he *hates* you. He means to ruin you and disgrace you before the Ton, the way he was disgraced to his family."

Blood thrummed in Christian's ears, blocking out all sound. That bloody arse! Putting the lives of dozens of people in jeopardy because of his own actions. The damn despicable fool. While Christian had thought the matter in the past, Wainsright had plotted this deception *for years*. His chest and arms tensed with the need to hunt Wainsright down and finish what the man had started almost a decade ago. It was time for the man to fully understand what pain he'd wrought.

Out of the corner of his eye, he saw Granville turn and kick a nearby chair, sending it crashing to the floor.

Twisden scowled. "It wasn't enough to terrorize dozens of young men?" he barked. "He brought about his own disgrace!"

Dale shrank further into the bed in the face of their anger. "I-I-I d-don't know. He wouldn't speak of Eton."

Christian choked back the lump in his throat. "What of the automatons?" When the man looked at him blankly, he clarified, "My inventions! Why steal them?"

Dale flushed scarlet. "The gambling. I couldn't stop. The money from Wainsright, from you…I kept losing. I'd almost win enough to pay you back for some of what I was taking, but then some lucky blade would come in and bilk me of my winnings. I tried to pay you back. I swear I did. I didn't feel right about cheating you for the lord. I thought, if I could sell them, I could win it all back."

"Of all the dicked in the knob schemes…" Twisden shook his head. He leveled a look at Granville, then pointed at Dale. "*This* is what happens to men who frequent the hells."

Granville looked away. "I'll stop," he mumbled.

While Twisden continued to glare at his friend, Christian focused on Dale. "Where are my inventions now? And how can I get the money back?"

"Here you are, my lords," Malcolm said as he entered the room carrying a silver tray with a crystal decanter of brandy and four glasses.

Dale's puffy eyes widened, and he sat a bit straighter.

Malcolm sat the tray on the top of the dresser, then poured each man a spot. Dale swallowed his drink in a single gulp and wiped his mouth on his sleeve. He held the glass out in a trembling hand, asking for more.

Christian nodded when Malcolm silently inquired if he should refill. The butler also refilled Twisden and Granville's drinks.

"The money?" Christian prompted.

"Wainsright closed all his sham investments and took the money. Carter…he has that fancy silver box. Took it from me in the scuffle."

"And the egg?" Christian pressed. Bellamy wanted it. Though after holding her in his arms last night, he wanted to beg her not to go.

"In my rooms. I hid it beneath the floor. There's a loose board beside the bed. Those fancy silver petals are in there as well."

"Tell us where you live," Twisden said.

Dale nodded, looking miserable. He gave them an address to a hotel in Charing Cross, along with his room key.

"Where can I find Wainsright?" Christian asked.

"I don't know. I swear I don't." Dale began to sob. Lines of pain bracketed his eyes and mouth, and he clutched his waist. "I'm sorry, Lord Huntington. I swear to you, I'm sorry."

Christian nodded, his ire only for Wainsright. "Twisden, make sure he's comfortable and have a tray sent up. And if either of you break any more of my furnishings, I'll drag you to Gentleman Jackson's saloon for a bout."

Twisden's lips twitched as he rubbed his jaw. "I still feel the last one. Your punch nearly knocked a tooth loose."

"What will you do?" Granville asked.

"I'm going to Charing Cross to retrieve my property. Then I'm going to find Wainsright."

"I'll come with you," Granville said.

Christian waved him off. "I won't be there long."

"Hunt, one of us should come with you," Twisden said.

Christian clenched his jaw, grinding his teeth in frustration, but he nodded. The fight between Carter's men and Wainsright was fresh in his mind. As much as he wanted to tend to the matter himself, he knew his friends were right. "Granville," he said.

The man nodded and moved to his side. Christian took a last look at Dale, then left the townhouse.

The rain had lightened to a drizzle, but the earlier downpour meant the roads were mired with mud. They slogged through the streets, maneuvering their horses around carriages and people scurrying out of the rain. Christian's ears and nose were cold and wet by the time they reached the hotel.

Dale's room was on the second floor. They gained entry with his key and stepped into a small, but tidy space furnished with only a bed, chair, desk, and small dresser. Christian strode to the left side of the bed, while Granville took the right, looking for the loose floorboard.

"The gall of Wainsright," Granville said. "To orchestrate this entire sham to ruin you. Why single out only you? We were all there."

Christian pressed down on a board, then tried the next. "It started with me."

Granville frowned. "If Gabriel hadn't been there…"

He didn't want to think about it. "It's not on this side."

"Here. Found it."

Granville had it pried open by the time Christian rounded the bed. A small compartment sat beneath the board. Inside lay the little, red enamel clock and a scattering of silver petals. He gently retrieved them. One of the hinges was damaged on the clock and part of the gold filigree looked to be falling off. He opened the little doors and stared at the golden dancers. Their hands were clasped in mid-dance. It reminded him of his dance with Bellamy. Would they have another before she left?

"You're smitten," Granville said.

Christian looked up.

"Lady Rothden's sister. I saw you dance with her at Lady Parling's ball. I think that's only the second time I've seen you ask a woman to dance."

His cheeks heated. Granville was one of his friends who'd hired the barmaid those years ago. How different last night had been. If he thought about it, he could still feel the satin of Bellamy's skin beneath his hands. Hear her cries of pleasure in his ears. He'd awakened with her in his arms, and it had taken all his willpower to release her so she could sneak back to her room.

Christian swallowed. He was more than smitten.

He was in love. But he wouldn't share that with Granville, or anyone else.

"She is special. Come, I want to return to Gabriel's and get out of the rain." He tucked the clock and the rose petals into his pocket.

Granville followed him back outside.

When they exited the hotel, the rain fell in sheets and the temperature had dropped a few more degrees. Christian turned toward where their horses were held, eager for dry clothes and a warm fire. Perhaps Bellamy would—

"William Dale," a man said.

Christian stopped at the mention of Dale's name.

The punch came out of nowhere. He stumbled to the side and spun. Four large men circled Granville and him.

"Carter sends his greetings," the burly man in front said. Then all four attacked.

⁂

"GOOD CHRIST, CHRISTIAN. What the devil happened?" Gabriel bellowed from the hall.

Bellamy was relaxing in the drawing room, reading an old issue of Ackermann's when she heard the commotion. Her heart started to pound. Gabriel sounded equal parts concerned and angry.

"*Whazit*?" Violet mumbled. She blinked slowly and sat up from the chaise where she'd dozed off after Patience left.

"Who did this?" Gabriel growled.

Christian mumbled something in response, voice raspy with pain.

Bellamy was out of her chair and halfway to the door by the time her brain registered his soft moan. She skidded into the hall and grabbed for the doorframe. The satin slippers she wore offered no traction when running on marble floors. She spotted Christian slouched near the front door. Blood ran down the side of his face, and he gripped his ribs.

Her chest grew tight, and her heart raced. She couldn't draw a full breath. Her vision wavered. In her mind's eye, she could see her father lying on a gurney, a similar pattern of blood on the side of his face, and suddenly the image tried to superimpose on Christian's face. *No. No!* She couldn't…couldn't lose anyone again. Bellamy blinked rapidly to clear the terrible vision from her mind. Christian was okay. Hurt but okay.

Violet moved to her side and took her hand. The comforting touch began to ease the stark terror thrumming in her veins.

She took a slow breath. Then another.

"…get some hot water and linens," Gabriel was saying to one of the maids. "I'll help him to his room."

"I don't need a doctor," Christian said. "Nothing is broken." He eased his great coat off his shoulders for the butler and winced when he removed his leather gloves.

"You look wretched. If you couldn't get a woman with a crooked cravat, you certainly won't get one covered in blood. Get ahold of yourself, man," Gabriel teased, clearly trying to goad his friend in an attempt to lighten the mood.

"I'm delighted to know this will not be a trend in the Bon Ton. Too painful."

Gabriel wrapped a strong arm around Christian and helped him to the stairs. They stopped when they saw Bellamy and Violet.

Now that Christian faced her, Bellamy saw the bruise forming on one cheek and the small cut on his lip. His knuckles were swollen and bloody. He'd put up quite a fight. "What happened?" She knew he'd gone to see the man who'd stolen from him, William Dale. Had they fought?

"Carter sent some men with a message for…" He groaned when he put too much weight on one leg.

"Save the telling for when you're lying down," Gabriel said.

Then, to Bellamy and Violet, "I'll take him up to his room and tend to his wounds. Can one of you dispatch a note to Zeph asking him to come?"

"I will," Violet said.

"I'll help." Bellamy swallowed. "I'll help take care of him."

Gabriel studied her for a moment, then nodded. She wondered what he was looking for in that serious gaze. But then Christian grimaced and all her concern went to him.

She followed them up the stairs, noting Christian's limp and the mud caking the knees and the hems of his trousers.

Gabriel helped Christian into the guest chamber and eased him down to sit on the bed. "Let's make you more comfortable, shall we?" He helped Christian out of his tailcoat.

Bellamy knelt to remove his boots and set them beside the dresser. When she returned to his side, Christian was out of his waistcoat and cravat. He eased back against the pillows with a soft groan and held his ribs. "I think they're bruised. One of the men got a hard kick in."

"Tell me what happened. Did you find Dale?" Gabriel asked.

"I did. Twisden and Granville located him and took him to my townhouse. He'd been shot in the scuffle at Vauxhall and the doctor was called."

Gabriel nodded. "What had he to say about the theft?"

Christian looked away, pleating the counterpane with his fingers. "He said Wainsright orchestrated everything and forced his hand. He stole my work in a poor attempt to sell them and use the money to win back part of what he'd stolen."

Gabriel's visage turned to stone. "Wainsright."

"He hasn't forgotten," Christian replied.

"Tell me everything Dale said," Gabriel commanded.

Bellamy listened as Christian recounted his conversation with Dale. In a way, she pitied the poor steward. His vice led him to ruin. What had happened at Eton with Wainsright? The secret locked the three of them onto this path of destruction and she worried what would happen next.

Seeing him injured…it made her heart flip uncomfortably in her chest. She hadn't been close to anyone in a long time. A small part of her was terrified that if she truly started to care for them, they'd go away. Like her parents. Like Lily, until Bellamy found her in this time. Maybe it was irrational, but she couldn't shake the fear.

A footman and maid entered with a steaming bowl of water and clean linens. They sat them on the table near the bed and departed.

Bellamy hurried to soak a cloth and wring it out before she sat on the edge of the bed and gently cleaned the blood from his face. It seemed to be from a small wound at his hairline that didn't look deep enough to need stitches. She picked up a fresh cloth and gently cleaned the rest of his face.

"Carter's men?" Gabriel asked.

"Granville and I went to Dale's hotel to retrieve the clock for Bellamy."

She sucked in a breath. "Did you find it?"

"We did. I had it in my pocket."

Had. Past tense. Her stomach dropped. She knew what was coming next.

His eyes met hers, then darted away. "When we exited the hotel, I heard someone call Dale's name. Carter sent four men with a message for him. They mistook me for Dale because I was leaving his residence."

"All this and the message wasn't for you?" Gabriel waved a hand at Christian's injuries.

Christian rubbed the swollen knuckles on his right hand. "Carter needs a better secretary."

Gabriel snorted. "Apparently."

"We fought back. In the scuffle, one of them tore the pocket of my greatcoat that the clock was in. Granville saw one of the men grab it." He lifted troubled eyes to Bellamy. "I must apologize although I know you will think me a fool. It is in Carter's hands by now."

God, the look on his face gutted her. She wanted to hug him and tell him that it was okay. But it wasn't. Was it? Bellamy couldn't decide if the relief she felt was because Christian's injuries weren't as bad as she feared or because she couldn't return home yet. She wrapped her arms around her waist.

Gabriel lay a hand on Christian's shoulder and looked at them both. "We'll find it. Violet will have a message dispatched to Zeph. He knows the alleys of London better than most. He'll find Carter."

Bellamy nodded. "What about Wainsright and Christian's money?"

The men exchanged a long look.

"Get some rest," Gabriel told Christian. "When you're on your feet, we'll finish this."

Christian reached up to squeeze Gabriel's hand, still pressed to his shoulder. "Once again, I am in your debt."

Gabriel shook his head. "There is no debt between brothers." Then he speared Bellamy with a look. "Remember what I said."

He referred to the day she'd been looking for Christian and Gabriel directed her to the workspace in the basement. *Do not hurt him*. Her head dipped. "I remember."

"See that you do." Gabriel gave Christian a faint smile and left the chamber.

"What must you remember?" Christian asked.

Her cheeks heated. "Not to be self-centered." His forehead furrowed in confusion, but she didn't want to elaborate. "Should I have a bath brought up for you? Warm water would soothe your aches."

Christian traced his fingers over her cheek. "If I were bold enough to ask you to join me, would you accept?"

Bellamy leaned into his touch. She wanted to. The temptation was so strong. But Gabriel's warning held her back. "I—I don't want to hurt you."

"My injuries are minor."

Her lips curled at his cajoling tone even though she felt disheartened. She didn't correct his assumption that she meant his wounds when she'd been thinking of his heart. At the same time, his confidence in himself was fragile. If she turned him down, wouldn't that also hurt him? What if he never pursued anyone else?

She pictured him dancing with another woman. Sharing one of those soft smiles that held that tantalizing mix of shyness and boldness. She hated the woman already.

Christian brought her hand to his lips and pressed a lingering kiss there.

Her heart hitched. Dammit, she wasn't that selfless. She'd give Christian everything she could until the moment she had to leave. With the clock stolen once again, who knew when that would be? "I suppose I could stay, to help you with your bath."

He grinned against her skin. "I look forward to it."

Bellamy left the room long enough to request that hot water and a tub be brought up, as well as a tray for his dinner. As she climbed the stairs back to his room, her thoughts returned to the conversation Gabriel and Christian just had about Wainsright. The man wanted revenge against Christian. For what? She couldn't imagine this gentle, shy man doing anything that would provoke this kind of retribution.

She returned to his room and closed the door. "Do you think you can get the money back from Wainsright?" she asked.

He plucked at a thread on the counterpane. "With Gabriel's help, yes."

She sat on the edge of the bed. "Why does he blame you for Eton?"

Christian went still.

"At Vauxhall, he said that being unarmed hardly mattered to a man like you. What did he mean?"

He huffed. "He meant that he did not appreciate receiving the same punishments he enjoyed dispensing." At her questioning look, he added, "Wainsright was several years older and our prefect."

She recognized the word but couldn't remember what it meant.

"A student who is given authority over younger students with the power to discipline as needed. Or wanted," he supplied.

Bellamy gasped and pressed her hand to her lips. The old scars on his back! "He disciplined you."

Christian avoided her eyes. "Older students often take younger students as their servants and force them to do anything and everything their 'master' orders. It's an accepted practice, and I imagine the headmasters are of the mind that such things make men stronger. They turn a blind eye when the authority is abused. And it was abused often by men like Wainsright."

Bellamy wanted to pull him into a hug, but she wasn't sure that he wanted her touch at that moment. He seemed to have closed himself off as he spoke.

"Some took young men who were…*prettier* as servants to attend to their needs." He flushed at what his words implied. "Others sought out lads they considered weaker, more…awkward."

Brilliant men like Christian who had trouble socializing with others.

"Refusal to do their bidding resulted in further torment from peers, or more punishment."

"You were his servant," she whispered, horrified by the image he painted.

"For almost a year. I hated him as I have never hated another. He and several others like him thrived on the power, knowing that no one would interfere for fear of exposing the accepted system and in doing so, looking weak to their peers." A dark smile crossed his lips. "His imperious sense of power made him blind to the one person who had no such fear."

"You?"

He shook his head. "Gabriel. One day, I had been ordered to bring Wainsright his meal. It was raining and the stones were slick. I lost my footing on the steps and dropped his tray. Shelby was enraged. He decided against dragging me to the birching block at the library for the public caning which was often used as discipline."

Her eyes filled. She couldn't stop the tear that slid down her cheek. A public caning in front of the school library was an accepted practice? God, how could people treat each other like that? She would never understand. Throat thick, she swiped at the tear.

"He caned me there on the steps. Instead of my…*ah*…arse, he aimed for my back which would cause more pain. After the fifth lash of the birch branch, I lost count. My blood was…" He shook his head. "Wainsright stopped, and I heard him cry out. I couldn't move to see what happened. Suddenly, Gabriel was there, helping me up and I saw that Wainsright lay on his back in a puddle of mud with a broken nose and wrist. I found out later that Gabriel had ripped the birch from his hand and struck him across the back with it several times before breaking his wrist and knocking him out." Christian met her gaze. "I believe I would have died had he not stepped in."

Tears streamed down Bellamy's face. She launched herself into his arms.

He grunted in pain.

"Sorry. I forgot about your ribs." She wiped madly at her wet cheeks, then threw her arms around his neck and held him close. "If he did all of that, how can he blame you?"

"At first, he told people his injuries were a result of a stumble on the path, and his cruelty continued to others. But Gabriel never let him forget the truth. He became a champion for the younger, weaker boys like myself. Once I was healed, I joined him.

"Three years after that night, we tricked Wainsright into exposing his cruelty publicly. The system has existed as long as it has because of secrecy. But with his actions made public he was disgraced at school. Even his fellow prefects in cruelty wanted nothing to do with him. He left soon after."

Bellamy sat back far enough to cup his cheek.

He wiped away her tears. "It was a long time ago."

"You still bear the scars." *Inside and out.* "And now Wainsright is back, licking a wounded paw because his reputation was dented." She was glad she'd kicked him between the legs in her struggle to get away at Vauxhall. Given the opportunity, she'd do it again.

"Bellamy. May I kiss you?"

She melted from the sweet way he asked. "Yes."

Christian leaned forward and pressed his lips to hers. The kiss started slowly, gently, but then grew heated.

Bellamy hiked her skirts up to straddle him, being careful of his injuries. She slid her fingers into his soft blond locks and kissed him deeply. Their tongues met in a hot glide.

He moaned against her lips. "I love the way you taste."

"I love the way you kiss." She also loved how he held her face like he was afraid she would pull away before he was done. How his eyes sparkled with excitement as he ran his hand down her side, close to her breast. She loved…*him*.

Bellamy's heart gave a dramatic thud. She sat back on his thighs, trembling, her heart thrumming so loudly in her ears that she didn't hear the knock at the door.

CHAPTER TWELVE

CHRISTIAN HELPED BELLAMY scramble off his lap so she could answer the door. Her cheeks were a lovely pink, her lips plump from their kisses. He ran his hands through his hair and down to gingerly rub his face. He'd told her about Eton and she…she hadn't called him weak or looked poorly upon him for not being able to fight off Wainsright on his own, as he had feared. Instead, she'd cried for him. Kissed him.

He hadn't told her that it wasn't only he who'd suffered. All the men of their group, Twisden and Granville, Edmund Somersby and Felton Seabright, even Noah Cradock, had all been servants to those tyrants. Only Gabriel and Zeph had escaped the caning. They'd brought Christian and the rest together with a mission to look out for the weaker lads. The remaining years at Eton were bearable for all, because of them.

Bellamy opened the door wide for a line of servants bringing up pails of steaming water and a bathtub. A maid laid out several drying cloths and soaps for him, and they departed. Bellamy closed the door and turned to lean against it.

Her eyes were a darker blue than he'd ever seen them, her nose a little pink from her tears. "Shall we get you into the bath before the water cools?"

His blood heated. He wanted Bellamy again. Last night, pumping inside her body had given him more pleasure than he'd ever thought possible. He was eager to repeat the experience to see if it could be as good the second, or even the third time. Except...she'd been hesitant about joining him in the bath. The reminder cooled his ardor. What if she didn't want to make love to him again and used his injuries as a polite way to refuse his advances? He swallowed.

"Christian?" Bellamy walked over to stand beside him.

He wanted to reach for her and pull her down to the bed with him. Strip that beautiful rose and gold brocade gown off her and pull the pins out of all that silky blonde hair. He'd never felt this *need* before. Christian *craved* her. Not only her body but her presence at his side. Her light laugh and teasing smiles. The way she looked at him was as if she saw the man he truly was, not the awkward, shy man everyone else saw.

"Christian?"

"Ah. Yes." He slowly pushed himself upright, barely holding back a wince as his ribs protested. He reached for the hem of his muslin shirt and pulled it over his head.

Bellamy helped him remove it, then set it on the bed. Her gaze locked on his chest.

Christian was pleased with his form. He exercised often with fencing and occasional trips to Jackson's Saloon for pugilistic pursuits. He kept his body strong in an effort to avoid the paunch many of his peers were prone to.

She slowly reached out and touched his bare skin. Her fingertips were light as they traced the muscles of his chest. Growing bolder, she ran her hands over his shoulders and down his chest, trailing her fingers through the dusting of his hair. "You have such strength," she said, in a low, breathy voice. "Not only here," she said as she brushed her palms back up his chest and down his arms, "but also here." She moved her right hand to lay over his heart.

He swallowed around the sudden thickness in his throat. The way Bellamy admired his chest rekindled the heat in his body. When she met his gaze again, he saw the desire he felt reflected back at him. It gave him the courage to draw her lips down to his for another heated kiss.

"The bath," she breathed against his mouth.

He nodded and reached for the fall of his trousers with trembling fingers.

Bellamy chuckled and brushed his hands out of the way. She swiftly unbuttoned them. "I know your leg hurts. Do you need help to stand?"

"No." Christian gingerly put weight on his ankle, letting it slowly adjust. During the fight, he'd landed on it wrong. It would sort itself out in a day. His pants slipped down to his hips the moment he was upright.

She grinned and helped him step out of them and his drawers.

Christian found himself standing naked next to a fully clothed Bellamy. The difference should have made him feel vulnerable. Instead, as Bellamy's eyes skimmed down the length of his body and appreciation flared in her gaze, his cock responded and any awkwardness burned away beneath the heat surging through him.

"Let's get you to the bath," she said in a low voice.

She slipped her arm around his back and walked with him around the bed to the tub. He eased into the water. The warmth soothed his aches, and he sighed in pleasure.

Her cheeks pinkened. "I should remove this gown if I'm going to help. Can't have it getting wet. How would I explain that?"

Christian grinned. "Indeed." He sat up and helped her loosen the ties in the back.

She slipped off the gown and laid it on the bed.

Her thin shift, stays, and stockings were all that remained. He wanted to peel them off her and guide her onto his lap. Instead, he waited until she returned to the side of the tub and pressed another kiss to her lips.

Intimacy with Bellamy was easy. He'd been so nervous at first, though she'd never made him feel awkward. Instead, she met his passion with her own, and Christian wanted more of it. He wanted *everything* with her.

She knelt beside the tub and helped him wash his hair, then lathered her hands with soap and ran them over his back. She traced each scar with a fingertip, making him shiver.

He never thought that he would want someone to touch them, and he didn't often remove his shirt in front of others. If he did, it was only in front of those who already knew about them. They were thick and ugly. Unsightly and—

She pressed her warm lips against his back, over one of the scars. He felt the feather-light brush of the edge of her mouth and sucked in a breath.

"Bellamy."

She kissed another. Then another. "You're so strong, Christian. I don't know how you survived the brutality and turned it into a mission to help others. In some ways, you remind me of Archer, my brother. He has that warrior spirit that doesn't give up. Most of the time," she added in a soft voice.

"You miss him."

"Yes. He came back from war injured. He shut Lily and me out. He barely speaks to us and won't see us. I'm afraid for him. He won't tell us the extent of his physical injuries, and I think his emotional scars are even worse."

Christian took her hand and pressed a kiss to her palm. "If he is as strong as you believe, then he will work through it. Trauma takes time to heal."

"He would like you," she said.

He wasn't certain of that but appreciated that she thought so.

Bellamy lathered her hands with soap and ran them along his shoulders and down his arms and chest. She explored him with her soapy fingers, lingering in areas that made his breath catch. Places he hadn't known were sensitive.

He sucked in a breath when she circled his navel, then trailed her hands lower to brush one finger over his cock from base to tip. Christian's hips bucked. Water sloshed at his sudden movement, making her laugh.

Bellamy washed his legs and tried to tickle his feet.

He chuckled and reached for her. She laughed and leaned out of reach.

"Careful. I don't want you to hurt yourself," she said, surreptitiously reaching for the foot nearest her.

Christian caught her hand and yanked her closer to capture her lips in a kiss. Bellamy laughed and braced her hands on his shoulders to keep from falling into the tub. Her eyes sparkled in the fading light from the window. "You're so beautiful," he said. "You light up when you laugh. I could watch you every day and never tire."

Her eyebrows furrowed, and she sat back. "Many people see the outer beauty," she said.

He heard the ache in her voice. The need to be seen as more. It was a feeling he understood well. "Do they also see the woman who loves her family? The one that takes care of others and is willing to help someone even at risk to herself?"

"I...I don't know."

He cupped her cheek. "I see her."

She leaned into his touch again, and he found he very much liked that. He pressed a kiss to her lips, then stood. Water sluiced off his body into the tub. He felt relaxed, and the aches diminished. He stepped out and dried himself.

Bellamy watched.

The heat he felt earlier returned in full force. His cock hardened for her. Christian held out his hand in silent invitation. He wanted her. His stomach fluttered with nerves as he waited.

She licked her lips. Met his gaze. Then she placed her hand in his.

Christian pulled her into his arms and claimed her mouth in a fierce kiss. He slid his tongue into her mouth, tasting her. She moaned and leaned into him. It wasn't enough. He needed her naked body against his.

"I want you," he whispered. "Let me make love to you again,

Bellamy."

"Yes. I want you too."

Her fingers fumbled with the laces of her stays. He helped, and soon they were sliding her chemise over her head, and removing her stockings, leaving her bare to his eyes. Those beautiful small breasts, the small strip of hair…he wanted to savor it all.

Injuries nearly forgotten, he took her hand and tugged her toward the bed.

"Wait. Is the door locked?"

He paused. They hadn't locked it when the servants left after delivering his bath.

Bellamy chuckled and went to turn the key in the lock. "Don't want any unexpected visitors."

Christian grinned and reached for her the moment she was close enough. He guided her over to the bed, urged her to lie down, and then climbed over her. The feel of her skin against his felt better than the softest silk. He propped himself up on one arm beside her head and traced her jaw with the other hand. "I never thought I'd have this," he said. He suppressed the desire to thank her, afraid it would sound awkward or too grateful.

She slid her fingers into his hair. "Neither did I."

He swallowed. "May I—"

"You don't have to ask," she said. "I'll tell you if you do something that I don't like."

Christian kissed her until they were both breathing fast. Then he kissed down her neck, lingering on the spot he'd found that made her arch against him. He sucked her breasts, loving the feel of her hard nipples against his tongue, and then kissed down her flat belly. He shouldered his way between her thighs. She was beautiful here, flushed pink with desire. He trailed a finger through her petals, reading her shivers and sighs.

"You can…you can kiss me if you want. Down there."

He needed no further encouragement. The book he'd read on the matter indicated that many women were too embarrassed for this sort of kiss. Not his Bellamy. She parted her thighs a little wider, letting him in.

Christian's first taste made him moan. He went for another, dragging his tongue through her folds. Bellamy arched against him. Her fingers speared into his hair and gripped tightly. He chuckled.

She gasped as his breath washed over her and rolled her hips.

Intrigued, he blew a soft breath over her damp skin. It made her grip his hair tight and moan. Encouraged by her body's responses, Christian learned what she liked. He kissed, licked, and sucked her folds, flicking his tongue over her nub, until she writhed beneath him. She'd let go of his hair with one hand to cover her mouth and hold back the cries of pleasure. He could feel her body growing tighter, her muscles tensing. Then she shivered and a new heat washed over his mouth and chin. He would never get enough of her taste, her passionate cries. He wanted to take her back to his estate where they could close themselves in his cavernous bedroom and she could cry out as loudly as she wanted.

Bellamy reached for his arms and tugged him up her body. She kissed him, tongue tangling with his. "I like the way I taste on you," she murmured.

His cock grew painfully hard at her words. Dear God, he might not make it into her body before he spilled.

She slid her fingers down his chest and wrapped them around his cock. She stroked him until he shuddered in pleasure above her. "Bellamy, I need to be inside you."

She guided him to her entrance. Christian didn't waste a moment. He didn't think he'd last if she stroked him again. He pushed into her hot core, slowly, allowing her body to adjust.

Bellamy wrapped her legs around his thighs.

The moment his hips touched hers, they bucked against him. She was all wet heat and silky walls, squeezing his cock tightly. He gasped out a moan, then pulled back and rocked back into her, hard.

"Yes, Christian. Like that."

He could do little else. He plunged into her, over and over, until her body captured his cock in a tight, rippling, hold and a tremor ran through her limbs. Wet heat touched his cock, buried inside her body, and set off his own eruption. He climaxed harder than he ever had.

Christian trembled above her. When he was spent, he lowered himself down beside her. He was reluctant to slide out of her body. She felt incredible.

Bellamy breathed fast beside him. When their eyes met, a beautiful smile crossed her face. She looked like an angel in his bed. Christian would pray to whomever he needed to keep her there.

Last October, when he'd traveled to Gabriel's country estate for a house party that he hadn't wanted to attend, he'd brought along his new clock project, hoping it would alleviate the boredom. He'd spent hours crafting the little egg with its red enamel and gold filigree, with the little dancers that spun together when the clock chimed the hour. It started out as a whimsical project meant to fill his time.

As he tucked Bellamy into his arms, her bare breasts against his chest, he realized that it had also brought him a woman he could love, something he never thought he would have. Christian placed a kiss against her temple and held her tighter. It also held the power to take her away again.

Once, he'd fought against men who abused their power on the younger, more unfortunate lads. This time, he'd fight to keep the woman he'd fallen in love with. Perhaps his Bellamy would choose not to stay. If she didn't, and if she desired it, he'd go with her to her time. If he could have her love, time and place meant nothing.

"WHAT DO YOU think of this one? The lavender would look lovely with your dark hair and blue-green eyes," Violet said. Her amber eyes sparkled as she held up a fashion plate and chattered on to Lily about the pearl trimmings.

"The pearls wouldn't be too extravagant?" Lily asked as she leaned over from her chair to squint at the drawing. She pressed a hand to her lower belly.

Bellamy smiled. They'd come to the dressmaker's shop for an outing in a thinly veiled attempt to avoid Aunt Josephine's small gathering of dowagers. Quite a few women were packed into the small shop, making the overly perfumed air smell stuffy. She perused the few ready-made gowns displayed while Lily and Violet bent their heads over the latest dress plates.

Violet threw her hands up in the air. "This is *Almack's*, Lily. The pearls will make you the most extravagantly dressed lady in the Ton. One must look one's best or not be allowed to enter."

Bellamy stroked a hand down the nap of some emerald-green velvet fabric on display. Lily and Violet were excited about a dance at the assembly hall next week. She hadn't been able to muster the same level of anticipation. Christian took up most of her thoughts.

He'd been in bed for two days, largely at her insistence. The small wound at his hairline had scabbed, and he seemed to breathe more easily. Even his ankle had healed. She'd tended to him, sat, and read to him, and even surprised him by bringing up some of his tools and gears for one of his projects.

They'd talked for hours. She loved listening to him talk about his projects. He'd start explaining a problem that he'd run into, then through the conversation, he would figure out how to fix it and would eagerly move to the small writing desk and scribble some notes down. He told her about his life growing up as the son of an earl, and the death of his brother. She sensed he'd been closer to his brother than his parents. He didn't speak of them much.

She'd shared her memories of growing up with Lily and

Archer and especially about the night that her parents died, and how everything had changed. The constant arguments with Lily, and how ashamed she felt for being such a brat during those awful years.

Now at the modiste's, Bellamy glanced over at her sister. As if she knew she was being observed, Lily lifted her head and met her gaze. They hadn't really spoken in the last few days. Bellamy had put off the conversation that they needed to have in favor of helping Christian and, in truth, she'd welcomed the delay.

Lily said something to Violet, then joined her. "Hey, Bells."

"Hi."

Lily smoothed her hand over the velvet. "This would look nice on you."

Bellamy nodded. "Thanks." *God, this feels so awkward.* "Lily…I-I'm sorry for what I said about you trying to be like Mom. I was angry, but that doesn't make it right."

"It's okay. I was mad too. Feels like we keep falling into the same old arguments."

"I don't want to do that anymore," Bellamy lowered her voice. Some of the ladies around them were looking in their direction. Probably hoping for gossip. "I don't want us to fight."

"Especially when we have an audience. Let's step outside for some cooler air."

"What about Violet?"

The young woman in question grinned, amber eyes lively, as she spoke to another younger woman, and pointed at a fashion plate. The poor girl she spoke with appeared to be wearing a frumpy brown sack, belted just under her breasts. She was pretty, but her clothes did her no justice. *If I didn't need to have this talk with Lily, I would love to help that girl pick dresses that would flatter her skin and figure.* Every woman deserved to look and feel her best, no matter what size, shape, or age she was.

"I'll tell her we'll be right outside. Knowing Vi, she will be happy to talk this poor girl's ears off about the latest fashions in dresses," Lily said, then returned to Violet and murmured to her.

Vi nodded, not taking her eyes off the dressmaker's book of fashion plates in her hand.

Bellamy smiled as Violet gestured at the plates and then the other young woman, pointing at her dowdy dress.

"She'll be okay for a few minutes," Lily said as she rejoined Bellamy.

They exited the shop and moved a few steps away from the door. People strolled along both sides of the street, some stopping to look at the shop window displays, while carriages rattled down the road in a constant stream of traffic. The cool spring air felt wonderful after the stuffy dressmaker's. Bellamy took a calming breath and faced Lily. She needed to resolve this tension between them. She wanted her sister back.

"I know I don't always make the right decisions, but I do try to take responsibility for them," she said.

Lily pursed her lips. "What about Christian?"

That threw her off. "What about him?"

Her sister gave her a pointed look. "The walls are thin. I've heard you *assisting* him a couple of times in the last few days."

Shit. Bellamy put a hand to her temple. Heat flooded her face. "Sorry."

"Don't be sorry unless you're still leaving, Bells. The man is smitten with you. Anyone can see that when he looks at you. If you still intend to leave, you're going to hurt him." Lily dropped her voice even lower. "I'm not trying to lay guilt on you, Bells. I just question if you thought through your actions when you decided to give in to that attraction."

She wanted to say that she had thought it through. She opened her mouth, but the words stuck. Had she, though? Had she *really* thought about what would happen if she left? Was she still leaving? If she stayed, what about Archer?

"Are you happy here?" Lily asked. "Or are you impatient to return home?"

At first, she'd been almost frantic to get home, afraid that if she didn't arrive in time to start her contract, they would drop her. She needed that money for the next chapter of her life, even if she hadn't quite figured out what that would be. But when she thought about it, she didn't *want* to model for Vivant. She'd just wanted the stability it would provide her, and the money for the future.

"I don't think modeling has made me happy for a while," she admitted. "The competition is brutal. It's hard to make friends with the other models because you never know when one of them will kick you down on their way to the top. Plus, there's the expectation to keep my weight as low as possible. I've eaten more in the last week and a half than I have in the last year and a half." She shook her head. "I'm not sure when I stopped worrying about how much I ate. It's nice."

Lily gave her an assessing stare, then said, "You care about Christian."

A soft smile touched Bellamy's lips. "I do. He's different from any man I've been with. He likes me as I am. Not as a beautiful, but brainless, trophy model on his arm."

"Christian wouldn't be like that. He needs someone who appreciates his brilliant mind and will love him for it." Lily studied her. "Will you?"

Her throat felt thick. "What about Archer?" she rasped.

Lily smirked. "I don't think he would fall in love with Christian. I doubt you'd have competition for his heart from our brother."

Bellamy shook her head and lightly elbowed her. "You know what I mean."

Lily took her hand and gave it a gentle squeeze. "When I struggled with the decision to stay here or return to our time, Zeph reminded me that love should play a part in any big decision. The path you see as the way forward might not be the only path available." Her mouth twisted in thought. "Although he's quite cryptic…he might have been talking in circles for the fun of it."

They laughed.

Bellamy liked Zeph even more now that she knew he'd helped Christian, Gabriel, and the other men protect those students who were younger and more vulnerable from any that would abuse them. She sobered at the reminder of all the pain Christian had suffered. He'd told her only of the single incident, which had to have been the worst, but she saw in his eyes that the year in Wainsright's service had been hell. It made her want to pull him into her arms and soothe away all the abuse and hurt. Heal him in body, mind, and soul, and protect him from any that would try to hurt him.

Including herself.

"I'm sorry for being overbearing. Now, and back then," Lily said. "I don't want you to get hurt, but I don't want you to hurt those I care for. I know you wouldn't do so intentionally. I just worry." She looked at her feet. "Back then, I had no idea what I was doing. I'd never had to pay bills or even buy groceries. It's a good thing Mom taught us to cook and clean, otherwise, I don't think the courts would have let you stay with me. If you'd gone into the system…with Archer overseas…I don't think I would have made it." She squeezed Bellamy's hand harder. "As difficult as those times were, I needed them. I needed you. Every time you went to a friend's house, the walls closed in on me. I know I was strict, but that was because I was afraid to be alone. I was afraid that if I let you out of my sight, you'd be gone too. In clinging to you so tightly, I ended up pushing you away. I'm sorry."

Bellamy pulled Lily into a hug and surreptitiously wiped a tear from her eye. "I understand. When Christian showed up two days ago covered with all that blood, all I could see was Dad lying on the gurney. I was so afraid of losing someone else that I—cared about, that I couldn't breathe."

Lily pulled back and linked their arms together. "I missed you so much, Bells. I'm glad we have this time. Strange as it is to us."

She chuckled. "I've missed you too, Lily. And Archer."

"I hope he'll be okay," Lily murmured.

Bellamy pressed her lips together. Somehow, she didn't think he would be. Not until he asked for help, something her stubborn, broken brother was unlikely to do.

"Let's get back to Violet. I do hope she hasn't ordered a new wardrobe while we've been out here. Gabriel would *not* be pleased."

"I'm afraid I must delay you a while longer," a familiar male voice said from behind them.

Bellamy's breath froze in her lungs and a tremor ran through her. She released Lily and turned to find Shelby Wainsright standing directly behind them.

He wore a peacock blue, embroidered waistcoat over tan trousers with a black tailcoat and greatcoat. In one hand, he held a walking stick with an ivory handle. In the other, a small pistol, partially hidden by his coat.

None of the passersby would see the weapon.

She stepped in front of Lily, shielding her as best she could. "Leave us alone."

Wainsright shook his head. "I find I have need of you, Miss Bennett."

She paled and her heart tripped into a gallop.

"I thought you would have fled by now," Lily said, poking her head around Bellamy's arm to glare at him.

What?

"We saw the newspaper this morning. Your shady dealings in India prompted a full review of your father's business dealings here and abroad. Your family is disgraced, and other lords are calling for action to be taken against you," Lily said.

His lips pressed into a hard line. His eyes flicked over her shoulder, then back to Bellamy. "Come with me quietly."

"Hell no," she replied. Stories of his cruelty to those he considered weaker were fresh in her head. There was no guarantee she could fight him off a second time if he grabbed her.

The click of the hammer cocking back was muffled by the noise of the street. Bellamy saw the movement all the same. She stiffened.

Wainsright stepped closer. "You misunderstand, Miss Bennett. It was not a request."

She reached back to put her hand on Lily's hip and eased both of them back a step to keep the distance between them. "You won't shoot us on the street in Mayfair."

"Won't I?" He smiled as a black carriage steered closer and came to a stop beside them. It blocked the view from anyone on the other side of the street.

"There are still people on this side. Do you think they won't hear? Let us go."

"Rothden and Lael are looking for you," Lily added. "The longer you stand here, the more likely they are to find you."

A slow, satisfied smile crossed his face.

Bellamy's stomach dropped. She hadn't expected him to be pleased with that knowledge. Whatever he had planned, she didn't want Lily or Violet anywhere near this man.

He moved closer.

Bellamy eased them back another step, only to stop short when Lily gasped and hit something at her back that gave a low, male grunt. *Damn, damn, damn.* Of course, the vile man wouldn't have come alone.

"What do you want?" If she kept him talking, maybe she could think of a way to get Lily out of there. Maybe someone passing by would notice. She spotted a couple of gentlemen walking in their direction. If she could get their attention, the distraction might give her enough…Two men walked around the carriage and stepped in front of the other men, distracting them. Bellamy glared at Wainsright. How had he organized this so fast? More importantly, how had he found her? Had he followed them here from Gabriel's?

"Come with me, Miss Bennett, and no harm will come to your sister."

She gulped. Trust him to play the one card that could force her to comply. Still, if she got in that carriage with him, the chances of her making it out of this nightmare alive were slim. Could she get the gun away from him? She'd practice disarming tactics in her self-defense class. Even if she could, what about the man threatening Lily?

Think, Bellamy. Her hands shook as she held them out at her sides. "Let Lily go. I'll come with you."

"What? No," Lily growled.

"Vi," she murmured back, hoping Wainsright wasn't familiar enough with Gabriel's family to know Violet's pet name.

Her sister tensed behind her. "Damn."

Wainsright studied her. "No harm will come to Lady Rothden."

"I don't trust you." *Uh oh.* She hadn't meant to use her "you're an idiot" voice. *Don't antagonize the man with the gun and a vendetta, Bells.* She took a calming breath. "Let Lily go. Once she's back in the dressmaker's shop, I'll go with you." A lie. She'd fight him like a wildcat to stay out of that carriage, but she couldn't do that until Lily was safe.

Wainsright looked between Bellamy and Lily, then nodded toward the shop just steps away. "Lady Rothden, if you would be so kind as to deliver a message to Huntington? Tell him that Miss Bennett and I will await him at the London Docks."

"I will not. She's not going with you," Lily said.

Bellamy clutched her sister's hand. She forced herself to look away from Wainsright but didn't turn her back to him. "Lily, *take the message.*"

"This is *not* thinking things through," she hissed.

Bellamy would have laughed if she wasn't utterly terrified. "I did. He needs me right now, so he won't kill me." She put on a brave front, but she was not at all sure that he wouldn't hurt her in other ways. "I'll escape," she mouthed. She wanted to beg Lily not to give Christian the message, but the fear in Lily's eyes told her she would call in the calvary the moment she could.

"I've already been afraid of losing you. This feels like it's almost certain," Lily said in a rough voice.

"I love you, Lily." She pulled her into a quick hug. "Get inside. Please."

Her sister reluctantly drew away. She glared at Wainsright. "If you hurt her, you're a dead man."

"I do love the fire in your family," he said.

Lily visibly shuddered at the lascivious look on his face. She took one more look at Bellamy and backed toward the door of the shop. At the last moment, she raised an eyebrow, asking without words if Bellamy was certain she would be okay.

She nodded.

Lily swallowed, then slipped inside.

Warmth at her back was her only warning that Wainsright moved behind her.

"I kept my word," he said in her ear.

Bellamy slammed an elbow into his chin as hard as she could, then spun around and kneed him. Wainsright groaned, leaning over and gasping for breath. Before she could run, the second man grabbed a handful of her hair and yanked her head back, then locked a meaty arm around her throat. She struggled to drop her head and body, but he held fast and gripped the wrist she tried to punch him with.

Wainsright snarled. He grabbed her feet and lifted her so she was suspended between the two.

"What goes on here?" She heard someone shout. one of the gentlemen from the sidewalk that had been delayed by Wainsright's brutes? "Unhand that woman."

His demand came too late. They dumped her into the carriage. Bellamy landed hard on her hip and pain rocketed up her side.

Wainsright climbed in after her and slammed the door closed.

Bellamy scrambled up off the floor onto the seat opposite him.

"Go for the door and I will shoot," he said, producing the small pistol again.

She sucked in a panicked breath and tried to calm her racing heart. At least Lily had escaped.

CHAPTER THIRTEEN

"THE DOCKS ARE a bloody big place. There are hundreds of men here. How are we to find your Bellamy?" Zeph asked as he checked over his pistol and then put it in his great coat. He adjusted his top hat down over his pale hair and took another look around the dock.

They crouched behind stacks of crates, Zeph on Christian's left and Gabriel on his right, watching as men loaded and unloaded dozens of ships around them. Large warehouses lined the docks, growing shady in the fading light of the setting sun, and the smell of rotting fish and sewage clogged the air.

Christian cursed. It had taken far too long to get here. Lily and Violet had returned from the dressmaker frantic and talking over each other. Gabriel calmed his wife long enough for her to relay Wainsright's appearance at the shop, and his message.

According to Lily, Bellamy protected her sister and Violet as much as she had been able. Once Lily returned to the shop, she'd watched from the window as Bellamy fought the two men. In the end, they still managed to kidnap her. Fortunately, Zeph had already come to meet with Gabriel over the matter with Carter when the women returned. They'd spent another interminable hour planning and considering contingencies, then dispatched messages to Twisden and Granville.

"She won't be far from Wainsright," Christian growled.

"He'll want to gloat, no doubt."

"What of Carter?" Gabriel asked as he also checked his pistol. The scowl on his face had only deepened from the moment Lily and Violet returned until his hazel eyes darkened with fury.

"He is often seen in this area. If Wainsright is here, I suspect Carter shall be as well," Zeph replied.

"We'll get Bellamy to safety first, Christian. Then Zeph and I shall track down Carter and your automatons."

Christian gut clenched. He couldn't face the possibility that when he had the clock back, Bellamy might choose to leave him. He needed her safe in his arms and far away from Wainsright.

"The man could come to an unexpected end," Zeph suggested.

A muscle moved in Gabriel's jaw. "We can't kill Wainsright, Zeph."

"Whyever not?"

Christian wasn't shocked by Zeph's suggestion—or his reply. Part of him wondered if Shelby's death wouldn't be for the best. The man took great pleasure in cruelty. Christian had no illusions that he would have matured out of it as he aged. Men like that crafted their cruelty into a weapon. *Killing Wainsright would make us no better of men than he.* He didn't think he'd be able to look at himself in the mirror the next day if they did.

"We're not murderers," Gabriel sputtered.

Zeph shushed him with an exasperated look. "We would put an end to the damage he inflicts on others. Even if we stop him today, what will keep him from returning in the future with a worse retaliation?"

Gabriel glared at him. "You can't seriously mean to—"

"We must ensure that he cannot return to harm those we love," Christian said. "He is a peer, which makes prosecution more difficult. However, I hope that his crimes in India will be enough to sway a magistrate to sentence him to prison."

Zeph eyed him, then turned to scan the dock once more.

Christian heard footsteps nearby and held his breath. A worker with a box on his shoulder stopped in front of the crates they hid behind to readjust his load. He whistled a lively tune, then strode away.

"By the tobacco warehouse," Zeph murmured.

Wainsright paced before the wooden structure, hands clasped behind his back. Another bulky man leaned against the warehouse, looking unconcerned.

Christian shifted, looking for Bellamy's lovely blonde hair and lithe body. He didn't see her near the two men, which meant Wainsright held her somewhere else.

"Christian is correct. He would want her close by," Gabriel said.

"One of these warehouses." *Blast.* There were too many to check. Wainsright's stiff movements indicated he was losing patience. "I'll talk to him." He turned to his friends. "Find her."

"Distract him as long as you can," Zeph said.

Christian nodded.

Gabriel clapped a hand on his shoulder, and then the two men crept out of their hiding spot and hurried away. After a few minutes had passed, giving them enough time to circle behind the warehouses, he rose to his feet and straightened his hat. The flintlock pistol was a comfortable weight in his pocket. It wasn't the only weapon on his person. Underestimating Wainsright would be a grave error. He flexed his fingers around the carved ivory head of his cane and walked down the quay toward Shelby.

Wainsright spotted him and stopped pacing. A slow smile spread across his face.

It hardened into a scowl several moments later when he realized that Christian strolled toward him unhurriedly as if he were out for an evening walk. He kept his face impassive. Inside, however, he seethed.

This man had terrorized Christian and dozens of young men at Eton for four years. Thick, ugly scars marred his back, a physical reminder of this man's brutality. That hadn't been enough for Shelby. He'd orchestrated this mad plan of revenge that threatened the lives of simple people who'd worked hard for the little they had and endangered the life of an innocent woman who'd done nothing more than accept Christian as he was and help him to become a better man.

Wainsright's face looked mottled with fury in the shadows. Workers hustled around, lighting the lamps as dusk settled over the dock.

Christian stopped in front of the man who'd brought so much pain into his life. The years hadn't been kind. His hair thinned on his head and lines sagged on his skin. His hips were wider than his shoulders and he carried that same paunch about the waist that Christian had worked so hard to avoid.

Once, he'd felt burning hate and disgust at the sight of this man. Now, he could barely muster pity. "Where is she?"

Shelby puffed his chest out. "You will see your ladybird in time." He gestured to the muscular man with dark skin and a bald, shiny head who stood at his side. "Mr. Hill will—"

Christian ignored him and stepped closer. "You will bring Miss Bennett to me immediately, along with the money that you stole. I offer this single opportunity to do what you know to be right, Wainsright. Refuse, and I will make certain that you never see a single day outside of the gaol."

Wainsright laughed and a bit of spittle caught at the corners of his mouth. The man was mad. "Let's escort our guest to the warehouse, Hill," Shelby said to his man. "I think it is time he sees the special festivities I've prepared."

Christian pulled the pistol from his pocket and aimed it at Hill. "I suggest you do not move."

"I must recommend the same to you," Wainsright said in a jovial tone.

Christian saw a movement in his peripheral vision and swung around to aim at the man sneaking up on his side. He was as wide as his colleague, with a scar that curled his top lip into a demonic grin. A click to his right sent a chill down his spine. Shelby had used the third man as misdirection, giving him enough time to remove his own pistol.

Christian considered his options. The pistol offered one shot. Could he hit Wainsright, avoid being struck by the man's gun, and also pull the sword free from his cane before either of the large men attacked? Granville would no doubt bet against his success.

He swept his gaze over the surrounding warehouses and saw movement. Gabriel crouched between the two closest warehouses. He signaled Christian, then melted back into the shadows. They'd found her.

Christian lowered his weapon.

Wainsright laughed and nodded at Demon Lip, who relieved Christian of the pistol. The other shoved him forward, making him stumble after Wainsright. The man led them to the warehouse where he'd seen Gabriel.

Demon Lip pulled open the heavy wood door and Hill shoved Christian inside. His feet were rooted to the floor and refused to move. A well-used birch block sat on the floor, exactly like the one in front of the library at Eton where Wainsright had publicly caned him so many times. In front and behind, shackles were bolted to the floor to keep a prisoner in place.

Christian lifted his gaze to Wainsright as his stomach rioted and bile choked his throat. "Feeling reminiscent?"

His nemesis snorted a laugh. "I thought it would fulfill me to take your money and the lovely Miss Bennett. But as I lay in bed last night, I realized that *this* would be far more satisfying. A parting gift."

Christian gripped his cane, knuckles turning white. "Everyone in Town knows of your fraudulent dealings in India. Should I be flattered that you risk the opportunity for freedom for this ill-fated revenge?"

Wainsright spluttered. "Ill-fated? Hill, strap him down. Jarod, bring Miss Bennett. I wouldn't want her to miss the evening's entertainment."

Christian took a steady breath. A shadow moved among the

crates stacked three deep along the back wall. Another shadow separated from the opposite side, and he saw a flash of white hair. He held the handle of his cane in a tight fist.

A low, feminine voice cursed, the sound cutting through the growing darkness. A couple of candles were lit near the door, otherwise, the cavernous warehouse was dark. Jarod dragged a struggling Bellamy forward.

Christian scanned her quickly, looking for any injuries. Her hair had come out of her pins and lay in a tangled mass down her back. Her dress was ripped at the shoulder and covered in mud. Otherwise, she looked like a hissing cat about to claw Jarod's eyes out. She was magnificent. He'd never seen a more beautiful woman.

Knowing she was unharmed settled the intense fear inside him, especially when Bellamy spotted him and smiled. That tilt of her pretty lips, given in the midst of struggling with a man twice her size, buoyed his resolve. Wainsright's days of terrorizing people were at an end.

Christian swung the bottom of his cane up into his opposite hand. With a quick turn of the handle, the wooden shaft separated. He unsheathed the rapier blade within and tossed the cane away.

Wainsright stumbled back and fumbled in his pocket for his pistol. He tripped on his own feet and fell into a stack of crates that jostled beneath his girth. As he struggled to his feet, one of his men slid a metal rod his way. Wainsright snatched it up and swung to meet Christian's blade.

Behind Christian, Bellamy yelped, and something heavy hit the floor. It took all his willpower not to look for her. He kept his focus on Wainsright as the man avoided more crates and moved into the open space.

Christian chased him, their weapons clashing in a flurry of strikes and the reverberating sounds of metal against metal. Shouts rang out around them and out of the corner of his eye, he saw Zeph trading blows with one of Wainsright's burly guards.

Wainsright parried the thrust of Christian's blade, then retreated a few steps.

Before Christian could follow, a heavy body collided with him, taking him to the ground. The sword was ripped from his hand. He rolled and gained his feet just as four men swarmed around him. Christian landed a few hard punches, but couldn't fend off all the assailants.

"Bring him," Wainsright said as he tossed the metal bar to the ground.

Two men spun Christian around while Hill and Demon Lip marched behind. An additional eight men were in the warehouse, fighting Gabriel and Zeph, as well as Twisden, and Granville who had come from the other end of the docks as planned.

His friends fought but Christian could see they were wearing down fast.

Hill marched Christian toward the center of the warehouse. He shoved him to his knees and kicked him forward. The edge of the birch block bit into his stomach. Demon Lip sank to one knee in front.

Christian bucked and fought to free himself from their grasp. Another man stepped up and slammed a fist into his cheek, dazing him. He grabbed Christian's hands and forced them into the shackles on the floor. Someone did the same with the back, locking Christian's legs to the ground.

One of the men behind uttered a rough curse. "Touch me again and it will be the last thing you do with those hands," Bellamy snarled.

Despite his awkward position, Christian chuckled. He wished he could see her face. See that fierce beauty and intelligent mind at work. Instead, he yanked at the shackles. The floorboards look decayed here. With enough pressure, the cuffs could break loose.

"What shall we do with these four?" another man asked.

"Rothden, Lael, and friends," Wainsright crowed. "How I had hoped you would join us. Once Christian has his turn, you will experience what you tried so valiantly to save others from." His voice turned hard. "I was helping those young men. They had to toughen up to survive in this world. Instead, you coddled them all. I heard Tanner leapt into the Thames last month after losing his estates in the hells. He might have lived had you not interfered at Eton."

Christian sucked in a breath. Tanner was one of the young men they'd protected. He hadn't known Tanner well—the lad was two years his junior—but he'd been far smaller than most of the other students. Too small to survive a caning by Wainsright.

"A sound idea, Wainsright. Perhaps you should try the same," Zeph taunted. He muttered an oath, and it sounded as if he was forced to his knees.

Wainsright's face turned red. He spun and swiped up a thin wooden rod.

"No," Bellamy yelled. "Get away from him."

Christian gritted his teeth and twisted the shackle on his right hand. The wood gave the slightest bit.

The rod cut through the air in front of Christian's face and came down across his hands. He hissed out a breath and saw welts begin to form on his knuckles.

"Those that try to escape get extra lashes," Wainsright said. His voice had softened to the tenor of a young man.

Christian looked up to see the gleam of fervor in his eyes.

"Did you know that women have the ability to take more pain than men?" The crazed man asked conversationally. "Maybe your Miss Bennett will want to become *my* Miss Bennett. If not, she can be our experiment to find out if what they say is true about a woman's pain."

Christian wrenched his hands back, trying to break the shackles. If he couldn't, Bellamy would be at the mercy of Wainsright's cruelty. He would never allow it.

A struggle broke out behind Christian, where Gabriel and the others were held. Another crate toppled and Bellamy swore.

"Don't just stand there," Wainsright bellowed at his men.

Christian used the distraction to work his shackles. Blood

welled where the metal cut into his wrists. He pushed the pain away and focused on breaking the floorboards. A pop, a snap, and his right shackle pulled free of the floor, splinters of wood scattering around his hand.

A solid, familiar form knelt at Christian's side and helped release him from the shackles. "What is happening?" he asked Gabriel.

"Bellamy caught Wainsright's man off guard. She slammed her hand into his face and unmanned him with a hard kick." Gabriel chuckled. "I think she broke his nose. It provided enough distraction for the rest of us to break free. Zeph and the others are keeping those ruffians occupied."

Christian felt a surge of pride in her. Once again, she hadn't dissolved into tears and huddled in fear. His Bellamy fought like a lioness even at risk to herself. "She is astonishing."

Gabriel helped him stand. "Indeed, although let's not tell her about Jackson's pugilism saloon just yet. I fear she'll have Lily and Violet there before the week is out."

Christian chuckled. Once he was steady, he found Bellamy crouched on top of two stacked crates, attempting to avoid Demon-lip. He started toward her.

"Hold," a man said.

"Good Christ," Gabriel muttered.

Christian slowly turned to see Carter swagger into the warehouse. His green satin breeches shone in the dim light and set off the delicate embroidery of his waistcoat.

Carter surveyed the state of the warehouse. He looked at Zeph. "I was hesitant to trust you."

"What goes on here? Carter, you've no right—" Wainsright sputtered.

Demon-lip and Hall edged their way through the chaos to stand at Carter's side.

Wainsright's eyes widened, and he sputtered "You work for me." They ignored him.

"The money?" Carter asked.

"If you think you're due a single farthing—" Wainsright stomped forward.

"I'll get it," Hill said.

Christian rushed to the stacked crates and held his arms up for Bellamy. She made a little noise of relief and then reached for him. He lowered her into his arms and set her on her feet. "Are you hurt?" He smoothed his hands down her sides and brushed a long lock of blonde hair over her shoulder.

"Your hands?" She took his hands and angled them to the candlelight. Red welts crossed the back of his palms, but they weren't bleeding. She raised each to her lips, pressing a kiss to them.

The feel of her soft lips on the back of his hands, showing him such care, touched his heart as nothing else could. Christian wrapped an arm around her back and pulled her against his chest. He breathed in her lilac scent until it soothed him.

"That's mine," Wainsright roared.

Christian spun and pushed Bellamy behind him. But Wainsright wasn't looking at him. He was fighting Hill for a black bag. Hill narrowed his eyes, then landed a punch to Wainsright's face.

Wainsright stumbled back, clutching his cheek. He glared at Carter, who appeared indifferent to the whole issue. A muscle in Wainsright's jaw twitched. He stood to his full height, then produced his pistol and pointed it at Hill. "I'll take that bag!"

Carter sighed. "Don't be a fool, Wainsright. That money does not belong to you."

Wainsright yanked the bag out of Hill's hands and edged to the door. His eyes found Christian in the shadows. They promised retribution.

The money. Christian glanced down at the bag in Wainsright's hand and realized the man's plan. He meant to humiliate Christian one last time, then take the entirety of the stolen money and flee England.

Wainsright aimed the pistol at Christian, pulled back the

hammer, and fired.

Christian kept himself in front of Bellamy, blocking her with his body. She screamed, but the shot went wide when Granville darted forward to shove Wainsright aside.

He wrenched himself away from Granville and fled out of the warehouse.

Christian chased after him. Wainsright dropped the flintlock pistol as he ran, having discharged its only shot. It didn't take Christian long to catch up with Wainsright at the quay. They grappled for a few seconds, until Christian hammered him with his fist, almost knocking him out. As Wainsright reeled, Christian grabbed the black bag out of his limp fingers.

But the man recovered quickly. He jammed a hand into his pocket and pulled out a second pistol, identical to the first. He cocked the hammer. "Give me the money, Huntington."

Christian drew himself to his full height and faced the man that caused him so much pain. After the events of the last few days, he didn't feel an ounce of fear standing in front of the barrel of the pistol. He had the money back to help his people and Bellamy was safe. Wainsright and his mad vendetta no longer mattered to him. "No. This is over, Shelby."

Spittle flew from Wainsright's mouth. "It's not done until you bend to me. I am *superior* to you." His hand shook and his finger trembled over the trigger.

Christian tensed. He'd lost both of his weapons, but he wasn't about to give up. He raised the bag to swing it at the pistol, intent to knock it out of Wainsright hand.

Wainsright squeezed the trigger.

Christian watched the movement. Time slowed until each heartbeat felt like a month. He wished he'd had the courage to tell Bellamy that he loved her. To ask her to stay with him.

The crack of a weapon discharging made him flinch. He waited for the pain. It never came. In front of him, Wainsright went pale. Then he staggered back a step. He touched his abdomen, and his fingers came away red with blood. Then he tripped over his shoes and fell backward into the water.

Christian spun. Zeph stood a few feet behind him with a smoking pistol in his hand. His friend dragged his gaze from the spot where Wainsright had fallen. He shrugged and put the weapon back in his pocket.

"Now we do not have to concern ourselves with retribution."

Gabriel and Bellamy rushed out of the warehouse. Granville followed, holding a limping Twisden upright while pressing a handkerchief to a cut on his own temple.

"What happened to Wainsright?" Gabriel asked.

"Went for a swim," Zeph replied. He winked at Christian.

Gabriel huffed. "Can he swim?"

"Not with shot in his stomach," Carter said from the doorway of the warehouse. He sauntered forward to join them. Six men followed and surrounded him in a protective semi-circle.

Christian let out a shuddering breath and tried to bring his heartbeat under control. When he could move without trembling, he opened the black bag; thousands of pound notes lay within. At least eighty thousand by the look of it. Relief flooded him, making stars dance in his eyes. He shook his head to clear them. That left…"What of my automatons?" he asked Carter.

The dandy pursed his lips and considered Christian. Then he snapped his fingers and held his hand out. Demon-Lips stepped forward and removed the little egg clock from his pocket. He gave it to Carter.

Bellamy let out a soft gasp. His heart clenched. Was that a gasp of joy or trepidation?

Carter ignored her. He admired the red enamel egg, Then his gaze met Christian's. "I will return this to you if you allow me to keep the silver music box."

That was unexpected. "If you plan to sell it, I will simply buy it from you."

A smile flashed on Carter's face, gone as quickly as it came. "I've no intention of selling it. There is someone I think would derive great joy from it."

Christian saw what appeared to be gentleness mixed with sadness. Who did Carter wish to give the music box to? No matter, now that he had the money back, he had no need to sell it. The clock was most important. With it, he could give the woman he loved the choice to leave him. White-hot pain stabbed his heart at the thought.

He swallowed around the lump in his throat and nodded at Carter. "A trade."

The dandy tipped his hat in thanks and gently set the clock in Christian's hand. He'd forgotten how much the little automaton weighed. He traced his thumb over the edge of the doors that opened, then looked up to give his thanks.

Carter, and his men, were gone. Half a dozen silver rose petals on the ground were all that remained.

"Can we go home now?" Bellamy whispered.

He dipped his head toward his chest. She could return to her time and never look back. He couldn't voice the words. Instead, he raised her hand to his lips and pressed a gentle kiss to her knuckles. "I would like nothing better, my love."

He tucked the clock into his pocket and then pulled her into his arms. He kissed her for long moments, telling her the only way he knew how glad he was she was with him, and that he never wanted her to go.

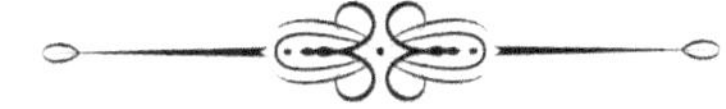

Chapter Fourteen

Bellamy stood in front of the fire in the drawing room at Gabriel's townhouse, trying to absorb the warmth into her frozen limbs that felt as if they might never be warm again. They'd returned a few minutes ago, and Christian and the men went to Gabriel's study to discuss how to report the events of the evening.

Lily and Violet had clamored to her, checking her for injury and taking turns between hugging her and scolding her for so foolishly going with Wainsright. She'd had to pry them off and ask for a few minutes alone to process what had happened.

Standing before the fire, she found she couldn't stop trembling. Couldn't shake the memory of Wainsright aiming that gun at Christian while he shielded *her*.

Then after, when Carter produced the enamel clock and laid it in Christian's hands, she hadn't been able to read the expression on his face. Did he want her to stay? Or, had their time together drawn to its natural conclusion? Did *she* want to leave? She searched her heart, wondering what to do. Could she give her life in the twenty-first century up for love as Lily had?

The thought of life without him was unbearable; she'd realized that when she thought Wainsright might shoot him, and that she might lose him forever.

What if he didn't feel the same way? She wrapped her arms

around her waist and stared into the flickering light.

"Sometimes it is difficult to know if you should move forward or stay where you are at in life," Zeph said as he joined her. His silver gaze was intense.

Bellamy sensed a deeper meaning to his words but couldn't quite grasp the thought.

"In time, I have no doubt that you'll make the correct choice." He offered a cryptic smile.

"I don't know what to do. If I stay, it means leaving our brother behind. He seems so broken. I'm not sure I can leave him on his own."

Zeph laid a hand on her shoulder. "If he's anything like his sisters, he'll find his way home."

She didn't know how to respond to that. What did that even mean? "I don't know how to thank you. For protecting Christian. He told me about Eton, that you've always been there for him. And tonight, at the warehouse. If it hadn't been for you, Gabriel, and the others, I don't know what would have happened."

His lips tipped at the corners in a small smile. "We are nothing without the people we care for. I learned that a very long time ago." He touched a finger to her chin. "Who will you be, Bellamy?"

She looked up at him, seeing fathomless wisdom in his silver eyes. "I…" *Don't want to be a model anymore.* "I want to be close to those that I love. I'll…figure out the rest."

"I know you will." With a nod, he walked away.

Lily entered the drawing room as he was leaving. He paused to kiss her cheek, then left.

"Is he always that…"

"Cryptic?" Lily supplied. "Yes. Always. He's like the Cheshire Cat. Sometimes I swear that he knows about the time travel. But how could he unless Gabriel or Christian told him? I know Gabriel didn't."

"Maybe Christian did."

Lily laid a hand on her stomach and rubbed it.

Bellamy cocked her head. "Is something wrong? You've done that a few times over the last…" Suddenly, the truth hit her, and she was surprised she hadn't realized it earlier. "Oh my God, you're pregnant!"

Lily's lips twitched. "We were waiting to be absolutely sure. Not like I can grab a quick pregnancy test from the drug store." Her smile turned dreamy. "Could you imagine another little Gabriel running around?"

"Oh heavens. No," Violet whined as she entered the room. "I insist that you have a little Lily instead. Or better yet, a little Violet."

Bellamy laughed, although it felt hollow. Her heart twisted with indecision. Lily's pregnancy added another layer of complication to her decision. If she left, she'd never see her little niece or nephew.

But what about Archer? Could he… what if finding his way home meant coming to them, here in this time? Was that possible? She tried to picture him tying a cravat and snorted. Not likely.

"Bells," Lily began. She twisted her hands together. "I know you only agreed to go with Wainsright to protect Vi and me. I saw you fight him outside the dressmaker's shop. I'm sorry for what I said."

"Lily." She took her sister's hand, feeling her throat tighten with tears. The day was catching up with her and her emotions were all over the place. She'd been in turns irritated with Lily, surprised and scared by Wainsright, angry at the men who grabbed her, terrified for Christian, confused about her future, happy for Lily and Gabriel and the birth of their first child, sad about Archer, and now ashamed for what her relationship with Lily had become. Any more emotions and she thought she might break.

"I know you're an adult. I know you're doing what you think is right. If you stay, I promise to try and stop acting like I'm the mom."

Bellamy wiped a tear from her eye. "I'll try to stop being your bratty little sister."

"I won't stop doing either of those things," Violet declared.

They laughed and Lily pulled Bellamy into a hug. "No matter what you decide, whether you stay or go, please know that I'm proud of you, Bells. I love you so much."

She sniffed. "I love you too. And you, Violet," she added before the young woman could insert herself again. She pulled her into the hug as well.

This felt good, being surrounded by family again. It had been so long, she'd forgotten what it was like.

Christian's laugh echoed from out in the hall. Her heart quickened at the sound. He seemed far more confident in himself since she'd first met him. He smiled more. Especially when he kissed her. His newfound confidence was so sexy on him, and she knew he'd only grow more confident and so much sexier. She wanted to watch him flourish. To see him become all that he could be and marvel at his new creations.

Her heart clenched. She couldn't do it. She couldn't leave. Not now. When she'd fallen in love with a man who needed her as much as she needed him. She loved him, and she'd never belong anywhere else.

Archer, you better find a way home to us, because Lily and I are staying.

Christian stopped in the doorway, silhouetted by the candlelight. She admired his wide shoulders and strong form. That blond hair and handsome face, with his stormy eyes, and the little bit of scruff on his jaw. His crooked cravat that made her smile and want to straighten it.

She released Lily and Violet and walked to him, wanting to go into his arms but not sure how he felt. He looked pensive when she reached his side. "Can we talk somewhere?" she asked him.

His face closed down but he took her hand in his and ushered her downstairs. Near his workshop was a door she hadn't noticed before. Christian remained quiet as he opened it and led her out into a small, gated garden.

She gaped in surprise. Moonlight washed the flowers in silver and in the back were a few rows of crops. The mixed scents of hundreds of flowers clamored together into a heady perfume.

Christian lit a lantern on a table by the door and then drew her onto the short path.

Bellamy took his arm and shifted closer to his warmth. She felt the light tremor in his arm, beneath his coat. Was he as apprehensive as she? Gathering her courage, she pulled him to a stop and kissed his cheek.

His eyes turned sad. "Bellamy, I…"

"I love you," she said.

Christian stiffened.

Oh God, had she misread the signals? What if he didn't want her to stay? Her heart started to hammer, and her stomach flipped.

He took a step closer and cupped her cheek. "Say that once again."

Bellamy gripped his coat in her fists and gathered her courage. "I—I love you, Christian. I want to stay here. With you."

Christian searched her eyes, then crushed his mouth to hers. "I love you, too," he said when they finally parted. "I was terrified that you would leave me."

"I couldn't. I wasn't happy there. I didn't realize it until you showed me a different life entirely. And I think, all along, I needed you."

He pressed another sweet kiss to her lips. "I would have followed you through time, Bellamy. I want only you."

She wrapped her arms around his neck. "Then I'll always be yours, Christian Albury. My reclusive earl."

"No one could tempt me away from that life but you."

"I don't want to tempt you from it. I love you as you are. Shy, brilliant, and strong. I want to see all the wonderful things you will create and watch everyone else realize you to be the amazing, powerful man I already know you are."

"What about your career? It is unusual for the wife of an earl to seek employment, but I would never wish you to be unhappy."

Her heart tripped when he spoke of marrying her, but she focused on his question. "I realized that I hadn't been happy for some time. It is hard to deal with the constant pressures of staying thin." She thought of the young woman in the dressmaker's shop that Violet had spoken with, the woman who desperately needed guidance in her clothing choices. "Everyone deserves to look and feel their best," she murmured. "Maybe I can use my experience to help others." She told him about the woman. "I'm not sure how to go about it. Do you think people would want that?"

He smiled. "I'm certain of it. I can only imagine how my life would have been different if I'd had someone like you to give me confidence."

"You have me now," she whispered.

Christian kissed her tenderly. "I will treasure you always, my love. And the little enamel egg that brought you to me."

She leaned her head against his chest and wrapped her arms around his waist. "What will you do with it?"

"Repair it and put it somewhere safe. Gabriel might kill me if Violet decided to use it to go husband hunting in the future."

She laughed. "As wise as you are handsome." She had no doubt that there was a man out there somewhere who would love Violet for the vibrant, mischievous woman that she was. "I hope Archer will be okay," she said.

"From what I know of the Bennetts, he will." Christian captured her lips in another kiss. "May I take you back inside and warm you up?" he murmured in her ear.

Her nipples tightened and she shivered in anticipation. "As long as you promise to never stop."

Christian cupped her face and smoothed his thumb over her lower lip. "I promise to never stop loving you, Bellamy. Now and forever, I am yours." He lowered his head and sealed his promise with a kiss.

Bellamy held him close as they kissed. Her nightmare, she was sure, was gone because of this man who understood her so well and loved her even more. And she'd stay with him, always. She'd finally found her family and her heart.

About the Author

Aurrora St. James has been writing romance since she was a teen. Fortunately for the world, those stories will never see the light of day. Now, she loves writing sexy, paranormal romances featuring tough and sometimes dark heroes, women who find their inner strength, and a touch of humor added in for spice. In particular, she enjoys writing both Medieval and Regency romances that whisk readers into the beautiful landscapes of history, where love can overcome anything.

When she's not writing, you'll find her reading, drinking coffee, making her own journals, or watching old B, C, and D-movies. She lives in the Florida jungle with her husband, a slightly crazy dog, and a cat that thinks he's a brontosaurus.

Social Media:

Website: www.aurrorastjames.com
Facebook: facebook.com/AurroraStJamesAuthor
Instagram: instagram.com/aurrorastjames
Pinterest: pinterest.com/ladyaurrora
Bookbub: bookbub.com/authors/aurrora-st-james
Amazon: amazon.com/Aurrora-St.-James/e/B00E46VJD8
Goodreads: goodreads.com/AurroraStJames

www.ingramcontent.com/pod-product-compliance
Lightning Source LLC
Chambersburg PA
CBHW070349200726
48294CB00003B/813

* 9 7 8 1 9 6 1 2 7 5 2 8 7 *